KARAH
QUINNEY

THE CLOUD FOREST

Special Note:
To report any problems or to join the mailing list please email Karah Quinney directly at karah.quinney1@gmail.com

K/P

KENNEDY PUBLISHING
TITLES BY KARAH QUINNEY:

The Whale Hunter
Pillar of Fire (Book One)
Sacred Fire (Book Two)
Sacred Path (Book Three)

The Great Land
The Seeking Star (Book One)
Shadow of the Moon (Book Two)
Light of the Sun (Book Three)

Sundancer
Legend of the Sundancer (Book One)
The Last Sundancer (Book Two)

Warrior
The Warrior's Way
Daughters of the Sun
The Cloud Forest – New Release

Published in the United States by Kennedy Publishing.

Library of Congress Cataloging-in-Publication Data
Quinney, Karah

THE CLOUD FOREST: a novel/Karah Quinney.

THE CLOUD FOREST
Karah Quinney

Thousands of years before written history the primordial land known as the Amazon Rainforest was simply called the Great Forest. The vast mountainous region that hovered over the lowlands was known as the Cloud Forest. This is the story of the inhabitants that banded together in their valiant struggle for survival, against all odds.

CHAPTER ONE

The sibilant sounds of the jungle ceased as a piercing cry filled the air. A flickering fire gave off brilliant flashes of light in the stygian darkness. Treetop denizens quieted, alert to the footfalls of a predator. Again the sound of a scream broke the otherwise vociferous hum of the jungle.

Near the fire, several men sat quietly, aware that their entire band stood in tense expectation. The women were huddled together outside of a well constructed dwelling, much like the other raised lodges that housed their people high above the ground.

Another piercing cry sounded from inside the lodge, and the women began to sway back and forth, keening softly together. On a woven leaf pallet, a girl strained to enter into the realm of womanhood by giving birth to her first child. Throughout the day she had alternated between resting on her haunches and swaying back and forth on her knees in an effort to bring her child forth. Her labor pains were so close together that she could barely form a breath from one moment to the next. Sensing the impending birth, a stooped older woman came forward, pressing one gnarled hand expectantly between the girl's splayed legs.

"He comes." The older woman's eyes were not unkind as she watched the young girl's belly harden and strain with another labor pain.

"Aieee!" Suyan screamed as the women brought her to a standing position, supporting her on the left and on the right. Without their help she wouldn't have been able to trust her shaking legs to hold her. She reached overhead, grasping blindly for the braided rope that hung from the strong birch rods of the lodge.

"Pull upon the birthing rope, and push your son from your body."

Suyan tried to listen to Agada's instructions. The other women of her band trusted Agada to see to the wellbeing of their families. She had assisted each of them with the birthing of their babies, just as she helped Suyan now.

"Push, girl!" Agada's jowls shook as she stood in front of Suyan. "Push the child free of your body."

Suyan swayed weakly as the women held her up, bearing her weight. "I can't!"

Her voice was almost too weak to be heard over the eerie keening of the women.

"Do you seek to steal the baby's soul?" Agada's eyes were wild as she stared at Suyan. "Push the child free!"

Suyan pushed, clenching her teeth together as she forced herself to bear down. Her limbs trembled from the strain, and her lungs burned with the need for air as another harsh pain seized her.

She felt as if her insides were being ripped from her body. Panicked by the burning ring of fire that spiraled up from between her legs, she tried to break free of the hands and arms that held her.

Agada cackled over the girl's weak attempts to escape the pain of childbirth. She touched the round head of Suyan's child, aware that the baby's shoulders were lodged in tight. One gnarled finger entered the girl's opening, turning the child's body with a skill born of experience.

Suyan screamed, aware only of the burning pain. She closed her eyes, unable to break away from the women that held her still as Agada probed her opening. She bent low over her belly, weakly dragging in another breath as sweat bathed her body. Another pain threatened to rip her apart and a woman came forward to press hard against her stomach with her forearms, forcing Suyan to bear down with a final hard push.

Silence, unlike anything that Suyan had ever encountered, surrounded the women as Agada pulled the child's body free. Exhausted by the prolonged labor, the women lowered Suyan to the woven leaf pallet, each of them forgetting her existence as they waited for Agada's pronouncement.

Suyan strained to hear the first sound from her child.

She had gazed into his face for a brief moment, seeing a cap of straight black hair and a round face with eyes that would be round and almond in shape. It had only been a moment, but her child's face was seared into her memory forever. Agada held up the child for her inspection and Suyan froze in denial.

He was perfectly formed, but his face and body were blue, and his eyes remained closed. "My baby!" She sobbed, reaching toward her son as Agada cradled the infant against her wrinkled breasts. "Give me my baby!"

She watched helplessly as Agada murmured in a guttural tongue, a language unfamiliar to Suyan. The woman quickly covered the infant's body with the very same cloth that his mother had woven in preparation for his birth.

"My son!" Suyan cried, reaching out toward her child even as the afterbirth slipped unnoticed from her body. "Give me my child."

Agada shook her head, her expression full of blame as she wrapped the long cloth around the child's body, concealing his face from sight. "You killed your child, Suyan."

"No!" Suyan's terrified scream filled the lodge as the other women turned angry eyes upon her. She stared at the bundled form in Agada's arms without comprehension, flinching under the lashing blow from the willow stick that one of the women held. Suyan screamed, but the other women surrounded her, lashing her arms and belly with small whip thin sticks. Blow after blow rained down upon her, one followed by another.

"See that she is punished," Agada threw the words over one shoulder as she left the lodge. Anger and betrayal caused Agada to stand with rigid stiffness as she cradled the lifeless babe in her arms. Suyan's screams followed her from the lodge as she reached the ground and walked with purposeful steps toward the men waiting near the central fire. For her part, Agada turned a deaf ear to the young woman's terrible cries. At seventeen seasons of age, Suyan had betrayed their village by stealing her child's spirit before he could ever know life.

Supported by two women, Suyan was drawn forth from the birthing lodge, having rested for three days without any knowledge of her child. She saw her mother standing next to Chota, her husband, and Esta stared at her with a bleak gaze, silently telling her daughter that there was nothing more that she could do for her.

Suyan stiffened as she caught sight of a hunched figure standing next to Chota and her mother. She recognized the man almost at once, he was a man that lived in the shadows, but he had come to them as a shaman, and just like the lengthening shadows, he was a man to be feared.

A shiver passed over her shoulders as his piercing black eyes burrowed into hers. She looked away quickly, but not before seeing his sharp, birdlike features darken angrily.

"Suyan," Chota opened his arms, calling for silence as the people of their small village gathered around. His thick palms, broad shoulders and round belly stood out in contrast to the thinner men and women of their village. "Your son has been given back to the jungle, and we have grieved for the child these past three days."

Stricken with grief, Suyan's knees buckled, but the women holding her by the arms forced her to remain standing.

"You have been overcome by a bad spirit." Chota's eyes burned brightly as he stepped toward her. "You are a danger to our entire village. We–"

"No, Chota." Suyan interrupted, barely recognizing the sound of her own voice, hoarse from weeping.

"Silence!"

Suyan stared past Chota's angry face to peer at her mother. Esta's head was bowed and her shoulders lowered in silent agony.

"We understand that you are not aware of the damage that you have done. You stole the life of your son before he could take his first breath."

The accusation ripped Suyan's heart to shreds. She wanted to speak, but Chota's harsh glare threatened dire things if she interrupted him once again.

"We have decided that you will be given another chance."

Suyan's head snapped up as she thought of her son, wrapped in his blanket, alone, and cold. Where had they placed him? Who had spoken words over him, so that he would know that he had been loved? Drowning in a haze of unending grief, she could barely comprehend what Chota was telling her.

"You will undergo another first fruits ceremony with the girls that have had their first flowering." Chota's pronouncement caused the people to murmur amongst themselves, and Suyan's eyes widened as her mother's husband watched her expectantly.

Images of naked bodies wreathed in sweat and the sickeningly sweet taste of the Ayahuasca brew came to mind, causing Suyan to sway. She squeezed her eyes shut, but the images remained, and she could almost feel the hands of others upon her. Open mouths and moans surrounded her in a swirl of color and unending sensation. She blinked, forcing unshed tears to seep in twin trails down her face as she shook her head in denial.

"No. Never." Suyan found her voice. "I will never undergo another first fruits ceremony."

"The bad spirit speaks!"

Suyan's head spun as the shaman stepped forward, issuing the condemning accusation. *Anyan.* She knew him by name, but other than the mystical power that he supposedly possessed, she knew very little about him.

"Suyan, you must do as he says!" Esta broke her silence, pleading with her daughter to accept Chota's decree.

She shook her head in abject misery. "Mother, I cannot."

"No!" Esta turned to her husband. "Please Chota, give her more time. She is still weak from childbirth. She doesn't know what she's saying."

Chota gestured toward two of the women, and Esta cringed as they led her away from her daughter. The bitter sound of her mother's weeping echoed in Suyan's chest. Her mother had known too much grief in such a short amount of time. Since the death of Abadu, her father, she had watched her mother drift through life, allowing others to make decisions for her. Becoming Chota's lifemate was one of the decisions that Suyan had fought against. Suddenly unable to stand, she slumped to the ground, and this time the women holding her arms released her as if they were anxious to let her go.

"I had hoped that she would become a woman with the birth of her first child." Chota turned to Anyan in expectation. "As you can see, she is not the same girl that my wife brought into our marriage."

"I can see that she is afflicted, cursed."

Anyan's inflammatory charge caused the others to back away, making sweeping signs to ward off evil as they widened the circle that had formed around the three of them.

"Perhaps you can beat the bad spirit out of her." One of the men interjected, eyeing the red welts left by the willow switches.

Suyan kept her head lowered submissively, although she knew that Chota was within his right to have her beaten again if he chose. She bit her lip, yearning for her mother's protective embrace, but also painfully aware that her mother couldn't help her.

"You have refused to undergo another first fruits ceremony." Chota continued speaking, momentarily distracted by the mosquitoes that hovered around his back and shoulders. "Others have said that you have a bad spirit trapped within you and that you are a danger to our entire village. No child is safe within the reach of your hands."

"Chota, I did not cause my son's death." Suyan lifted her head, inhaling sharply as he turned his back upon her.

"You denied him life!"

She trembled violently from the harsh blow of his words. "No."

"I will ask you again, and this time you should think carefully before you give me your answer. Will you align yourself with the

Wuyari Village and give yourself over to the first fruits ceremony?"

Suyan's memory of the ceremony itself only came to her in shattered dreams and nightmares. Within the Wuyari Village the girls that came into their flowering time were offered by their families as a gift to their people. It was a long held tradition, and the girls that took part in the ceremony were given protection and standing. In the beginning, Suyan's mother had wholeheartedly encouraged her participation. Suyan had even anticipated becoming a woman in the Wuyari way prior to taking part in the actual ceremony. Just like the girls in her village, she desired a child of their shared blood, a son that she would raise on high before becoming the lifemate of a strong hunter.

Other young women had already given birth to sons and daughters, earning their place within their small village, but she had failed. She had been given into the first fruits ceremony twice now, and her body had only quickened with life after the last ceremony. Her failure to produce a healthy child marked her as different and separate from the other women.

Responding to Chota's question, she shook her head in misery. "No."

"Then you will remain a half-woman, an abomination." Anyan stepped forward, standing over her as his voice grew louder with each word. "You are cursed!"

The villagers moaned, stricken by the pronouncement from Anyan.

"There is yet hope for this young woman. Allow her to accompany me to my place of dwelling. I will force the bad spirit to flee from her, and then I will return her to you restored." Anyan turned away to gather an offering that would appease Chota. "I will offer you a fair trade for the young woman. I know that you will miss her help within your lodge."

"Chota." Suyan pleaded with her mother's husband. "Please, let me stay!"

Ignoring her extended hand, Chota eyed the offerings that Anyan thrust toward him. Resolved, he turned to face the villagers. "I have decided that Suyan will go with the shaman. He offers the only hope of restoring my wife's daughter to her true nature." Chota sucked his teeth, bending to speak to Suyan. "You are fortunate. He is a man that touches power."

Despite her anguish over the loss of her child, Suyan shuddered in denial. She feared Anyan almost as much as she feared opening her body to the men of her band during another first fruits ceremony.

"Don't seek to sway me with tears." Chota's angry tone hardened as he waved his hand in front of her face. "I expected you to do your duty. You were to carry new life and offer your son to our band as a future hunter. Instead, you stole his soul, denying him life."

The condemning words resounded in the silence of Suyan's mind, and she felt her heart shatter.

"I have made a good trade." Chota announced, entirely content with his decision. "Anyan will have the care of you for a time. He will see that the bad spirit within you is expunged, and I will take everything that he has offered in return."

Chota was satisfied that his wife's daughter would be taken away from their village to be cured by the shaman, and he would have the abalone shell necklace and hanging baskets that the shaman had promised him. The fine arrowheads and darts for his blow pipe were already the envy of the other men. Satisfied by his decision, he turned away from the girl that had betrayed him with failure even though he had fed and clothed her since the day that he had taken her mother as his wife.

CHAPTER TWO

Suyan raised her hands over her head to ward off the blow from Anyan's walking stick. She shuddered as he turned toward her with his weapon raised menacingly. From the first day that they had left her village, he told her that it was his right to beat her in the hopes that the bad spirit within her would flee. A sound from the jungle caught Anyan's attention, distracting him, and just as quickly, he turned away.

Her breasts ached as much from the lack of her son's suckling mouth as they did from the many scratches that had been inflicted upon her from the willow switches wielded by the Wuyari women. The other women of her village had shunned her, refusing to acknowledge her tearful pleading even as Anyan led her away from the Wuyari Village. She knew that her mother would have opened her arms to her, if only Chota would have allowed them to see each other again.

Darkness shrouded the jungle, making visibility difficult. They were surrounded on all sides by numerous trees, tangled vines, and scurrying creatures, but she had never felt more alone. Cold shivers moved over Suyan's body, despite the stifling heat. Anyan's eyes took on a terrible darkness as he began to speak to someone unseen, absently dropping the walking stick that he held in his hand.

"Is that so?" Anyan asked, lowering himself to the ground as he began to build a fire.

Suyan closed her eyes tightly shut, certain that the spirits listened whenever Anyan spoke.

The first few days away from her band had been the most difficult. Despite her failure to bring new life into her band, she had loved the Wuyari people. Anyan forced her to march deep into the jungle that first night, and despite her weakening condition, she had hoped to find a new beginning with the mystical shaman revered by the people of her band.

Upon closer inspection, it appeared that Anyan was only slightly older than Chota, having known over forty seasons of life. His skin was deeply scarred, and his black hair hung in lanky swatches over his shoulder blades. While he had the use of both hands, she couldn't help but notice that he was missing three fingers on his right hand. Unlike the hunched older man that he had appeared to be at first, she saw that he now stood straight and tall.

Suyan had learned during their first night alone that he was shrewd.

Having marched far away from her band, Anyan made certain that they weren't nearby to hear her cries for help when he bound her arms above her head, staking her to a young sapling. She hadn't known what to expect from him then, but now she knew that she was completely at his mercy as he watched her out of sharp, dark eyes. With her heart pounding with fear, she shivered uncontrollably as he began a whispered conversation with spirits that she couldn't see.

Challa. His brother.

She had learned that name quickly, listening with growing dread as Anyan told his dead brother about the good trade that he had made.

"I have finally won something rare and valuable, Challa." Anyan laughed to himself, scratching sharp yellowed fingernails over his shoulders. "Look at her, do you see what I see?"

Cushioned only by dense undergrowth and matted leaves, Suyan struggled with the ropes binding her wrists. She rolled onto her side to see Anyan, but when she finally caught sight of him, she wished that she hadn't looked. He stood naked next to a small fire, while smoke rose up to twist around his lean form. His male member hung between his legs uselessly as he stroked his hands over his body.

"She will give me a son." Anyan's voice had become thin and urgent, wheedling in its intensity. He tilted his head as if listening to someone unseen, and she couldn't still the trembling that consumed her body. "You promised that if I went deeper into the jungle, I would find her, and now she is here."

He stared down at his male organ, and his nails left thin trails of blood along his abdomen as he waited for his manhood to respond.

"I will fill her belly with my seed," Anyan continued his one-sided conversation with his brother before taking several purposeful steps toward Suyan. She trembled violently, kicking her legs in an attempt to forestall him. "My brother says that you are like a piece of fruit hanging from the aguaje palm tree." He laughed harshly, and his laughter remained with her long after it faded away. "He says that you are ripe for the plucking."

"No, I'm still bleeding." Suyan forced the words from a throat that was parched and dry; she could smell the sharp scent of her own fear as she held his gaze. "I recently gave birth."

Anyan tilted his head at an odd angle, listening with rapt attention to something that she couldn't hear. Suyan couldn't control the shivers that caused her body to quake.

"Challa says that women need time to heal after childbirth." The disappointment in Anyan's eyes made Suyan's heart pound with fear. "All will be well. I will simply wait."

Suyan struggled to keep up with Anyan as he walked at an unhurried pace, despite the sharp-edged fronds that snagged her bare skin or the thorny vines that hampered her attempts to follow him. She felt almost smothered by the humid air, or perhaps it was the terror that she had suffered since leaving her village that threatened to choke her, making breathing exceedingly difficult.

Life with Anyan was a constant struggle for survival, and as he walked forward with purpose, she could only wonder where he led her. She slept only when she was too exhausted to stay awake, and it was as if Anyan purposely led her in circles. They hadn't stumbled upon anyone else, and any thoughts of escape quickly fled as Suyan realized that she had been marked as cursed by her village. Anyan assured her that even if they happened to encounter other people they would turn away from her in fear.

"Anyan," Suyan called, clearing her throat as she struggled to speak. "Where are you taking me?"

He turned to peer at her out of birdlike eyes that were sharp and piercing, and she immediately regretted calling attention to herself. She never knew when he would try to press his attentions upon her, and she remained in a constant state of fear.

"We will live in the Agali Village."

The low moan of fear that came from her throat captured his attention.

"No." Suyan shook her head desperately as he began to turn away. "Anyan, I can't go to the Agali Village. You must know that they once held me as a captive." Suyan swayed in place, repulsed by the memory of her captivity, along with the suffering experienced by the other young women that were taken. "They would have killed us if the Saika warriors hadn't saved our lives."

Visions of that terrible time swam through Suyan's mind, and she shuddered as Anyan shrugged carelessly.

"No harm will come to you while you are within my care. I am now their shaman."

Suyan wavered on her feet. She had been beaten, bound to assure her compliance, and half starved. Yet, Anyan said that she wouldn't suffer harm.

Tired beyond bearing, she glanced around, noticing again how isolated and alone they truly were. Their only companions were the stinging insects, flying birds, and troops of monkeys that kept to the safety of the treetops.

"You can't take me to the Agali Village. I'll die there. I need–"

"Silence!" Anyan shouted, but just as quickly his eyes grew distant and flat.

Suyan knew better than to breathe a sigh of relief. She had come to learn that while his eyes saw the spirit world, they also saw the world of the living. She had no doubt that Anyan knew exactly where she was standing, and she swayed in place as a wave of tiredness assaulted her.

His eyes twitched, and he was with her again, but this he watched her suspiciously. "Challa says that you will leave me tonight while I sleep."

"No," Suyan barely recognized her own voice. Her tongue felt thick in her mouth, and her limbs were unbearably heavy. "You said that you would help me, and I need your help."

"Are you certain?"

Suyan noticed that Anyan's voice had become reed thin and expectant, like that of a young child, and she couldn't suppress a shiver.

"I won't leave you, Anyan." The hopelessness of her situation left her feeling vulnerable and exposed as fatigue threatened to bring her to her knees. She wiped sweat from her brow and licked her dry lips, yearning for fresh water.

Anyan peered into her eyes, and Suyan struggled to remain still as she held his gaze. "I know you won't leave me."

Instead of relaxing, Suyan's shoulder's tensed in awful expectation. She had seen him this way once before, during their first night alone.

"Please, Anyan…" Suyan tried to tell him that she needed water, but the words wouldn't form on her lips.

"Challa never lies."

Surprised by the dire certainty in his voice, Suyan took an uncertain step away from him, but dizziness caused her to stumble and fall. She felt Anyan's hands on her arms as dark stars flooded her vision and darkness swallowed her whole.

"Childbirth fever." Anyan growled angrily as he ran a wet strip of hide over the young woman's fevered brow. He had seen such things before, although he didn't know what to do to help the woman that he had chosen as his mate. "Challa, you and I both know that she could die."

He looked around for his brother, finding the jungle surprisingly silent. The absence of his brother's youthful voice frustrated him, but he knew that Challa would return when he was needed. In his mind's eye, Challa remained forever young, captured in time at the age of sixteen seasons. He considered it a mark of his shamanistic power that he could see and hear his brother clearly, even though Challa chose to hide from others.

"Suyan?" He pressed his lips against her mouth, enjoying the warmth of her skin until he realized that she was impossibly warm. "You must wake up."

His hands fisted as he stared at her unresponsive features. With one long fingernail he parted her lips, touching the tip of her tongue. He raised her head and pressed his waterskin to her lips, allowing the water to flood her mouth. "No!"

He shouted angrily as the water trickled in rivulets down the sides of her face.

"I need you to drink."

Aware that water would wash away the burning sickness inside of her, he shook her roughly, hoping to wake her, but she remained lost in an unnatural sleep. He had no doubt that he had pushed her hard over the past three days, but he had expected her to keep up with him so that he could bring her back to the village that he called home.

Anyan searched the heights of the canopy above for the sun. He stood to his full height, dragging Suyan to a sitting position. Her round breasts nearly burned his palms as he touched that which belonged to him.

"This is the woman that I have chosen for myself." He addressed his brother as Challa finally returned, his winsome smile securely in place and his eyes bright with mischief.

"You have chosen well, Anyan, but it is a shame that she won't live to bear your son. You will never be a father, and you will never be accepted by any village."

"Lies!"

The jungle suddenly grew quiet as Anyan lifted the young woman over one shoulder and stared at his brother.

"She will die if you don't find someone to help her."

"I can help her." Anyan grumbled. "I am a shaman, and I will say whether she lives or dies."

Challa's laughter rang in Anyan's ears until he thought he would scream.

"Don't mock me!"

"I would never mock you, my brother."

"Then tell me that she will not die."

Silence was his only answer.

"It matters not at all, Challa." Anyan's lips thinned into a sneer as he considered his options, absently rubbing the calloused nubs on his right hand where his fingers used to be. "I know of one that can send the burning sickness from her body. I will take her there and she will be well."

"She will leave you."

Unwilling to respond to his brother's dire prediction, Anyan lifted Suyan over one shoulder as he changed direction, walking steadily through the jungle at a rapid pace. His steps never faltered as he moved over fallen trees, decaying vegetation, and gnarled roots. With each step, he thought of the existence that had been stolen from him long ago, and he knew that with Suyan as his wife he would have all that he had ever desired for himself. He would make her well. He wouldn't allow death to claim her.

In the silence of the jungle, a lone hunter paused in mid stride, aware that he was no longer alone. Most of the day had been spent descending the rough terrain while silently communing with the creatures of the jungle.

Something unknown had disturbed him in the midst of a vivid dream, and he had awakened from sleep while darkness still cloaked the land. Drawn from the high places of the cloud forest as if by an unseen hand, he was filled with a sense of urgency. He left the secure cavern walls that he called home, traveling by instinct and touch until the first flush of dappled sunlight filtered through the trees.

By midday, he was ensconced by the vivid green triple canopy of the jungle, surrounded by moist heat and humidity. He was naked except for a loincloth and the familiar rattan strips that he wore tied above his knees. He carried his blow pipe and several poison tipped darts, an obsidian hunting knife honed by his own hands, and a small pouch containing fire making supplies. The wet moisture of the jungle coated his skin, telling him in a silent whisper that it had rained recently and would do so again.

Suddenly, he stopped his hurried stride and inhaled sharply as his nostrils flared, searching the air for the scent of a two-legged predator amongst the alluring fragrance of newly opened flowers. His wide, heavily calloused feet were at ease on the jungle floor, and he didn't make a sound as he walked toward the cry that was at odds with the common jungle sounds.

From one moment to the next, he shifted from the guise of a lone forest dweller to that of a stealthy hunter.

Unlike past hunts, he wasn't accompanied by other men in search of worthy prey. This hunt was different because he hunted a man instead of an animal. His nostrils flared again, but he stood perfectly still, sensing the world around him with a technique taught to him by his father.

Mal cun uk. He chanted silently, calling upon the process that allowed him to orient himself within the dense jungle foliage. He instantly sensed home, aware of which path would lead him directly back to the heights of the cloud forest, but that wasn't the direction that he chose to follow.

Mal cun uk. The word resounded in his mind, sweeping along through his spirit until it mingled in his blood, and he sensed the approval of the spirit world. All around him the forest was alive, pulsing, pounding in uncountable ways, alert to his physical and spiritual needs. The man called Unsa took several quick steps that were silent, predatory, and fluid.

If the forest bent to shield him, no one saw but the long-tailed macaque and the familiar barking deer who stood undisturbed by the man that walked through their midst. He was as much a part of the jungle as they were, with as much right to tread upon the compact undergrowth in search of water, food, and shelter.

Unsa straightened as first his ears and then his eyes told him that he had finally found the person that caused every survival instinct to shout in alarm. While his shattered dream might have drawn him from his beloved cloud forest, hovering high above the jungle, he was consumed by a very different sort of purpose at present. The need to kill drew him forward, and the desire to destroy had him reaching for his deadly blowpipe.

CHAPTER THREE

Anyan reached the outskirts of the Saika Village, battling against the memories that returned to rile his anger and outrage. He had once dwelled amongst many of the people sheltered by the lodges nestled close together near the foothills of the Great Mountain. He had walked amongst them as freely as any man of their shared blood, but events had conspired against him, making him an outcast.

Suyan moaned pitifully as he swung her limp body into his arms. He had hoped that her fever would break and that she would open her eyes and look at him with appreciation glimmering in their dark depths. She believed in his shamanistic power. She shivered with morbid fear whenever he spoke to his dead brother, but he also noticed the awe in her expression.

He had chosen the perfect wife for himself, and she would give him sons to carry his name into the future. But first, he would need to ensure that she lived.

"Suyan." He jostled her in his arms, watching with rapt attention as her eyelids fluttered, and she gave a weak cry of alarm.

One taste of her dry, cracked lips told him that she still burned with sickness. He had taken the time to lift her woven grass skirt, and the blood that flowed from between her thighs hadn't surprised him. Anger over his inability to cure her on his own caused his fingers to clench around her tender flesh.

"Where am I?"

Her voice cracked, grating upon his ears as he stared down at her. The glossy, black hair that had attracted him to her was now dull and lifeless. Her skin had a sickly cast to it, no longer richly touched by the sun. Yet, he wasn't willing to let her go without ensuring that she would return to him as a willing companion.

"The bad spirit that lives inside of you is punishing you for seeking my help."

"What?" Suyan blinked, her eyes tinged with a desperate fear. "Please Anyan, you said that you would help me."

"And I will." Anyan ran his hands over her shoulders, cupping her breasts despite her whimper of protest. "You will return to me after you have seen the Saika healer."

"The Saika Village?" Suyan's head lolled to the side, but Anyan slapped her cheeks lightly, rousing her.

"Suyan, listen to me carefully," Anyan's voice was a low rasp. "You will seek help from the Saika healer and then you will come to this very place and wait for me. Only then will I remove the bad spirit that has caused you so much harm."

Suyan blinked with dry eyes as Anyan laid her upon the jungle floor. "Please help me."

"Remember what I have said or you will never see your mother again." A fluttering of wings in the treetops warned Anyan that he risked discovery, and he turned away without another glance as he left the young woman behind.

Unsa held his blowpipe to his mouth, ready to take the shot that would end Anyan's life. The man's long flowing cape identified him as nothing else could, even at a distance. But the sight of a woman held over one of Anyan's shoulders stopped Unsa from sending his poisoned dart flying through the air.

He ran forward, losing sight of his prey as the jungle foliage hid him from view. Relying upon his keen senses and familiarity with the forest, Unsa picked up speed, unwilling to lose the opportunity to bring Anyan down.

Jumping over a fallen tree and then skirting a mass of liana vines and knee high buttress roots, Unsa's piercing gaze picked up the finest details. He saw Anyan lean over the young woman's prone form, and anger burned low in his belly.

Mischief maker. Deceiver. Outcast.

These were the words that defined Anyan. Unsa had been content to allow him to remain lost to the jungle until stories of his mischief making had trickled into the Saika Village. The stories were brought to him by the Maki warriors, battle-hardened men that fought to keep peace within the jungle.

One misstep gave away his presence as the fluttering of wings overhead announced his arrival.

"Anyan!" Unsa shouted, unwilling to lose the opportunity to take down his prey.

He needed to end Anyan's life the same way that he would end the life of a venomous snake. He charged forward, inherently recognizing that his capacity for violence had reached its peak.

Unsa never broke stride, plunging deep into the jungle, which was almost impenetrable. Silence engulfed him, but it was a living silence, one filled with the inhalations and exhalations of the treetop denizens, slithering creatures, and abundant wildlife. He searched his surroundings, but his quarry was nowhere to be found.

A sound from the left caused Unsa to whirl in place, bending at the waist to avoid the blow that had been aimed at his head. He caught his first sight of Anyan as he used his blowpipe to block the blow. Anyan was clothed oddly for a man of the jungle, wearing a long flowing robe dyed a deep red.

"I will see you dead!" Anyan's wild eyes were narrowed into evil slits of pure menace as he knocked Unsa's blowpipe away.

Unsa wasted no time with speech.

He reacted to the threat by slashing out with his obsidian knife that sprang into his hand faster than the eye could follow.

Shedding the guise of a much older man, Anyan deftly arched away, forsaking the sturdy log that he carried for his own knife.

"Death to you, Unsa!"

Aware that Anyan sought to bate him, Unsa forced himself to remain calm and detached. All of his training, all of his time spent with the warriors of the Great Forest came into play as he silently reminded himself that a warrior must remain detached in order to fight without distraction.

Anyan lunged, striking like a viper, but Unsa was ready. He attacked simultaneously, leaning away from the reach of Anyan's knife, while twisting his body so that his weapon made contact.

He felt the obsidian blade slice across Anyan's ribcage and chest, growling low in his throat when Anyan turned away at the last moment, causing him to miss his heart. Unsa's feral snarl caused the winged creatures to take flight as he saw that Anyan was merely wounded. Blood ran in rivulets from the cut, but it wasn't enough. Nothing short of Anyan's death would satisfy him.

He blocked the flying debris with his forearm, rolling instantly to his right as he barely escaped a deathblow from Anyan's bone knife. He faced his adversary again, but this time Anyan surprised him by flinging dirt into his face.

With his free hand, he wiped his burning eyes until they were clear, but he saw no more of Anyan. The moment that Unsa was distracted his adversary had taken the opportunity to run headlong into the jungle. In an instant, the jungle had swallowed him whole, allowing him to disappear just as quickly as he had arrived.

As Unsa returned to the clearing, his focus was absolute, but the prone form of the young woman immediately captured his attention. He glanced at her distractedly, pulled between the desire to chase after Anyan and the need to help the unconscious woman at his feet.

Black hair obscured her features, but then she moaned and shifted in place, stopping him in his tracks.

A harsh breath left his lungs the moment that he recognized the woman's face. "Suyan?"

The Saika Village bustled with activity, but no one was too busy with their daily tasks to ignore Unsa as he walked through the village carrying an unknown woman in his arms. The village rested at the foothills of the Great Mountain, sheltered by its craggy peaks and towering height. Each lodge had been constructed with painstaking care, using the bounty of the jungle to develop sturdy shelters that would withstand the seasonal rains, heat, and humidity.

As he walked, Unsa's face was a mask of calm, but inside his stomach churned. The last time that he had seen Suyan she had been a girl of fourteen seasons, barely budding into womanhood. Now she was a young woman, and somehow she had come to harm at Anyan's hands, he was certain of it. Carrying her wasn't a burden, although he jostled her slightly to shift her more comfortably in his arms.

"Unsa, what happened?"

He glanced over to see Orchid striding toward him. As the leader of the Saika Village, she deserved his respect and consideration despite the circumstances. Without breaking stride, he acknowledged Orchid with a nod of his head. He would need to speak with her later about the dire implications surrounding his dream, but for the time being his concern was for Suyan. "I need Lark's help."

Orchid's crestfallen expression barely registered as she immediately led the way to her sister's lodge. He hurried after her, aware that the Saika villagers were crowding in behind him. Any newcomer was an oddity to be watched carefully until their position and status was known.

"He's brought a blood moon girl into our village."

Unsa barely heard the frightened murmurings. The moon had been blood red last night, and there were those that found omens in many things. Suyan's appearance at the edge of their village after a red moon wouldn't sit well with the Saika people.

"The shaman has come down from the cloud forest with a blood moon girl."

Word spread like an unstoppable fire, traveling from mouth to mouth as Unsa lengthened his strides, reaching Lark's lodge within a matter of moments. Orchid scratched on the entrance flap of her sister's lodge, and Lark's singsong voice called for her to enter. She ushered Unsa ahead of her, before turning to address their people in a calm, authoritative voice.

"Everything is well in hand. Go about your day, and I will speak to you as soon as my sister has had time to help the woman."

Unsa ducked under the lodge entrance with Suyan in his arms. Lark's eyes widened in surprise, but she recovered quickly, beckoning her son forward. The boy sat silently beside a small fire that lit the inside of the lodge. At nearly six seasons of age, he was the image of Lark's husband, River. He took a moment to study the boy, noticing that Stone's eyes, nose, and ears were just like his father's, along with the cut of his jaw. A dark cap of black hair had been sheared above his eyebrows, but allowed to hang long across his neck and shoulders, while bright, inquisitive eyes noticed every detail.

"Stone, go find your father." Lark's quiet request brought about an immediate reaction from her son.

He ran past Unsa with a quick grin, eager to accomplish the important task that his mother had given him.

"What happened?" Lark asked as Unsa laid the woman to rest upon her sleeping blankets.

"I found her at the edge of the jungle." Unsa's dark eyebrows drew together in concern. "She burns as if there is fire in her blood."

Lark's hands moved fluidly over the young woman, sensing the sickness within her even as Unsa described the problem. "You have learned many of the ways of healing, Unsa."

"Yes."

"Yet you brought her to me."

"Don't you recognize her?"

Lark was busy examining the woman's body for injury as she ran her hands gently over the small, whip thin welts that were angry and red in places. "Someone beat her." She glanced at Unsa and his features tightened, and then she brushed long strands of hair away from the woman's face, looked closely at her features. "Suyan."

Orchid entered the lodge, drawing their attention as Lark removed Suyan's palm frond skirt. Fully naked, Suyan moaned, tossing her head from side to side as Lark tried to soothe her. She caught sight of the caked and drying blood on Suyan's inner thighs, and she glanced at Unsa, suddenly aware that like the men of her village he would find a woman's bleeding to be something unclean.

However, Unsa surprised her, as a shaman and dreamer he had taken the time to learn from her over the seasons, and he didn't hesitate at the sight of blood.

"Her belly is loose."

His quiet comment only solidified Lark's growing suspicion. "She has given birth recently."

"Childbirth fever." Orchid supplied, surprising them both.

Lark silently nodded, checking Suyan's eyes, mouth, and gums with a critical eye. She sighed as she considered the countless women that were stricken with sickness shortly after giving birth. Over the seasons, their village had lost enough women to illness after childbirth to know that it could strike at any time.

"Lark?" Orchid leaned closer. "Is it really our cousin, Suyan?"

"Yes." Lark answered, distracted by Orchid's presence. She needed to focus her full attention on the ill young woman. She couldn't allow emotion or anything else to cloud her judgment. She lifted a clay bowl from the edge of the small fire, using a water soaked hide to wet Suyan's lips, wincing at the cracked and peeling skin. "I need fresh water."

Orchid stooped low, grabbing an empty waterskin as she backed out of the lodge.

Unsa shifted, his brow furrowed with concern. "What will you do for her?"

"I will give her willow bark tea to bring her fever down. I will make certain that she's clean and comfortable and determine the cause of her bleeding." Lark placed a padding of moss under

Suyan's hips, gently urging her up as Suyan murmured incoherently. "You are safe now, Suyan."

"Lark?" Suyan's eyes fluttered open as she struggled to speak.

"You're safe, Suyan." Lark repeated, leaning over her younger cousin. "You recently gave birth to a child."

Tears pooled in Suyan's eyes, "My son died."

Unsa shifted in position drawing Suyan's gaze. He stared at her grief stricken features for the longest time before looking at Lark. "Tell me what you need, and I'll see to it."

Unsa waited outside of Lark's lodge as she worked to make Suyan more comfortable. When they were alone, she asked him if he wanted to remain with her while she checked Suyan over carefully. Declining with a shake of his head, he left quickly only to stand outside of her lodge in a daze as the Saika people milled about, keeping up the pretense of working while remaining completely aware of their surroundings.

"Unsa."

He turned as he spied River walking toward him with his hand on his son's shoulder. Lark's brother, Sappa, and his friend, Pago, hurried toward him and he moved forward, acknowledging the concern on their faces.

"Sappa and Pago, I hope you haven't gotten into any mischief since I've been away." Both young men gave him wry glances, neither willing to deny or confirm his suspicions.

"Unsa, what happened?" Sappa was the first to ask. "We heard that you brought a sick woman into the village."

"Lark is tending to an injured young woman."

"Is it true that the woman is Suyan?" River asked.

"Yes," Unsa said. "It appears that she was left at the edge of our village." He locked eyes with River, silently letting him know that there was more to be said.

"Lark will do everything that she can for her."

"I know."

"Is there anything that we can do?" Sappa asked.

"We'll help Lark as much as we can." River said. "For the time being, you could help Orchid gather fresh water and bring it back to our lodge."

Sappa and Pago quickly ran off to do as they were bid, and Unsa quickly described his fight with Anyan to River.

"I told Lark that I would gather a few of the plants and roots that she might need."

River grunted, watching Unsa with keen eyes. He noticed the blowpipe that Unsa carried over one shoulder and the unique, obsidian hunting knife strapped to his waist. "Were you hunting when you found the young woman?"

It was Unsa's turn to grunt noncommittally. He knew that he was unlike the other men that were chosen as dreamers and mystics; he had chosen a different path in his youth by hounding River until he trained him to walk as more than a hunter. River had made him into a warrior, teaching him everything that he knew.

"Unsa, you don't have to remain alone in the cloud forest." River's voice was low, but unerringly kind. "You're welcome within this village at any time."

"Our people fear me." Unsa's voice was clear, but his eyes were dark with an emotion that River couldn't name. "You should not enter your lodge until your wife purifies it and invites you inside. I must go."

River stood with his son as Unsa walked away, casting his gaze forward. He knew that Unsa would return with the requested items, but he was still surprised by how the villagers cleared a path for the young man that had once been a frightened boy not much older than his son.

"What will we do, Father?" Stone asked.

"Your mother is renowned for her skill with healing." River answered, looking into Stone's inquisitive face. "If anyone can help Suyan, it's Lark. In the meantime, we will keep busy and wait."

CHAPTER FOUR

Lark bathed Suyan's fevered brow. Once word spread that the blood moon girl was indeed ill, the Saika Villagers kept their distance. Orchid had returned with several roots and plants given to her by Unsa, reluctantly entering her sister's lodge.

"Will she die?"

Lark's eyes flashed impatiently as she glanced at her sister. "Do not speak such things where she can hear you, Orchid."

Her sister bit her lip with a petulant frown. "She sleeps."

"She mourns the loss of her son." Lark responded. "She is grieving, just as any mother would be. We don't know why her son died or how long she has been ill. I only know that she gave birth recently."

Lark had removed a darkened piece of what she suspected was afterbirth from Suyan's body. Somehow the young woman had survived this long without succumbing to the fever raging within her body.

"What does her sadness over her son have to do with whether or not she will live?"

Lark tried to stymie her irritation with her sister. At nineteen seasons of age, Orchid possessed a dark beauty, with sun burnished skin and dark sooty lashes that framed her onyx eyes. Her thick black hair hung in infinitely small braids to her waist, swaying with every motion, but Lark saw that Orchid's eyes were guileless, and she sighed wearily.

"The will to live sometimes brings us through things that we might otherwise never survive."

Orchid smirked knowingly, "But isn't it your healing ability that will help Suyan?"

"The plants and roots found in the Great Forest are good for healing," Lark answered. "But it is Suyan's will to live that will see her through this illness. Her spirit is suffering under the brunt of terrible grief. I can see it whenever she opens her eyes."

Orchid raised a hand as if to touch their cousin, and Lark waited with a spark of hope growing in her heart. "You two were once very close."

"I killed for her." Orchid's open gaze disappeared as memories of a darker time came back to her and she was a young girl again, stricken by the horrifying thought that she would have to take the life of an Agali warrior if she wanted to live. In the end, she chose life over death. Shaking her head to dispel the memories, she stood, ready to flee.

"Orchid," Lark called after her sister, concern shadowing her normally bright brown eyes.

"I must calm the hearts of our people and then I will return."

Lark watched Orchid leave and she was left with the memories of the many girls that had been taken from their families and villages by the Agali warriors. They were both left with invisible scars even though Orchid and Suyan had been rescued from their terrifying ordeal. Lark understood why Orchid was at times secretive and pensive, while Suyan had been deeply grieved by the subsequent illness and death of Pira, the young girl that she had befriended during her captivity. Lark shook her head, determined to leave the past where it belonged. She focused her attention upon her young cousin as Suyan fought for her life.

Unsa wasn't surprised that the Saika Village fairly hummed with activity. After finding Orchid and giving her a basket full of the various plants and roots that Lark had requested, he approached the village fire circle. The presence of River, Sappa, and Stone drew him forward as nothing else could.

Sappa glanced up, aware that Unsa wanted to speak with him as he tilted his head toward the jungle.

"Unsa, is there something that you need?" Sappa asked.

He weighed his words before speaking, "You will become the leader of this village by the time of the new moon."

"Yes." Sappa's voice brimmed with excitement. "I have made my first kill, I have become a man in the eyes of my people, and I am ready to walk as their leader."

"You're barely fifteen seasons."

"I am ready." Sappa countered. "My sister thought to talk me out of taking on the responsibility that she has shouldered for far too long."

"Lark?" Unsa questioned.

"No," Sappa's grin was infectious. "Orchid."

Unsa nodded. "That might not be a bad thing, Sappa. You have much growing to do. You could enjoy more time with your friends, more time to be a boy."

At this Sappa scowled. "I am a man, Unsa."

There was silence between them as Sappa's declaration resounded in the air. Unsa shifted toward the youth, watching him carefully. "I take it that River has continued to train you?"

"He is the best at training the other men. I'm grateful for his direction and help."

"But have you learned the warrior's way from him?"

Sappa sighed. "He says that I have more to learn. Orchid says that I need more time and now you question whether or not I should become the leader of this village."

"I have never questioned it." Unsa said as he caught sight of Orchid lingering just outside of the men's fire circle. She speared him with a glare that beckoned him to her side, but he finished his thought. "You will take your place as our future leader when the time is right."

Leaving Sappa to contemplate his words, he approached Orchid. He wasn't surprised to see that she wore the full raiment of her standing as the current leader of the Saika Village. It was common to see her clothed in a woven dress that clung to her figure, falling just above her knees. Her jade jewelry sparkled as she raised a hand to brush a stray strand of hair away from her oval face.

"What ails you, Unsa?" Orchid asked without greeting him. "Why have you come from the heights of the cloud forest?"

He gestured for her to walk alongside him as he led her away from the prying eyes and ears of their village. It was a long time before he spoke again. "I am uneasy. I have had a terrible dream."

Orchid's face blanched, but she took the seat that Unsa indicated, sitting gracefully upon an overturned log at the edge of the jungle. Overhead the sun was setting, finding a place to rest while the moon rose. Orchid usually enjoyed the sight of the clear blue sky and the varied sounds of the jungle, which were as familiar to her as the sound of her own voice. However, Unsa's dreams were legendary and could either bring about good tidings or bad omens of things to come.

"You know the ways of the spirit world best, Unsa." Orchid swallowed. "Whatever you have to say will affect the way that I lead our people. Tell me your dream."

"I don't always understand the ways of the spirit world, Orchid."

"But you're a shaman, a dreamer…"

Unsa held up a forestalling hand. "I was born with a keen intuition that often reveals itself through dreams. I am a man that was chosen, just as you have been chosen. What is given to me is not mine, just as these people are not yours. It is mine to protect, mine to defend, and my burden to bear." Unsa's dark eyes narrowed. "Perhaps one day you will understand what I mean, but for now you should know that I have come to you with a warning."

Orchid swallowed, uncertain whether or not she truly wished to hear whatever it was that Unsa wanted to share. Villages had fallen and crumbled based upon Unsa's inspired dreams.

Desperate for a reprieve, Orchid interrupted Unsa with a pleading glance. "Tell me the story of how you became a dreamer."

Unsa hesitated, but her expression asked for understanding. "You know the story well."

"I wish to hear it again."

Unsa sighed, "I was chosen when I was slightly younger than your brother. I had the same dream seven nights in a row, and I eventually told my mother and father about the dreams."

"What did they say?"

"My father consulted a wise man, someone that knows the jungle and the ways of the spirit world. He was told that I had been chosen to be the dreamer belonging to my people."

"Our people."

"Yes."

Unsa nodded, continuing his story. "I ran away because I was afraid. I didn't want to be different from the other boys. I wanted to be just like them, and I thought that if I could learn to control my fear I would eventually be able to bear the responsibility given to me."

"And did you?" Orchid's tone was breathless. "Did you learn to control your fear?"

Unsa took a long time answering. He didn't want to frighten Orchid, but as the leader of the Saika Village, he needed her to heed his dream. "I learned once long ago that fear is the thing that breeds courage."

A smile touched Orchid's lips, "River often says the same thing."

"It's true."

Unsa and Orchid sat in silence for a time, each lost in their own thoughts. All around them the jungle frothed with activity, cloaking them in a cocoon of clamorous sound.

"I'm ready," Orchid suddenly spoke. "I'm ready to hear whatever it is that you dreamed."

"My dream was interrupted, but I saw enough to know that something terrible is coming." Unsa's eyes were piercing even in the semi-darkness. "Your brother will be betrayed before he ever becomes the leader of this village."

Lark rested outside of her lodge, surrounded by her husband's strong arms as her son slept nearby. The weather was clear and warm, perfect for a good night's rest, but she was wide awake, staring into the darkness as her thoughts whirled.

"What if Unsa's dream is true?"

Orchid had returned to the village fire, summoning River and Ransa to her side with a hand sign taught to the elite warriors belonging to her husband.

River pulled his wife closer, comforted by the touch and feel of her smooth skin even as he comforted her. "Be at ease, Lark. We must remember that Unsa's dreams don't always happen exactly as he remembers them. Your brother is protected by the men of this village. He's sleeping peacefully right now in Ransa and Yama's lodge."

At the mention of her mother, tears formed in Lark's eyes. "My mother has already lost her children once." She remembered the seasons of separation that had taken her and Orchid away from Yama, leaving them in the care of their beloved grandmother. Their reunion had been the changing point in her life, but the time apart had taken its toll on Yama. "She can't go through the loss of a child again, River."

"You and Orchid were returned to her," River soothed. "Remember her joy upon being reunited with her daughters."

"I remember."

"Then you should know that a mother's love is an enduring love, but she won't lose Sappa."

"How can you be so certain?" Lark reached back to stroke River's hair away from his face. She loved his sharp features, even when they were stern and unmoving.

"I know that your brother will be fine because I'm here." He pressed a kiss to his wife's brow, wishing that they were ensconced in the privacy of their lodge so that he could remove her grass skirt and look his fill at her smooth skin and womanly curves. "I won't let anything happen to the people that I have sworn to protect."

Lark nodded, inhaling deeply as the fear that she had carried in her chest like a burning stone began to dissipate.

"How is Suyan?"

"She's resting, but I won't know more until she's awake and able to talk to me." Lark had given her water and broth to drink, rubbing salve over the small whip thin lashes that covered the girl's body. "River, someone beat her shortly after she gave birth."

He grunted, but she could feel the coiled tension in his body. "Did she tell you how her mother fares?"

"She wasn't alert enough to tell me much of anything." Lark had spoken to her mother and answered the same question when asked by Yama. "I can only hope that my mother's sister is alive and well."

"We will have more answers tomorrow. Tonight, you and I will watch over our son and Suyan. We will rest and face the worries of the future when the sun rises."

Lark smiled. She thought of teasing River about his high handed ways, but she couldn't find the desire to spar with him verbally. Instead, she leaned into the quiet assurance that he readily offered, relying upon his strength without reservation.

Two days passed without any sign of Suyan, and Anyan seethed with anger and betrayal as each moment extended into the next.

"I told you that she would leave you."

He spun in place, surprised to see Challa sitting on a log, watching him with an amused expression upon his face.

"She hasn't left me, I brought her here." Anger caused a bitter taste to form in his mouth as he spoke, and he stroked a hand over the shallow cut on his chest. He had done what he could to treat the injury, but he needed someone else to see to his care. "I have no choice but to return to the Agali Village. With their help, I can see to it that Unsa is killed, and Suyan will be returned to me."

"You have lost again, Anyan." Challa laughed harshly. *"First the Saika Village sends you away, injured and alone. What makes*

you think that the leader of the Agali Village will bend to your will?"

"I am their shaman." Anyan's chest swelled as he spoke. While few villages had the privilege of caring for their own shaman, he had recognized the need within the Agali Village, and by guile and cunning, he had filled that need. "They will listen to me."

"No one will listen."

Challa's voice was eerily sad, and he looked over to see that his brother's smooth and youthful face had morphed into the gruesome face of death.

"You're nothing, Anyan."

"No!" Anyan shouted.

"You're no one."

Anyan stood to his full height, taking a threatening step toward his brother, but Challa turned away, blending into the shadows of the jungle. With a determined grimace, Anyan regained control of himself and turned toward the Agali Village. He didn't need Challa's permission to seek his future in whatever way he saw fit.

"I will have everything that I desire." Anyan vowed, almost daring his brother to return and tell him otherwise. The only response was the natural sounds that rose up on all sides, making him feel utterly alone despite his surroundings. He reasoned that if he hurried, he would find shelter overnight and reach the Agali Village at sunrise. Within a few strides, Anyan disappeared into the gathering darkness.

Orchid and Unsa stood together overlooking the Saika Village with River at their side. Silently, Ransa joined them, casting a questioning glance toward all three. They remained quiet, lost in their own thoughts as the sun rose to bathe the jungle in gossamer light, displaying brilliant shades of amber coupled with ochre.

"Anyan is crafty." Unsa was the first to speak. "He is one to be watched, but he is not a man to be given a second chance."

"We will watch Sappa carefully, but Unsa, we need you." Orchid replied. "This village needs you."

River cleared his throat, meeting Unsa's gaze directly. "If you go off hunting Anyan, you might walk right into whatever trap he has laid out for you."

"I'll be cautious."

River growled low in his throat, a clear warning that Unsa decided to ignore.

"Sappa will become the leader of this village very soon," Ransa inserted. "The men are planning a hunt for the celebration that will take place when he is recognized as our leader. My wife and Lark have organized the women to prepare various meals that will satisfy all. You should have a part in the leadership ceremony."

Unsa stood undecided. Everything within him said that he should continue his search for Anyan and end what he had begun long ago. He couldn't help but think that Anyan might pose the greatest danger to Sappa.

"Tell me that you will offer a blessing during the hunting ceremony." Orchid made it clear that her words were a command instead of a request.

"I will stay long enough to see what Suyan has to say about her time with Anyan." Unsa replied. "And I will offer my help at the hunting ceremony."

Orchid nodded and River's shoulders relaxed marginally. "Perhaps you can join us on the hunt. It has been too long since you ran through the jungle with us."

Unsa's expression didn't waver. "I would like nothing more, but you will have enough support without me."

"Unsa," Ransa drew his attention. "I want you to know that Yama and I understand that you were only trying to protect Sappa from danger by sharing your dream, but we have decided not to tell him. We are concerned that it would only frighten him."

"You are his parents," Unsa replied, meeting Ransa's gaze. "It is your decision." The older man seemed relieved that he thought as much, but he wasn't finished. "Sappa has become a man in word and deed. Perhaps you should consider sharing this with him."

"No." Orchid said, bringing all eyes back to her. "I think it's best to keep Sappa in the dark until we discover the threat. Why ruin his joy at such a pivotal time in his life?"

"River!" Lark's piercing cry caused River to pivot as his wife appeared on the rise leading to their village. Her flushed face and stricken expression spoke of an unknown calamity. "All of you must come quickly! Several of the adults and children are ill."

CHAPTER FIVE

The Agali Village

Anyan enjoyed the comforts provided by dwelling within a large settlement. Ayusha had been the first to welcome him upon his return, seeing to his injuries with her own hands as he told her of his travels. He kept his interest in Suyan a secret that he would share only with his brother, and he delighted over the cordial deference shown to him by the former Agali leader's wife.

"Anyan," Ayusha's clear, crisp tone drew his undivided attention. "If there is anything else that you need, please let the serving women know."

Her reverent smile made it clear that she believed in his shamanistic power, and she held his ability to commune with the spirit world in high regard, likewise encouraging the Agali people to believe in him as well.

"I will see to it that you're treated with care." Ayusha soothed the ire that he felt over his current circumstances.

"And I am at your disposal." Anyan replied, knowing full well that the surviving Agali villagers would be lost without someone to commune with the spirit world on their behalf. With the fall of their village from their former lofty position, they had lost many of their men, including their trusted mystics.

It was by chance that he had stumbled upon them during his journey through the jungle as an outcast. He had been badly injured by men from the Saika Village, and Ayusha had taken it upon herself to see that he was waited upon with care until he was well.

"Anyan, is there anything else that you need?" Ayusha waited for an answer, smiling coyly as his gaze skimmed over her lithe frame.

"Not at this time," he dismissed her along with the serving women, glancing down at his body with growing remorse. Since being sent as an outcast from the Saika Village his flaccid manhood no longer responded to the sunrise, nor did he have a physical response to Ayusha's nearness or her intoxicating touch.

At forty-six seasons of age, he bemoaned the loss of his former prowess, certain that his hopes for the future were outside of his reach until he had come upon Suyan. She had stirred something within him, even with her pregnant belly and cumbersome gait. Unbeknownst to the people of Chota's band, he had hidden in the forest and watched her for many days. He remembered her from his time spent with the Saika Village, many seasons ago.

He would have gladly taken her and the child that she carried if her mother's husband would have allowed it. But from careful observation, he learned that Chota would prove to be unreasonable. The Wuyari leader would have arranged a marriage within their village for Suyan once her child was born healthy and whole. If not for the calamity that had befallen the young woman, she would already be another man's wife. She was barely more than a girl the first time that Anyan had seen her, and he had wanted her from that moment until now.

"I always get my way in the end, Challa." Anyan turned, expecting to see his brother, only to be disappointed as he realized that he was alone. Fists clenched with determination, he braced himself against the empty, hollow feeling that was always with him unless Challa was nearby. "It doesn't matter if you've gone away for now, I know that you'll be there when I need you." A cold smile graced his lips. "You always are."

The Saika Village

"I don't understand how so many could have been stricken with sickness." Orchid's eyes swam with tears as she shook her head back and forth. Sappa placed one hand upon her shoulder in a show of silent support.

"Many are blaming the blood moon girl," Pago replied with an unapologetic glance toward Sappa.

"Don't call her by that name," Sappa snapped, leaving Orchid's side to stand face to face against his friend. "She's my cousin."

Pago quickly bristled, scowling in irritation. "I can call her anything I want."

"Enough bickering!" Orchid's sharp voice startled both young men. "We should focus on those that are sick. Lark and Unsa are doing everything they can to help. You should both do the same."

"What can we do, Orchid?" Sappa asked.

Orchid smiled kindly as she ruffled his hair, much as she had when he was only a boy. She spared a glance toward Pago who looked at her with an expectant expression. Her brother and his friend already showed the promise of the strong men that they would one day become. "They'll need fresh water, and perhaps Pago gather a few of the women together to make a rich bone broth. We will need enough to feed several people."

"Will that help?" Sappa asked.

"It can't hurt." Orchid cleared her throat, unwilling to mention that Lark had informed her that a bone broth might help fight off the illness. She reasoned that it didn't matter where the information came from as long as the results were beneficial to their village. "We will find our way through this together, Sappa. Go with your friend, and remember to remain within the village boundaries."

As Sappa and Pago left, Orchid watched her brother with sad eyes. They were so close to the leadership ceremony, and they didn't need anything to take away from the occasion that would finally assuage her mother's grief over the loss of their father.

Sappa would be protected by the people of the village, even though he sought to find a way to protect them. She could only hope that Lark and Unsa could find a way to battle the unfamiliar sickness that had caused several to become ill.

She glanced over her shoulder, surprised to find that she was alone for the time being. The forest beckoned and she took a few hesitating steps toward it as she tried to determine whether or not it would be safe to venture away. It was true that she had warned Sappa against doing the very same thing, but she was capable of taking care of herself.

Biting her lip as she made her decision, she took the last fateful steps away from her village, disappearing into the depths of the jungle without looking back. Once she was well hidden by lush green foliage and trees so tall that she couldn't see the sky through the green canopy overhead, she ran toward her intended destination.

Orchid came to a stop with her heart pounding in her chest as she glanced about. The person that she sought had to be here. She waited with bated breath, suddenly aware of her own vulnerability and uncertain about her decision.

Unsa went from lodge to lodge, visiting the villagers that had become ill so suddenly. In each lodge it was the same, one or more family members had been stricken with bouts of vomiting, loose bowels and fever. The people blamed the blood moon girl for their sickness. *Suyan.*

"She isn't to blame. Her illness is a result of a recent birth." Unsa answered one man who sought to cause trouble as others gathered close to listen in. "She lost a child."

Suyan's symptoms weren't the same as the Saika villagers that were ill, but he left that unsaid. Many of the villagers would be shocked to know that a woman who was bleeding had been allowed inside of their healer's lodge. There was a special lodge for the women of the village whenever their flowering time was upon them. Women would disappear for three to seven days or longer, reappearing when all signs of their flowering passed.

Several of the men believed that their arms would weaken at a pivotal moment in battle or during the hunt if they came into contact with a woman while she bled. The disparity in their beliefs came from many seasons spent scattered throughout the jungle, living apart from the people of their shared blood.

"Suyan once belonged to this village."

"But no longer." One of the men supplied. "Her mother chose to seek a mate outside of our village, and she took her daughter with her."

"Unsa."

Lark's voice stopped him from responding. He turned to face her, suddenly aware that his fists were clenched and his chest heaved with anger. "What is it?"

"Suyan is awake. Perhaps you would like to speak with her?"

Unsa nodded, leaving the village fire for the relative peace of Lark's lodge. River stood just outside of the lodge watching over his son who had also been brought low by illness. "How is he?"

"Stone is strong." River's jaw clenched as he looked at his sleeping son. "His mother says that we must wait and see how he responds to the healing brew that she gave him."

Unsa nodded once, silently willing strength into the child. He knew how much Stone meant to River and Lark. In the six seasons that they had been married, they hadn't conceived another child.

He started forward, but River stopped him with a hand on his shoulder. "If there was anything that you could do for him, you would do it, wouldn't you?"

Unbidden, pain flashed through Unsa's spirit. It was always the same. He wasn't like everyone else because of his dreams and his position as their shaman. Even though he felt isolated and set apart from the others, he couldn't blame River for asking for his help when the life of his son was at risk. "Your wife taught me everything I know about healing."

Despite his calm assertion, he noticed that River didn't move a muscle. "If there was anything that I could do for your son, I would do it."

Satisfied, River finally nodded and stepped aside as Unsa ducked under the lodge entrance without another word spoken between them.

A hand snaked out, grasping Orchid about the waist as she barely managed to stifle a scream. "Carrum!"

She recognized the broad set of his shoulders and his muscular build as he stepped in front of her. Before she could say anything further, his mouth brushed over her lips, and a quiet moan escaped her throat. He took full advantage, pulling her body flush against his as he dipped his head to gain full access to her mouth. He bit teasingly at her bottom lip before pressing for more.

The flush of pain and pleasure completely overwhelmed Orchid's senses and she melted against him. Enraptured by the exciting thrum of satisfaction that she felt when her fingers swept over his stomach muscles and they trembled beneath her touch.

"You risked everything by coming here to meet me."

"I know." Orchid's eyelashes hid her gaze from him until he raised her chin with one hand. "But it's worth the risk, Carrum. I only wish my family knew you the way that I do."

Carrum's tone was mild, but his expression hardened. "They would never accept me, Orchid."

"You have been my only solace, my only companion, and confidant during such a difficult time."

"It doesn't have to be so difficult. Can't you see that?"

Orchid shook her head. "I only wish that there was a way that we could be together."

Carrum hesitated. He knew that she wanted him to tell her that they could be together any time they chose, she had only to come to him. However, that wasn't the case. "My village would never accept you, Orchid. Not in this way."

"Then how?" Tears brightened Orchid's eyes as she looked upon the man that she was denied. Carrum was everything that the young men of her village were not and could never be. He was strong and wise, and he had always supported her decisions.

"Orchid, we've been over this before. Your warriors brought about the destruction of my entire village. They overran the high places that we claimed for ourselves." Carrum's voice thickened. "They killed my father."

"Carrum–" Any objection that she had died on her lips as she noticed the glistening sheen of unshed tears in his eyes. She brought her lips to his chest and neck, kissing him desperately in hopes of easing his pain. "I lost my father and mother in different ways, Carrum. I understand your pain."

"But your mother was returned to you and your father died long before you ever truly knew him."

His words stung. Her relationship with her mother wasn't what she had hoped it would be. She had never even imagined that she would see her mother again, let alone come to live within the same village. Over the seasons, Yama had tried to strengthen their relationship, but they were different, vastly different.

"I'm sorry, Orchid." Carrum cupped her face in both hands, inhaling the fragrant scent of the flowers that adorned her hair. He kissed her again, reveling in the way that she leaned into him, giving of herself in a way that communicated her need. He knew that he could take her, mate with her in secret, binding her to him forever, but for the time being, he held his lust deep inside, refusing to allow it free reign. His lips grazed her breasts and his hands encircled her waist, roaming over the lush swells of her hips. "I want to make you my woman in every way, Orchid." He panted with need as she opened her passion filled eyes to stare at him with rapt fascination. "I'm desperate with the need of you."

Buoyed by his admission and his passionate restraint, Orchid smiled. "I feel the same way."

"I know that you do." He kissed her again, this time savoring the feel of her lips and tongue. "I want you to be my wife, Orchid. I want to show everyone, my people and yours, that we belong together."

"They will say that you can't possibly love me." She forced the words out, unwilling to bring him further pain, but desperate to make him understand. "You held a knife to my throat in front of the men of my village and threatened to kill me." Orchid's eyes brightened with tears at the memory.

"I never would have harmed you." Carrum's voice held anger over the reminder of the past. "You know that I was desperate to save my mother's life. I would have said anything to get them to let us go without harm."

"I know." Orchid hugged herself, missing his embrace as he backed away from her.

"Do you?" Carrum's dark eyes narrowed as he grabbed her arms, tempering his strength when she winced. "No one has ever meant as much to me, nor will they ever mean as much to me as you do." He released her as he once again moved outside of her reach. "At times, I wonder if you truly love me or if you simply seek a diversion while your village prepares to make a child their leader."

Her sharp gasp gave away her anguish. "No. It isn't true. My village suffers even as we speak. There are several that are sick." Seeing that his interest was piqued, Orchid hurried to continue. "A girl came to our village and then the next day several children and older ones became ill." When his stony expression didn't soften, she clung to him. "I love you, Carrum. Only you."

Carrum hesitated, lured by the apology that he read upon Orchid's face. "My mother is pressuring me to take a wife. What will I tell her the next time that she asks me why she doesn't have any grandchildren of her own? How can I face another day, another night without you?"

The familiar agony pierced Orchid's heart. She felt the same way.

She loved Carrum and despite everything that had occurred in the past, he had proven himself to be loyal and true. He was the one that she wanted to spend the rest of her life with, and she wouldn't have anyone else. The only thing that kept them from a shared future together was the past.

"There is something that I need to say Orchid." Carrum's jaw hardened as she watched him searchingly, unable to hide her concern. "I can't meet you like this anymore. I risk losing the respect of my people each time that I journey away from them to meet you. Like you, I am the leader of my people. I am the one that they look to when food is scarce, when disaster befalls my village, or enemies threaten our wellbeing. They believe in their hearts that I am a direct descendant not only of Talud, but of our sun god, Agali."

"Carrum, please…" Brought to the edge of reason by his sudden decision, she struggled to speak over the tears clogging her throat. "I can't lose you. There must be a way for us to be together. There must be something that I can do or say that would allow us to become husband and wife."

Carrum hesitated, and Orchid's breath feathered in and out in the silence.

"Carrum?" Orchid pleaded. "Tell me what to do, and I'll do it. I vow it on my father's memory."

CHAPTER SIX

Suyan sipped from the clay bowl that Lark pressed upon her. She was almost too stunned to believe that she was back within the village belonging to her mother and father. It was difficult to believe that the Saika Village was also the village of her birth. So much had changed since her father's death and her mother's remarriage.

At a sound from the entrance, Lark called out in welcome and Suyan shifted tensely. A dark shadow filled the entranceway and then Unsa entered, watching her expectantly.

She barely withheld a gasp of recognition at the sight of him. His face had filled out from the slender features that she remembered, and he was much taller. He no longer wore a thin stick through the septum of his nose, but his chin had been pierced by three hollow bones, which appeared to be as much a part of him as his flesh and blood. But if anything was different about Unsa, it was his eyes. They no longer held the familiar edge of fear that had stalked him in his youth. Instead, his eyes were stalwart and resolute. She shivered as he focused his full attention upon her, never once breaking contact as Lark backed away.

She wanted to tell Lark not to leave her, but she sensed a shifting of power between the pair. Lark was the healer of their village, a privileged position in and of itself, but Unsa was their dreamer, their shaman. A kernel of fear built in her stomach, and she pressed both palms against her belly, unconsciously reminding herself of her loss.

"I am sorry for the death of your son." Unsa's words startled her; it was as if he heard her thoughts.

"Thank you."

"You were brought here by Anyan." Unsa knelt at her side, taking a position that should have made her feel more comfortable, yet it didn't. His very closeness was threatening, even if it wasn't his intention to frighten her. It was like sitting next to a wild animal of the jungle while waiting for it to pounce or turn away. Suyan had the feeling that Unsa would never turn away.

Since Unsa was already aware of the circumstances that had brought her within the boundaries of the Saika Village she saw no reason to qualify his statement with an answer.

"How?"

Her eyes flew to his, meeting his gaze almost against her will. "What do you mean?"

"The last time that we saw you, your mother was by your side, and you were both going to join her new lifemate's band."

"Chota," she supplied the name with a grimace of distaste.

"He still lives." Unsa knew it to be true by the way that Suyan used Chota's name. If he had perished then she wouldn't have spoken his name at all. "What about your mother?"

Tears filled Suyan's eyes as she nodded. "She was alive the last time that I saw her."

"And Anyan?" Unsa asked. "Why were you with him?"

Suyan battled tears as she thought of her child, lost, cold, and alone. She didn't know why she was still alive when all she wanted to do was die so that she could be with him. Unsa stared at her without blinking, waiting for her answer.

"They have said that a sickness has come to this village, is that so?"

"Yes."

Unsa's response condemned her, and she swallowed the urge to retch. "Then I am to blame."

Surprise flitted across his stoic expression. "How so?"

"I'm cursed, Unsa." Suyan's tears fell relentlessly as she choked out the words. "I killed my son, and now I have brought death to the Saika Village."

Lark had been summoned to soothe Suyan when the young woman continued to weep inconsolably. Her sister entered the lodge without waiting for permission, and Lark saw that Orchid was stricken to learn that Stone was also ill.

"Where were you?" Lark asked her sister. She kept one eye on Suyan who slept fitfully, even after drinking a mixture of chamomile and valerian root.

Orchid stared at her sister. "I went to visit the sick."

"Impossible." Lark said, "I was with those that are sick."

"Well perhaps I arrived just after you left." Orchid shifted uncomfortably, aware that her sister was truly angry with her. "How is Stone?"

"He seems to be responding to rest, and he's finally keeping his food down."

"Good."

Orchid's relief was evident, and Lark thought about how wonderful Orchid was with her son. It was obvious that Orchid loved Stone and spent as much time with him as possible.

"Lark, I searched for Sappa, but I couldn't find him." Orchid stroked both hands over her hair, bringing the long mass to hang over her breasts as she waited for her sister to answer.

Lark rubbed her brow in frustration. "Sappa, Pago, and many of the other young men are preparing for a hunt in preparation for the leadership ceremony."

"Of course," Orchid's smile was forced. "I have been distracted by the illness that has plagued our village, and the arrival of the blood moon girl."

"You shouldn't call her by that name. She is our cousin," Lark reminded her, mindful of the strain in her voice. "You two were once very close."

"Suyan has much to answer for Lark."

"What do you mean?"

Orchid frowned. "Our people were well and healthy before her arrival. Many of the villagers blame her for the sickness that has befallen us."

"Her illness came from childbirth."

"Who can say?" Orchid shook her head. "Is it true she told Unsa that she was cursed?"

Unwilling to answer, Lark pressed her lips together, relieved when River ducked under the entrance flap of their lodge. One glance from him soothed her spirits immensely, and her face brightened.

He pressed a kiss to her lips, inhaling the scent of lavender as he met his wife's eyes. "How is Stone?"

"He's fast asleep." Lark answered. "Will you join us soon?"

"Yes, I'll gather my things and be right with you."

Orchid drew their attention, her expression one of deep concern. "Lark, we need to discuss Suyan and figure out what we plan to do about her."

"That is a discussion that can wait until tomorrow morning." Lark tried to reign in her temper as Orchid narrowed her eyes. "Where is your pity, Orchid? She's a grieving young woman who just lost her child."

"She was found in the company of Anyan."

"I won't argue with you." Lark answered. "But I would expect more from you than hasty assumptions."

Orchid huffed, "River, perhaps you can talk some sense into my sister."

River held Orchid's gaze unflinchingly. "I think it would be best if you returned to your lodge, Orchid. Lark needs her rest, and we would both feel better if we could be with our son."

"He's my only nephew. I'm worried about Stone just like you are."

Lark's expression grew strained at the unintentional reminder that she hadn't been able to give River another child. If Orchid noticed her sister's stricken expression, she chose to ignore it, but

River's gaze hardened. "I doubt that anyone could measure the concern that Lark and I feel for our son."

Orchid opened her mouth to say more, but River turned away, guiding his wife outside with a hand cradled at the small of her back. "You need your rest."

They both watched as Orchid gathered her things and left without another word.

"I'm worried about her, River. She has no one to confide in, no one who truly understands how difficult her life has been." Lark sat next to Stone, stroking his hair as she pulled his blanket more securely around his shoulders. "But Orchid is a grown woman, and I'm more concerned about our son and his wellbeing than anything else."

Her husband didn't respond. Instead, he spread out their sleeping blanket so that she could rest next to Stone, and he cradled her in his arms as she cuddled their son close.

Unsa returned to speak to Suyan the next day, and he found her sitting upon her sleeping pallet, staring blankly at the walls of Lark and River's lodge.

It bothered him to see the bleak stare in her eyes. He remembered her as a girl with shining eyes and a round, glowing face. It seemed to him that she had given up on life with the death of her child, and he was concerned by the nightmares that plagued her. He wondered what had happened to her during the time that she had been away from their village, but he held back his questions.

"You're well enough to leave this lodge, Suyan." Unsa held out his hand, but he kept his tone firm. "Come with me."

"I'm safe right here." She spoke without turning to face him. "I can't hurt anyone if I stay where I am."

"Lark has a sick child to care for right now. Would you increase her burden?" Unsa asked. "Wouldn't you at least like to relieve yourself outside of the confines of this lodge?"

At the stark reminder, Suyan's bladder protested, and she grimaced. "I'll go with you so as not to be a burden, but I won't stay long."

Unsa didn't respond as he led the way from the lodge. She caught a glimpse of River and Lark as they huddled close to their son. The boy seemed to be alert and awake, but she couldn't be certain. She began to wonder if simply staring at him would bring about the return of his illness. She knew nothing of curses and bad spirits other than the whispered rumors that had run rampant in Chota's village.

Unsa led her close to the jungle where she quickly took care of her needs, alert for any sound that would tell her if Anyan was near. She hadn't forgotten his promise, or his threat that she would never see her mother again if she refused to return to him once she was well.

When she stepped free of the jungle fringe, Unsa was there, waiting for her. He seemed to be as tall and fierce as the distant mountains. Despite her dire outlook, her interest was piqued. She knew that Unsa had taken to the high places shortly after she and the other girls returned safely to the Saika Village. Even as a boy, he had been enamored with the cloud forest that hovered in the distance, standing like a silent sentry over the jungle.

Unsa led her forward, touching her elbow to indicate that she should follow him. "Why do you believe that you're cursed?"

She glanced longingly at the safety of the many lodges scattered in the distance. She wanted nothing more than to hide and weep out her grief. "I killed my son."

The stark expression on her face pierced Unsa's heart. No matter what she said, he couldn't believe that the gentle young woman he remembered could ever harm a child. "Explain exactly what happened."

"I killed my child." Each word came out louder than the last, echoing her startling admission from the previous day.

"How?"

Unsa's steady gaze surprised her.

"Aren't you afraid of me? Shouldn't you speak an incantation to ward off the bad spirit that has taken hold of me?"

He stared at her without blinking until she looked away.

"Explain."

She took a shuddering breath. "My baby came out of my womb without taking his first breath." She swallowed painfully as she lifted her hands with her palms facing the sky. "I stole that from him."

"How so?"

Suyan fumbled for an answer. "I don't know. The pain was so great, so terrible that somehow I wished my child dead. Do you believe me now?"

Unsa didn't respond either way. "How did you come to be with Anyan?"

Suyan shuddered. Even the mention of Anyan's name caused fear to dance over her backbone. "Chota, my mother's husband, thought that it was best if I went with Anyan after…" She couldn't bring herself to say anything more.

"Why?"

"Anyan promised to help me get rid of the bad spirit that caused me to harm my son."

Unsa's stare became harder and more difficult to turn away from. "Why would the people of your mother's village believe that Anyan was capable of ridding you of a bad spirit?"

At this, Suyan looked up sharply. "Because he is a powerful shaman. He belongs to the Agali Village, and he knows the ways of the spirit world."

CHAPTER SEVEN

The Agali Village

Carrum saw his mother before she saw him, and if he didn't know better, he would have thought that she was a young woman of tender age. Ayusha's bare back was adorned by esoteric images painted in red, a sacred color to the Agali. Her breasts were bare, covered only by the lush flowers that hung from a beaded necklace.

She smiled at him, showing startlingly white teeth against her sun burnished skin. "My son."

As always, Carrum responded to the unmistakable pride evident in his mother's voice. "Mother."

He bowed his head to her, aware that she would look him over critically upon first glance, as was her way. Everything about his appearance would meet with her approval. He felt and saw her gaze flow from the crown of his raven black head of hair, to the sight of his muscular chest and strong legs, which were bare except for a decorative waist covering, dyed a brilliant shade of red. He wore a jade armband on each forearm, and his ears were pierced, encircled with gold orbs in the way of the Agali men from times long lasting until now. As her eyes brightened, he knew that she momentarily saw his father instead of her own son.

His mouth tightened briefly, snapping her attention back to the present. "Are you well?"

Ayusha's lips turned up in a patient smile. "How can I be well when our people have become a shadow of who we are meant to be?" Her dark eyes narrowed into angry slits as she took a few steps toward him, stroking his arms with motherly pride. "You're the image of your father. I see Talud whenever I look at you."

Pride caused Carrum to lift his chin, but his mother's next words caused anger to flare within his chest.

"But your father knew how to obtain anything that was within his reach for the taking. I fear that this is a trait of his that you do not share."

"I am my father's son." Carrum growled. "Do you doubt my loyalty to our people?"

"Of course not, my son." Ayusha turned away. "But you have the look of a man that has bad tidings instead of good." She turned back to him expectantly, a look of hope replacing her earlier melancholy. "Or have you come to tell me that all is going exactly as planned."

"Almost." Carrum met Ayusha's stern gaze, fully aware that hadn't wrung a promise from Orchid, and her full cooperation was of vital necessity. "Mother, she isn't ready."

"To think that our future rests in the hands of a young woman that was once under my control." Ayusha laughed, but just as quickly her eyes flashed with hidden fire. "We are the last of a sacred line descended from Agali. Tell me, have you forgotten your purpose? We don't have time for anything to be left undone. Look and see what our people have become!"

Carrum turned to watch their people as they went about their daily tasks. They wore the red colors of the Agali Village, but other than that there was nothing to distinguish them from the forest dwellers. The rough lodges that had been built were shoddy at best, capable of keeping out the rain and little else. Each structure was placed close to its neighbor, obviously a temporary shelter built to keep its occupants safe from the elements.

"The Saika Village stands in the path that leads to reclaiming our former glory. If we don't control them, they are a threat to us." Ayusha intoned. "A threat that must be destroyed."

Carrum noticed a burial pier being erected by several men at the entrance of their settlement. He turned to his mother in question, "Has someone died?"

Silence met his abrupt inquiry, but he felt the heat of his mother's presence as she came to stand behind him, placing her face against his forearm, stroking the jade bands that his father had once worn. "We are preparing a sacrifice as a fitting gift for Agali."

Carrum stiffened slightly, but Ayusha's stroking hands soothed his tense shoulders.

"Can you doubt that our sun god has been angered by these last seasons when we have been scattered amongst the jungle?" She clasped her son's hands as she held his gaze. "By chance we were able to find several of the villagers that were driven from our home, and by chance we have continued to survive."

"The men have worked tirelessly to provide for our women and children. It is possible that we will have enough to see us through another rainy season, if we all work together."

"And is that enough for you, my son?" Ayusha asked, releasing her hold upon him. "Is chance and possibility enough to secure your position as the leader of our people?"

Carrum's jaw hardened with anger. His mother had a way of making him feel less than a man, undermining his place as the rightful leader of the Agali Village. "Who have you chosen?"

"Hanuq's youngest granddaughter will pave the way for our entire village." Ayusha's brow furrowed and then smoothed. Hanuq had been a man knowledgeable about the celestial beings and their ways, but he had perished shortly after the battle that ousted them from their home. "Hanuq would have been honored, and his granddaughter will not suffer. She will be welcomed by those that have gone before us."

He heard the fervent tremor in his mother's words, and he thought to himself that while Hanuq's granddaughter might not suffer pain, she would suffer death. She was a girl of only eight seasons, beautiful, and perfectly formed. She was also a fitting choice for Agali. Without recognizing her true purpose, he had held her upon his knee only yesterday at the evening meal. "What would you have me do to ensure our future?"

Ayusha's light laughter floated over him, soothing his anger while at the same time stoking the flames of revenge that burned in his heart. "Everything within your power."

Lark allowed River to lead her away from the village, although she noticed that he kept the sturdy lodges in sight. She held her husband's hand, leaning into his strength even as he helped her over a fallen log. Their son rested comfortably with her mother watching over him, and Lark trusted Yama to see to Stone's care.

"I would do anything to see you smile again, Lark."

"I'm only tired, River." Lark soothed. "The last few days have been extremely trying."

River turned to face his wife, stroking her thick hair, smoothing it away from her face as he looked at her. "But is there more to your tiredness than you've said?"

Happiness danced in Lark's eyes as she nodded. "I haven't wanted to say anything until I was certain."

River grinned, anticipating her admission. "Didn't you think I would notice that you haven't visited the women's lodge regularly?"

Lark's smile wobbled slightly before blossoming fully. "I wanted to be certain."

"And…" River prompted.

"And I am certain now that I carry your child." Lark barely uttered the words before River crushed her to his chest, touching her chin lightly as he caressed her face and captured her lips in a passionate kiss.

"When?"

"Six or seven moons from now." Lark whispered between kisses. "Our child will be born at that time."

"Stone will have a brother or sister to teach." River smiled, mirroring his wife's joy. "And I will have another son, or perhaps a daughter that looks exactly like you."

"Yes."

Lark closed her eyes as River kissed her soundly, enjoying the throaty purr of pleasure that escaped her lips. They broke apart for air, laughing quietly together as they shared in the secret of the child growing in her womb. "I don't know why it has taken so long. After Stone was born, I hoped that I would conceive again immediately, but when it didn't happen, I despaired over whether or not we would be blessed with another child."

The light in Lark's eyes dimmed slightly as she remembered her sister's hurtful words about her inability to have another child. She had been very close to confiding in Orchid, even before telling River, but something had stopped her. Now she was glad that she had given River the chance to be the first one who knew about the new life that she carried. She acknowledged that sisters shared many things, but there was no bond as sacred as that of a husband and wife.

River's embrace tightened and then he stepped away, cupping her face in both hands. "I don't want to hurt you."

"You won't hurt me," Lark answered. "I need your arms around me now more than ever."

"Our son will continue to improve in health and this child will be strong just like you."

Lark looked at River's lean form with his broad shoulders and muscular torso, and she almost laughed at the irony. "River you're the one with the strength of two men."

"No," River shook his head. "I meant the strength inside of your spirit, Lark. I have never met anyone as strong as you are inside, where it counts." River kissed her again, drawing forth the laughter that brimmed just beneath the surface. "You are my heart, Lark."

She marveled over the warmth of her husband's arms as he whispered sweet words into her ear, thrilling her with the passion that existed for them alone. Lark looked into his eyes, realizing not for the first time that no matter what was happening around them, with River at her side, she was exactly where she wanted to be.

Orchid stood hidden by the fringe of the jungle, her grass skirt and bare torso effectively making her invisible in the shadows unless one looked closely. Two empty waterskins dangled from her hands as she stared at her sister, wrapped in River's arms with her head resting upon his shoulder.

As she watched River touched her sister's chin, tilting her head up so that he could look into her eyes. The love evident in their every touch was clear to see, and Orchid blinked away tears of longing as Lark leaned into River's unyielding strength, accepting his kiss, his possession.

Orchid was suddenly keenly aware that the people of her village expected her to choose a mate from amongst them as soon as she handed the position of leadership over to her brother, but the mere thought was repulsive.

She knew that there were strong men within the Saika Village, but they didn't have the position or standing that she now held. How could she lower herself by choosing a man from amongst her people as her husband?

Several seasons ago, loneliness had driven her into the jungle, and it was there that she had stumbled upon the surviving Agali villagers. They could have killed her, but Carrum had held up a staying hand, taking her into his embrace.

Long ago, he told her that he didn't blame her for going along with the warriors of her village after the attack upon his people. She had been confused, angry, and hurt. Ayusha hadn't spoken to her, but her eyes had held only sadness as she looked upon Orchid, not anger.

Carrum had walked her back to the boundary of her village that first day, leaving her with a lingering touch upon her shoulder, but he had also placed his mark upon her heart. The Agali people meant no harm to the forest dwellers, it was simply their way to honor their sun god, and despite what her sister thought, she knew that the Agali people had sought to honor them above all.

Orchid's hands fisted around the dangling waterskins, and she lifted her chin proudly, ignoring the fact that Lark and River indulged in stolen moments of passion while she remained alone.

She hardened her heart against any stirrings of regret. As soon as the opportunity presented itself, she would take the necessary steps to ensure her future happiness. She would see to it that everything fell into place exactly as she intended.

CHAPTER EIGHT

At Orchid's request, Unsa gathered the men together in preparation for the upcoming hunt. They would need to scour the jungle in search of deer, tapir, and peccary. "We will send out groups of three or four together."

"Yes." River agreed.

Ransa grunted, never one for many words.

"The women and children will bring in many fish while we're gone." Sappa spoke up, where he sat next to Pago.

Unsa could see the excitement in the faces of everyone present, but especially Sappa. The young man understood that once the hunting was complete they would hold his leadership ceremony.

Nestled within a clearing with the other men, Unsa stared up at the endless sky arching over them, noticing that it was sometimes protective and other times threatening. He was surprised to see the figure of a man walking toward them. He knew that every able-bodied man within their village was accounted for and present. Unsa stood to his full height, waiting in expectation as the man drew closer.

It was as if the shadows of the jungle had encircled the man, giving his skin a rich, deep brown hue, while his strong features appeared to be cut from stone. His eyes took in the group of men, before settling upon Sappa.

"Ajaya, you are welcome amongst us." Sappa stood, walking to stand beside the newcomer. "I didn't expect to see you."

"I couldn't miss an occasion of such immense importance." Ajaya's eyes brightened as he looked at Sappa, recognizing the changes that were evident in the young man after such a long time apart. "I see that you have grown into the man your father knew you would one day become. You look so much like him."

Sappa nodded, "My mother has said the same thing many times." He stared into the distance, and Ajaya's lips turned up at the corners. "Have you brought others with you?"

"My people prefer the high places," Ajaya answered. "We are in the midst of rebuilding all that was lost to us for generations."

"I understand." Sappa spoke with a wisdom that was noticed by all, but he seemed unaware of their admiring glances as he turned to gesture toward the other men. "Will you join us?"

Ajaya addressed the group of men, "I would like to speak to Sappa before you begin your ceremony."

Unsa nodded, walking to clasp Ajaya's wrists in greeting. "You are welcome amongst us. We know that your journey must have been tiring. Please eat and drink while you're here with us."

"Shaman," Ajaya said. "It is good to see you amongst the people that need you most."

Unsa blinked, disconcerted by the knowing light in Ajaya's eyes. The man hadn't changed in the six seasons since he last saw him, but he spoke to him with as much familiarity as he always had in the past. It also occurred to Unsa that Ajaya knew more than he should for a man that dwelled high up in the mountains.

"We won't begin our ceremony until Sappa returns." He watched as Sappa led Ajaya away, the older man walking with the aid of his spear and Sappa brimming with youthful exuberance as he walked beside the man who had been his father's closest companion.

"You don't wear your father's necklace?" Ajaya asked, watching Sappa's face with steady eyes that took in every detail. The young man shrugged his shoulders, and then tilted his head to look up at him.

"My sister still wears the necklace," Sappa explained. "She is the leader of our people at this time."

He saw that Sappa wasn't in a rush to take anything away from his sister, but his eyes brimmed with excitement at the thought of possessing his father's prized necklace.

Ajaya placed one hand upon Sappa's shoulder, allowing the youth to lead him up a steep incline to a hill that was as familiar to him as the jungle and the mountains above. Sappa carried a waterskin and a small sack of food given to them by one of the village women. Their passage through the Saika Village had been noticed by all, but Ajaya insisted upon leading Sappa to this very place, and he hadn't stopped until they reached the familiar hill.

"This is the place that belonged to your father." Ajaya found a dry place to rest his weary bones, and he sat with an ease that belied his true age of over sixty seasons of life. "Your father here whenever he needed to think. He said that he felt closer to the sky, here upon this hill."

Sappa nodded. He shifted as he tried to keep his expression even and calm. Yet, his heart beat furiously as he stood in the presence of a man that he respected and admired above anyone else.

Ajaya had been his father's closest friend and confidant.

While his mother had kept Umbra's memory alive for him, Ajaya made his father real in ways that Sappa couldn't define. He hadn't seen the man since he was a boy, and he had truly believed that he might never see him again after so much time had passed. Yet, standing before him now, it was as if the past was only yesterday.

"Sit," Ajaya spread his hand in a gesture of welcome. "Be at ease. Remember, I have come to you, the future leader of the Saika Village."

Sappa sat, crossing his legs as he balanced his hands upon his knees, watching the enigmatic man with great interest. "I am honored that you have chosen to visit our village before the leadership ceremony."

Ajaya smiled with ease. "Your village is a prosperous one, but you are wrong in your assumption that I came to see anyone but you. Sappa, you have the look of a man that has made his first kill and seeks to return to the forest in search of food for his village."

Surprised by his insight, Sappa nodded, struggling to find his
voice. "I would like nothing more."

Ajaya drank from his own waterskin, but he accepted a portion
of the food handed to him by Sappa. He chewed a strip of dried
venison, enjoying the taste as he stared at their surroundings with
an appreciative eye. Sappa couldn't find the desire to eat, not when
excitement buzzed in his stomach like a swarm of bees. The
silence between them lengthened, but it was a comfortable silence,
and he felt as if he had known Ajaya all of his life. He realized that
the converse was true; Ajaya had known him from the day of his
birth until now.

"I am an old man, but I remember the days of my youth."
Ajaya's eyes grew distant. "I promised your father that I would
share the stories of our lives with you as you grew into manhood."
His onyx eyes darkened as he spread his hands wide and then
clasped them together. "The time for that is now. The jungle and
all life within it has held its breath in expectation of the moment
when you would stand in your father's place."

Sappa's gaze snapped to meet Ajaya's eyes as the older man
leaned toward him and lowered his voice. "Imagine your father
sitting in my place; he is an older version of yourself. You have his
features, but try to see yourself as I see you. Like a torrent that
becomes a swift flowing river, you are an extension of the man that
I once knew. Listen closely to all that I will share with you, and in
this way you will accept your father's blessing through the words
that I will impart."

Sappa leaned in close to Ajaya so that he could capture every
word and hold it close, and in his mind's eye he saw not Ajaya, but
Umbra, his father. He was bathed in sunlight, strong and proud,
sitting directly across from him with the proud eyes of a father
watching his son.

In this way, the young man sat beside the wizened older man on
top of a hill that had always belonged to his father, and he received
the blessing meant for him on the day of his birth.

Unsa welcomed Sappa back into the fold of their group, noting with surprise that the young man walked with more confidence and there was a new light in his eyes as he searched his surroundings.

"Sappa, where is Ajaya?"

"He has returned to the high places." Sappa's expression was difficult to read, but Unsa thought that he saw a hint of sorrow there.

Unsa digested Sappa's words, realizing that Ajaya had completed his purpose and returned to the place that he called home, unwilling to spend even one night away from his people.

"Light the fire." Unsa said, gesturing toward Sappa. It was an honor to be chosen to light the fire at a hunters' gathering and Sappa accepted the honor with a quiet nod, displaying humility, a rare trait in a young man chosen to lead others.

Unsa noticed that Pago looked on with pride shining in his eyes, and he approved wholeheartedly. Sappa would need close friends in the days and seasons to come. His hands were fluid and quick as he used a hot coal to light a bundle of dried kindling. As requested, the coal had been taken from Sappa's lodge where the small fire inside always remained alive.

Dressed only in a breech cloth, Unsa was unadorned except for the white shell necklace that hung around his neck. He observed the reverent silence that had fallen over the men, aware that they watched him expectantly. It occurred to him that even though he often felt excluded from the intimate family circle of the Saika Village, in this one thing his presence was essential.

"I cannot give you a blessing to ensure that your arrows fly true and that your spears remain straight and unbent. I cannot bless the flight of your poisonous blow darts or enhance the skill of the hunter inside of you, but I can ask a blessing on your behalf." Unsa raised his hands over the fire. "Stand together as one."

The men stood in a circle extending from the reach of his right and left hands. "Together we are stronger than we would ever be alone. This circle is only a small part of the whole. The women and children that rely upon us make up more than half of our numbers. I ask a blessing on behalf of the men standing in place, acknowledging their position within the Saika Village."

The men chanted in acknowledgement together as one. They lifted the hollow reed poles that they carried and hit them upon the ground in repetition, eagerly voicing their agreement.

"Sappa, you will lead the first group of men on the hunt. You will depart at first light." The men cheered. It was an honor to be chosen first and Sappa had proven himself to be an able hunter, having recently made his first kill. "Choose the men that will accompany you."

"With respect," Sappa addressed Unsa. "I need only one more." He turned to his right, facing his friend. "I choose Pago."

A moment of uneasy silence passed between the men, but Unsa addressed Sappa. "Are you certain?"

"Yes." His answer was resolute, and it didn't escape Unsa's notice that several of the men grumbled over Sappa's choice. No matter which of the men he would have chosen, one or more of them would have felt slighted by his decision. It showed careful forethought and planning on his part to choose Pago, his closest companion.

"It is good." Unsa replied. He quickly divided the other men up into five groups, allowing those that were too old or ill to bow out. More than half of the men would remain within the village to see to its safety and defense while the others were away. River and Ransa decided to remain behind.

Unsa painted signs of protection and strength upon the faces of each man that would participate in the hunt, effortlessly blending the mystical with a physical ritual that would complete the spiritual process associated with the hunting ceremony. When he finished with the last man, he turned to face Sappa.

"A gift for you." Unsa said, handing him a parcel, wrapped securely. "May it bring you good fortune during this hunt, and the others to come."

Sappa accepted the gift, staring at the outer covering in silence as if he could see through the hide to the contents within. Slowly, he unwrapped the hide covering, barely stifling a surprised gasp of astonishment as he stared at Unsa's gift.

"Obsidian knives."

Unsa heard the stunned wonder in Sappa's voice, and he nodded. "The longer knife is used during the hunt, and the shorter knife can be used after." *Or for fighting*, though he left that thought unsaid.

The other men began to speak amongst themselves, marveling over the rare knives. Pago's eyes gleamed with excitement as Sappa stepped forward to thank Unsa. He knew that the location of the obsidian used by Unsa, River, and the Maki warriors was a well kept secret, and he had no doubt that Unsa's gift meant more than his words revealed.

"But only you, River, and the Maki warriors have knives made of obsidian." A young man named Tupin stood up, leaning closer as the other men crowded around. "Sappa isn't a Maki warrior."

"This is my gift to Sappa, your future leader." Unsa stared at Tupin until he backed away with a sullen expression upon his face.

The men sat around the fire, marveling over Unsa's gift to Sappa and telling stories about past hunts deep into the night as the moon rose overhead.

Sappa laughed and talked with an easy confidence that Unsa found admirable in one so young. All around him, the other men were caught up in the excitement of the hunt, lingering over old stories nearly forgotten. This was the way of the Saika Village since times long lasting until now and before long, they would venture into the murky depths of the jungle in search of worthy prey.

Orchid's shoulders tensed as several children ran past her. She breathed a sigh of relief when they merely shouted a greeting before continuing on. The need to see Carrum again had driven her from her lodge and then the village itself. She cast a furtive glance over her shoulder as she took one step into the moist, humid jungle.

The dim forest ensconced her, soothing her worries if not her heated flesh. She wet her lips in indecision, but her footsteps took her deeper into the jungle. It was as if she couldn't resist the pull of her emotions, which urged her to go to the one man that she should by all accounts fear.

But she didn't fear Carrum.

He was her solace, and she believed in her heart that they belonged together. She thought to herself that all would be well if only she didn't have to deceive her family and hide her feelings from others. If only...but that was as much as she allowed herself to consider the future. She knew that Carrum would be disappointed that she hadn't made a decision, and she hoped that he wouldn't doubt her desire to be with him.

She stepped over several fallen logs, hollowed out and aged by the changing seasons. Orchid knew the jungle just as well as any hunter, and she didn't need anyone to recount the ways of the forest to her. During the rainy season the rivers would flood and the torrential rains would drown out any animal or insect that didn't scurry into the highest reaches of the jungle. As the leader of her village, she knew how fragile life could be. They lived at the whim of the merciless forces of nature. It was for this reason that she couldn't find the strength to deny herself the one man that soothed her heart.

Carrum.

After walking without cease, she stopped and a half smile graced her face as she sensed him before she saw him, but it was often that way between them.

"Orchid."

He was there to her left when she turned, and her heart thumped madly as she took in his appearance. His hair skimmed his shoulders, and his muscular chest was bare. Around his waist was a bright red loincloth that hung almost to his knees in length. The familiar jade armbands that adorned his forearms nearly sparkled as dappled sunlight filtered through the trees. She closed the distance between them, touching his face with one hand, feeling the warmth of his skin and the tension that moved through him. Orchid leaned forward to kiss a trail along his jaw, ending at his pierced ears, which were encased with golden shells.

"I didn't think that you would meet me again." Carrum murmured, seeking the warmth of her lips before she could respond.

"I couldn't stay away," Orchid replied, thrilled by the firm length of his body as he pressed against her. Taken off guard, she flinched when he grabbed her shoulders and drew her away from him. "Carrum?"

"You merely seek a distraction." Carrum's eyes narrowed. "I can tell that you're no closer to making a decision now than you were when we last saw each other."

Orchid wanted to tell him that his accusation wasn't true, but she knew that he saw the truth in her eyes. She was caught in an impossible position, and she couldn't decide what her next step would be.

"There is no future for us, Orchid."

This time Carrum's words were filled with finality, causing Orchid's heart to lurch painfully in her chest. "Don't say that!"

She leaned forward to kiss him, but he pulled away. "You know that it's true." Carrum made a slashing motion with his hands. "I have honored you, Orchid. I haven't taken you as my woman out of a sense of honor and responsibility. Do you think that I don't yearn for you? Do you think that I don't crave your touch?"

"No…" Orchid's eyes widened as Carrum stepped forward, pinning her against the tree at her back.

"I yearn for you night and day, Orchid." Carrum swallowed. "At times, I think I'll go mad with the desire that I have for you."

Unable to move, unable to do anything other than melt under the searing heat of his gaze, Orchid shivered, arching toward him as he swept his head low for a shattering kiss.

All of her senses were set ablaze as he clasped her hands and held them in one hand. When they broke apart, they were both panting with desire.

After several moments had passed, Orchid finally found her voice, and she couldn't look away from the possessive gleam in Carrum's eyes.

"You don't have to wait any longer."

Sensing her full capitulation, Carrum moved against Orchid in a way that he never had before. Orchid felt him shift, and pleasure radiated throughout every fiber of her being. She met his hips, cursing the barrier of her palm frond skirt, and as if hearing her thoughts, he ripped the garment away. Orchid gasped at the abrupt contact, shivering despite the heat, thrilled by the scent of their sweat slicked skin as Carrum covered her with his body.

This was what she had always wanted, a man who was as passionate about her as she was about him, someone who couldn't live or breathe without standing in her presence from sunrise to sunset. Orchid marveled at the play of light over his chest and abdomen as he looked his fill, enjoying the sight of her naked flesh. She knew that she was beautiful, but she had never given herself to a man, until now.

He kissed and stroked her until she rode a wave of desire so strong that she cried out her need, scattering the birds in the treetops until he covered her mouth to muffle the sound. There was a moment where she could have resisted, but she thought briefly of her sister and her husband. They took what they wanted from each other without suffering the pain that she had suffered by depriving herself of the same joy.

Her thoughts scattered as she felt the strength of Carrum's desire when he lifted her high. She was ready for his possession when he finally took her, and even though there was a moment of shattering pain it wasn't enough to make her regret their coupling. Before long, she moved with him as they mated for the first time, joining their bodies together as one. Carrum controlled her every movement, stretching out the pleasure of their mating until she panted from exertion and strain, and when she closed her eyes, lightening flashed behind her eyelids. Thrilled by the freedom that she found with him, she listened to the roar of blood in her ears as he bit into her shoulder, chaffing the flesh, marking her as his woman, now and forever.

"Say it, Orchid." Carrum didn't give her time to recover as he brushed aside undergrowth with his hand, while lowering her to the ground.

She knew what he wanted to hear, and as she opened her body to him again, he sheathed himself inside of her, and she gave all of herself with passionate abandon to the man that had conquered her body and soul. "I am yours, Carrum."

A piercing scream filled the air as the sun set over the Saika Village. Lark and River rushed from their lodge, leaving Yama with their son.

In the center of their village, a woman held her son in her arms, keening in a mournful howl. "My son!"

Lark broke free of River's hold, rushing to the woman's side. She knew her at first glance; both the woman and the boy had been ill since the first day that sickness had come to their village. "Let me see him, Pellar."

"No!" Pellar reared back, pushing Lark away in her attempt to protect her son. "You said that he would be well. Tell me that he's merely sleeping. Tell me!"

Tears of regret sprang to Lark's eyes as the child's head fell back limply without his mother's supporting hands. Pellar's son was only four seasons of age, and she had promised his mother that she would do all that she could for the boy. Over the past few days he'd been plagued with loose bowels, unable to hold anything inside no matter how often his mother pressed broth and tasty treats upon him. It was clear to see that the child was no longer breathing as his mother stroked his face, breaking into a series of grief-stricken cries.

"Pellar please let me see your son." Lark saw that Pellar's gaze was far off, as if the woman was caught in the memories of the past. Her attention shifted to River, who helped her to her feet.

"Are you injured?"

"No, but my sister should be here. Where is Orchid?" Lark peered over River's shoulder, glancing around helplessly as she searched the gathering crowd for her sister. "Orchid should be here." She pressed her lips together in irritation, but her eyes softened as they focused upon the woman and child. "River, she doesn't want to let the boy go."

"Then let her hold him." River placed one hand upon Lark's shoulder in comfort before she went to join the grief-stricken woman. Others quickly followed his wife's lead, and he silently watched as Lark knelt beside the mourning woman, and wrapped her arms around Pellar and her son.

After a time, Pellar's eerie keening ceased, and Lark suddenly raised her head, staring at her with stark eyes. "Pellar, where is your daughter?"

Unsa wasn't certain how to help Suyan, but he knew that she wouldn't heal within the Saika Village. The people continued to blame the sickness that plagued their village upon her, and he had caught more than one youth referring to Suyan as the blood moon girl.

Suyan's eyes were wild as she scrubbed away the last remnants of sleep. She had dreamed of the first fruits ceremony again. In the dream, countless hands had touched her body, taking from her that which she would never willingly give. She had been naked to the waist, and lying upon her back with several other girls as the men danced around them. The bitter taste of the Ayahuasca brew made her want to gag, but the sound of the drums and the chanting from the women forced away her will and strength.

"I have to leave."

"Suyan." Unsa soothed, blowing steam over her sweat slicked body. "You had a bad dream."

"No." Suyan shook her head, Unsa didn't understand.

It was real.

He reached for her hand and she flinched, seeing the injury that she caused him without meaning to do so. He tried again, and this time she accepted his touch, comforted by the warmth of his hand and the steady gaze that looked at her with quiet acceptance.

"If it wasn't a dream, what was it?"

"A memory."

Unsa stiffened, aware that any memory that would put such stark fear into Suyan's eyes had to be immensely painful. The sweat lodge that he had erected for her benefit had done nothing to erase the hollow sadness in her eyes. He had chanted over her until she fell into a fitful sleep and even his most well versed protective chants had not stopped her from waking in terror.

"Perhaps you will lessen the sting if you tell me what it is that you remembered."

Suyan shook her head back and forth. She didn't want to talk about the things she had endured in an attempt to gain acceptance amongst Chota's band. Unsa hadn't judged her unfairly, even though many people in the village had somehow known at first glance that she carried a stain, a mark that made her a danger to everyone.

"I need to leave."

"Where would you go?" Unsa asked.

"Anywhere but here."

Unsa opened the lodge entrance, releasing the steam, relieving their sweat soaked bodies in one fluid motion. "I have tried everything that I can to help you, Suyan."

She nodded, aware that Unsa had selflessly given of his time, trying his best to rid her of the curse that afflicted her. "It is the bad spirit within me, fighting to maintain control. That is the only reason why your chants and incantations haven't worked."

Unsa shook his head. "No, I don't believe that you're afflicted with a bad spirit."

A piercing cry sounded from the midst of the village, breaking the intensity of Unsa's gaze. Suyan stiffened, the hope in her eyes fading into uneasy acceptance. She recognized the mourning cries that followed that first terrible scream of anger, denial, and the loss of hope.

"If that is so, then why is everyone around me dying?"

CHAPTER NINE

"I couldn't help him." Lark wept freely in the quiet of their lodge. She kept her right hand upon her sleeping son while the other rested upon River's chest. His heartbeat assured her that he was healthy and whole, vibrating with life. "We could have lost our son, just as quickly as Pellar lost her child."

"Stone is alive, and he has recovered from the sickness that brought him low."

Lark wiped her eyes, glancing over at her son with the wonder and awe that all mothers felt for their children. Quiet sobs caused her to shudder as River gathered her into his arms.

"Lark, stop." River's voice was firm but soothing. "This can't be good for the child that you carry. You must find comfort in helping Pellar with her daughter."

He glanced at his wife's red tipped nose and swollen eyes as helplessness moved through him in waves.

"Ha'ini," Lark whispered brokenly. "Her name is Ha'ini, it means bright smiling one."

"She's resting comfortably in her mother's arms."

"But she is still ill, River. There is still the danger of Ha'ini succumbing to this sickness, just like her brother. I only wish that I had been able to help Pellar's son." Lark ran her hands over her face. "There should have been something that I could have done for him. What is the use of my knowledge and skill if I cannot save one small boy?"

"You would have saved him if it had been within your power to do so."

"And what about her daughter? If she dies, what comfort will that be to me?" Lark rubbed one hand over her face, distractedly.

"Our people are saying that I gave more of my time and care to Stone when I should have been sitting with the sick."

River smoothed his wife's hair away from her face. "You are his mother."

"I am the village healer." Lark's features crumpled as she gave in to tears again. "What is my purpose if I cannot heal the sick?"

River shook her slightly. "We must think of the living and figure out a way to help those that are ailing."

"Mother, I'm thirsty." Stone rolled over, unaware that his parents were embroiled in an emotional discussion.

Lark sat up quickly, grabbing one of the waterskins that hung upon the lodge wall. "Here," she urged. "Drink slowly."

Stone took a small sip and then grimaced. "No. I don't want it."

Lark glanced at River and then back at their son. "You must drink if you're thirsty."

"I don't like the taste." Stone shook his head.

Lark sniffed the contents of the waterskin, detecting nothing out of the ordinary. Aware that she wouldn't be able to rest until her son had something to drink. She got to her knees and then gained her feet as she quickly walked to the small fire that they always kept burning in the center of their lodge. "Try this."

She handed Stone a clay cup full of warm water that had been heated upon the stones of the fire.

"Better?" she asked.

He nodded, settling in to rest again as his mother stroked his forehead.

"His fever is nearly gone."

River nodded. "See, there is already improvement where our son is concerned. I am certain that others will follow."

Lark relaxed slightly, resting her fist upon her chest where her heart ached for Pellar. She couldn't help but wonder what would become of the woman if she lost her daughter in the days to come.

River opened his arms, and she went willingly to his side, but her eyes remained upon their son. Silvery light from the moon cast an eerie glow around their lodge, filtering inside from the opening at the top of the dwelling. Despite the warmth of her husband's embrace, Lark was aware that somewhere nearby, Pellar watched the same moon hanging overhead while holding her daughter close, but she was without her son forever.

Sappa led the way, confident that he and Pago would be able to find worthy prey before sunrise. The jungle was his home, and he recognized, not for the first time, that this was how he'd been born to travel. The humidity coated his skin like a blanket, familiar and welcome, while sunlight filtered down from the upper canopy lighting his way through the underbrush.

Since his blessing ceremony with Ajaya, he saw things in a different light. It was as if the older man had clothed him in a blanket of wisdom, and something had settled over Sappa, changing the way that he interpreted the world around him, reshaping the way that he viewed life.

Pago remained three steps behind him, but he was aware when his friend paused, standing in place. Sappa stopped instantly, alert to the slightest sound. The unexpected call of a black stinger was at odds with their surroundings and Sappa turned toward the sound.

"Everyone knows black stingers don't travel this far inland." Sappa was unsurprised when a troublesome young man from their village stepped from behind a stand of trees, but he instantly bristled. "Tupin, I'm surprised to see you here."

"I decided to join you."

The words were uttered in an offhand tone, but they were also a challenge if Sappa had ever heard one.

Tupin was an able hunter. At seventeen seasons of age, he was adept at stalking prey, expertly instructed by his father and grandfather who were both skilled hunters. He was also Sappa's greatest rival within their village.

Pago stepped forward as if to intervene, but a hard look from Sappa stopped him.

"I would like nothing more." Sappa responded.

Tupin smiled, but his eyes were cold. Standing taller than Sappa and Pago by a full head, he enjoyed the dominance that his height gave him over the others. He was lean and muscular, with rattan strips tied around his knees and ankles. Like the other two young men, he was completely naked except for a strip of rattan tied at his waist which held his hunting knife. Sappa took in the sight of Tupin's blowpipe and quiver of darts with a grimace. Tupin was deadly accurate with his blowpipe and everyone knew it. He also carried a bow, slung across his back along with a quiver of arrows with arrowheads made of monkey bones.

"I wonder which of us will bring in the most from this hunt." Tupin threw the words over his shoulder as he took the lead, leaving Sappa and Pago to trail behind him. "If you or Pago should bring in more than enough to split between a handful of children, I'll be surprised. Even with your new knives, you're no match for me. Sappa, have you learned how to send your arrow flying and notch a new one into place in time to make a kill?"

Sappa's face flushed as he silently stared at Tupin. Everyone knew that he had trouble with the use of his bow and arrows. While he could often hit a stationary target, hitting a moving target during a hunt was a different matter entirely. Hunters were trained to notch another arrow into place with calm assurance and accuracy. Pago had mastered the technique, but Sappa was still learning. It was just like Tupin to exploit a weakness wherever he found it.

"Don't worry about me, Tupin." Sappa responded. "You would do well to worry about yourself."

"Sappa," Pago snapped angrily, keeping his voice low. "Why are you allowing him to join us?"

Before Sappa could answer, Tupin turned, spearing Pago with an angry glare. "Tell me, future war leader, have you learned to find your way alone in the jungle yet?"

With that question he laid bare Pago's greatest shame. Sappa opened his mouth to answer for his friend, but Pago beat him to it.

"No, but I can still hit an animal between the eyes from a greater distance than anyone else in our village, including you."

Tupin shrugged, unimpressed as he easily moved out of earshot.

"Between the eyes." An unwilling grin twitched upon Sappa's lips. "Have you lost your wits?"

"Of course not, it's true. I can shoot between the eyes of any animal foolish enough to cross my path."

"But you can't find your way out of the jungle after you've made a kill. If I were to leave you now, you would be lost until someone found you."

"True," Pago acknowledged, "But I would eat well while I waited for rescue."

Unbidden, a harsh burst of laughter came from Sappa, and he was joined by Pago. Tupin stopped up ahead and scowled at them, a clear reminder that their silence was all that stood between them and the success of their hunt.

As darkness fell, the three young men decided to find a place to wait out the darkest part of the night. However, it went without saying that they would rise well before the sun made its appearance. They methodically cleared an open space, sitting with their backs against each other for support. Only those foolish enough to trust the deceptive ways of the jungle would have chosen to sleep nestled against a tree. There were too many dangers awaiting the unwary, and they knew better than to let down their guard. Nearby, the buttress roots of a large tree were crawling with leaf eating ants that were capable of overcoming smaller prey and causing pain and injury.

Despite sitting with a possible enemy at his back, Sappa inhaled deeply, forcing himself to relax. He was asleep almost the moment that he closed his eyes.

Howler monkeys awakened them before dawn, and all three young men stood quickly, shaking off the remnants of sleep that clung to them. Sappa drank deeply from his waterskin, checking to see that Pago was well as his friend did the same. Much to their dismay, Tupin had chosen to stalk off into the jungle with the expectation that they would follow.

"What choice do we have?" Pago growled, taking the position of follower with an angry glance his way.

They lengthened their stride, catching up with Tupin as Sappa saw him stop walking only to stand beside a towering tree. He turned to face them, expectantly holding up a familiar plant.

Sappa barely suppressed a groan.

"What is it?" Pago asked without moving his lips as Sappa came to stand abreast with him.

"He has an ebony plant in his hand." Sappa knew that Pago despised Tupin, but he hadn't been able to back away from the challenge offered by the other young man, and he wouldn't back away now. "If he uses it, we have to as well."

Pago hissed in a breath, grabbing Sappa's arm to hold him in place. "No."

"It's a direct challenge to our manhood." Sappa replied, stepping past him with a forceful yank of his arm. "If he decides to use the ebony plant, so will I."

The drippings from the ebony plant mixed with water would burn with a pain that was blinding in its intensity, but it was also known to heighten the senses and empower hunters with stealth and cunning.

Pago slapped his thigh with impatience as they started forward. "Again, I'm curious as to why you ever allowed him to join us."

"What are you afraid of Pago? The men of our village have used the ebony plant to increase their powers in the hunt for generations. It won't kill us."

"But it might blind us."

Sappa leaned toward him, whispering, "Together we're strong, remember?"

Pago faltered, obviously surprised by Sappa's unexpected response. "I thought you knew better than to trust a snake."

Sappa kept his thoughts to himself, but his tense shoulders told their own story. Before long, Tupin stopped walking, bracing his weight against a towering tree, and he took the opportunity to respond to his friend's angry assertion.

"Your reasoning is skewed, Pago."

"How so?"

Sappa lowered his voice. "I know better than to run when a snake crosses my path, and as my future war leader, you should know the same."

He left Pago behind, certain that his friend would either catch up or become lost in the jungle.

When he found Tupin, the young man faced him squarely, a disbelieving glint in his eye. "I must admit, I'm surprised that you're willing to take the juices of the ebony plant."

"Why?" Sappa asked.

"Because your sister shields you from all trouble and pain." He saw that his words had the desired outcome, and his lips twitched with mirth. "I'm amazed that Orchid even allowed you to leave on a hunt. Everyone knows that she favors you above others, and she treats you like the child you are."

"Don't speak of my sister."

Sappa had no doubt that Tupin thought to use Orchid as a sparking point between them. He had noticed that Orchid favored him, but it had never bothered him until now. He was a man, and he saw no reason to defend his manhood. He glared at Tupin, unwilling to back down now that the other young man had openly challenged him.

"We'll see if you actually go through with this or not," Tupin sneered. "I think you'll go running back to your sister while I finish the hunt for you."

Sappa's hand clenched against his spear. "Say one more word about my sister, and I'll give you the fight that you seek."

He wasn't surprised when Tupin backed down. Despite the difference in their ages, Sappa's fighting ability was well known, and he never issued an empty threat. He had been trained by River and Unsa since boyhood, often sparring with the Maki warriors whenever they visited the village, and he firmly believed that he could take Tupin in a fight.

"He's right, Sappa." Pago said, lifting a hand to brush the hair from his eyes as he stepped forward.

"What are you talking about?"

"You've had everything handed to you." Pago shrugged. "It's no wonder that you can't set your arrows in place fast enough to bring down an animal."

Sappa glared at his friend. "Is this about you becoming the war leader for our village?"

"And what if it is? At least I've worked for something in my life."

Sappa shoved Pago, taking him by surprise. "You don't know what you're talking about."

Pago punched him in the stomach, and he bent at the waist, sucking in gasps of air. "Of course, I know what I'm talking about."

"No, you don't."

"You have no idea what it's like to want something more than you want your next breath." Pago glared at him. "I'm your friend, but unlike Tupin, I'm actually trying to help you."

Sappa stared at him, while they both breathed hard in an effort to regain their breath. "What exactly are you saying?"

"The next time that you have a chance to make a kill, don't focus on the speed with which I can shoot one arrow after the next, focus on your own abilities and do whatever works best." Pago held his gaze. "Not everything in life will be handed to you. Some things you'll simply have to work hard to obtain."

Sappa turned away from his friend and went to find Tupin. He was tired of bickering and almost certain that if he stayed, they would eventually to blows with one another.

He found Tupin on his haunches with the leaf funnel held above his head so that the drippings from the ebony plant ran into his eyes.

"What are you doing?"

"I'm increasing my chances of success." Scowling with irritation, his face reddened, contorting with pain as he squeezed his eyes shut, holding the plant out to Sappa.

Pago made a noisy entrance, silently bending to one knee as he raised his face toward Sappa. "I'm next."

"Are you certain?"

Pago grinned, "No, but you are, and that's good enough for me."

With their earlier disagreement forgotten, Sappa made quick work of the task as he dripped the dark liquid into Pago's eyes. He swiftly bent to one knee and splashed the burning liquid into his own eyes before fear could paralyze him.

As the first fiery wave of pain struck, he was glad that he was on his knees. The burning continued on and on as Sappa bit back a moan of distress that threatened to break free at any moment.

He couldn't see, but he also couldn't hear any sound coming from either Tupin or Pago. In a moment of startling clarity it occurred to him that they were at their most vulnerable, three well-armed and able-bodied young men, effectively blind amidst the dangers of the Great Forest.

CHAPTER TEN

At first light, Unsa approached Lark's lodge with Suyan at his side. He scratched once upon the entrance flap, unsurprised to find River and Stone together. River came outside at his behest, standing quickly as he scanned the village with a glance.

"Lark has gone to tend to Pellar's daughter."

"And your son?"

River hesitated, unwilling to sound overconfident, but heartened by Stone's recovery from illness. "He has shown improvement since last night."

Unsa nodded, glancing uneasily toward Suyan. "It is best for Suyan if I take her away from here. The people are angry; they are suspicious of anything that they don't understand." *Or anyone.* But he kept his thoughts to himself, aware that River already knew his feelings on the matter.

River nodded. He had no doubt that Unsa was aware of the growing unrest within the Saika Village. Ever since the death of Pellar's son, the people of their village were divided over whether the blood moon girl was the cause of the sickness plaguing them.

Even Orchid had kept her distance from the young woman who was related to her by blood. They had shared so much, as captives of the Agali Village when they were little more than children.

At the time, Orchid and Lark had wept with sadness when Suyan and her mother left to join Chota's band, but with Suyan's mysterious return, Orchid had been nothing short of cold toward her. It would be better for all if Suyan was taken away from their village, if only for a time.

"Where will you go?"

Unsa's gaze answered River's question as he looked into the mists rising toward the heavens.

"The cloud forest is more your home than the jungle has ever been."

"They are linked. One is the same as the other." Remembering the way that Ajaya left to return to his people, Unsa couldn't help but see the similarity between them. The cloud forest called to him as nothing else ever had. "We are all connected, River." Unsa answered, openly holding River's gaze. "The people should know that I will not take kindly to any interruptions while I try to help Suyan."

River's jaw ticked angrily. "They are your people, too." He didn't like the warning that he heard in Unsa's voice. "When will you return?"

"I will return when I'm needed."

River noticed the way that Unsa held on to Suyan's hand. The shadows in the young woman's eyes stopped him from addressing her. Her gaze was weary and broken. She seemed more comfortable with Unsa than anyone else, including Lark or Orchid. He was aware that the pair had known each other since childhood, but it surprised him that Unsa had taken responsibility for Suyan's wellbeing.

"Will you be here for Sappa's leadership ceremony?"

"If I'm needed."

River watched Unsa turn away, but he stopped him with a brief touch upon his shoulder. "Unsa, I know it's difficult for you to believe, but you're as much a part of this village as I am, or anyone else for that matter."

Unsa nodded once before turning away with the young woman shielded protectively by his body.

River had the suspicion that Unsa wanted to save Suyan, just like Lark wanted to save those that came to her for her healing gift. Sadly, he thought to himself that sometimes it just wasn't within their power to save anyone. It was a hard lesson, but one that Lark had already learned. In time, he had no doubt that Unsa would do the same.

Sappa's blood rushed through his body as his senses swirled until he felt strong and powerful, buoyed by a sense of almost overbearing euphoria. The slightest sounds resounded in his ears, and his sight was crisp and vivid, enlivening his senses with an abundance of color.

Pago was within arm's reach, having recovered from the painful burning associated with the ebony plant. At a sign from Tupin, they stopped in their tracks. He didn't know how long they had traveled in the early morning light, but he knew that his senses were alive in a way that he had never experienced before.

Tupin's hand sign was unmistakable, but the familiar stench that assaulted their nostrils also identified their prey. Peccary.

Where there was one peccary there was often a larger band to be found nearby. The strong musky odor emanating from their prey caused all three young men to grab the bows slung over their backs. Arrows were notched simultaneously, and they were instantly alert to even the slightest movement.

Out of the corner of his eye, Sappa saw Pago's right ear twitch, a trick that he had learned in his boyhood. He wondered distantly if the ability to move his ears actually heightened Pago's senses. Sensing movement to his right, Sappa shifted in a motion that would be imperceptible to anyone watching. His eyes were in constant motion, searching the underbrush for signs of movement, but the jungle was unerringly silent.

With an expression of annoyance, Tupin gestured that he would once again take the lead, but Sappa remained standing in place as Tupin moved deeper into the jungle.

Sappa's entire being vibrated with intensity, and his senses hummed with the desire to make a kill. At his side, Pago waited with a patience that surprised him.

He inhaled deeply, closing his eyes once before opening them quickly, turning his head to the left as the rattling bushes and shrubs announced the presence of a band of peccary.

Whirling into motion, Sappa released his first arrow, sending it toward one of the rotund creatures even as he sensed that he would miss his target. In Sappa's peripheral vision, he saw Pago sending arrow after arrow flying toward their fleeing quarry. Pago didn't wait for his first target to fall as he took aim and released, again and again, all within the span of one exhalation of breath.

Remembering their earlier discussion, Sappa bent to one knee while adjusting his bow as he sent another arrow flying through the air. This time, he hissed in a breath of shock as he felt the rightness of the moment. The peccary fell, but as it rose to its feet injured but alive, Sappa ran forward, grabbing a round, smooth rock from the ground as time slowed. His fingers tightened upon the rock and he hit the peccary with the full force of his strength, shouting once in triumph as it finally fell. When the stampede was past, there were six fallen animals and another in its death throes.

"Tell me that you didn't make a kill with a rock?" Pago asked with an amused grin.

"I thought you said that I should do whatever works best."

They looked up just as Tupin returned, empty-handed and angry at the sight of their spoil, including Pago's many kills. Sappa barely withheld a whoop of astonishment as he noticed that one of the fallen animals, brought down by Pago, had an arrow buried between its eyes.

The Saika Village

Lark held Pellar's daughter, Ha'ini, in her arms as she watched the child closely. She didn't have to be a reputed healer to know that the little girl was deathly ill. Her once round cheeks were sunken, and her eyes appeared hollow and listless. She cradled Ha'ini close to her heart, aware of Pellar's weighty gaze upon her back.

"Can you do anything for her?" Pellar's voice resounded with pain; it was as if she had already given her daughter up for dead.

"I will need a strong bone broth," Lark responded. "Do you have anything here to make a broth that will nourish your daughter?"

"Last night, I prepared the broth as you directed." Each word was forced from Pellar's lips, but Lark ignored the hostility that radiated from the bereaved woman. She could only imagine how she would feel if her child's life hung in the balance.

Lark accepted a small wooden bowl and began to trickle a tiny amount between Ha'ini's parched lips. At three seasons of age, she was too young to suffer the debilitating bouts of sickness, runny bowels, and vomiting that had plagued her almost constantly from the onset of her illness.

The little girl no longer cried for her mother's touch, and Lark almost wept over that realization. She handed Ha'ini over to her mother, despite the yearning inside of her that urged her to keep the child close to her heart. "Hold her close. Sing to her, and perhaps she will accept more nourishment."

Lark left Pellar cradling Ha'ini in her arms, blinking away angry tears as she looked up at the wide expanse of sky. "Grandmother, I need your help."

She only wished that Agama was here to help her. Lark surrendered to the feeling of complete helplessness that washed over her, she allowed it to consume her momentarily and then she let it go. Ha'ini's spirit hovered near death, and she didn't have time for Lark to wallow in self pity. Lark looked up at the sound of boisterous shouting and cheerful greeting coming from the village entrance. Despite the dire circumstances facing their village, Lark smiled, catching sight of Sappa and his companions returning from a successful hunt. They carried the evidence of their success between them, and she noticed that their faces were alight with good health. Lark stood utterly still, stricken by an odd sense of rightfulness as her thoughts coalesced and settled into place.

Sappa and Pago struggled to contain their excitement as they were greeted by their village. Tupin carried a heavy burden upon his back, having agreed to transport their spoil if he could claim his part in the kill. Pago had refused his offer with a vehement denial, but in the end, he agreed with Sappa that they would need help. As it was, Sappa was almost bent over from the weight of the animals tied between them. He had even considered ridding himself of the burden in his arms, but as the young village children ran forward, Sappa handed the squirming young peccary that he carried over to an adorable little girl who walked with a slight limp.

"For you, Irari. Keep him healthy and well fed." Sappa accepted the child's hug as she threw her arms around his leg, squealing with delight as the other children gathered closer to inspect the baby peccary.

He raised his hands as the villagers cheered, announcing that they were the first to return from their hunt. The women came forward with offers of help, but Sappa waved them away.

"It is our privilege to butcher the meat that we have brought back with us. Only then will your help be needed." The kindness in his words, didn't escape the notice of the women and Pago poked him in the side as several of the younger girls looked at Sappa with worshipful eyes.

"Sappa!"

He turned to find his sister, Orchid, running toward him with her arms outstretched. He was glad to see her, but he held up a forestalling hand. It wouldn't be fitting to allow his sister to embrace him in front of their entire village. He stood to his full height, realizing that he was more than a head taller than Orchid. "It is good to see you, Orchid, but I must go with the men and help them with their burden."

"But Sappa..." Orchid reared back in surprise as her brother turned away.

"All is well, Orchid." Lark stepped forward, placing a bracing hand upon her sister's shoulder. She was still upset with Orchid for her disappearance the day that Pellar's son died, but Orchid had made many excuses about the need for time alone to contemplate the future, and Lark hadn't pressed her.

"But he shunned me, Lark." Orchid raised hurt eyes to stare at her sister. "I am the one that he has always turned to when he wanted to share anything of value."

Surprised, Lark reared back, turning her head to look at her sister. "Orchid, that isn't true."

If Orchid heard her, she didn't respond. Instead, she narrowed her eyes and pursed her lips with frustration. "He gave the baby peccary away without even considering that I would have liked to keep it."

Lark was distracted by the crush of villagers as they began to clap their hands and stomp their feet, welcoming the men. It bothered her that Orchid wanted to claim Sappa's affection and attention for herself, even though Sappa's gesture would go a long way to helping Irari with the other children. However, she also realized that the deeper emotion behind Orchid's reaction was pain. With that thought in mind, she softened her voice as she patiently tried to reason with her sister.

"Look and see, Orchid. Sappa has become the man that we have always hoped he would be. It is not a time for sadness, but for rejoicing."

Lark turned to Orchid, expecting to see realization dawning in her sister's crystalline eyes, but Orchid had turned away with a dejected cast to her shoulders. The need to go after Orchid warred with the desire to find River and share her discovery about their water source. With a sigh of regret, Lark went to search out her husband allowing hope to grow in her heart for the first time since sickness had come to their village.

CHAPTER ELEVEN

River and Lark sat in the quiet enclosure of their lodge with their young son sheltered between them. Stone had rallied only this morning, and he was resting peacefully, although they refused to leave him by himself.

"You think that the water is somehow causing the sickness?" River asked while bathing Stone's brow with a wet woven strip of cloth. "How is that possible?"

"I don't know, but I noticed that Sappa and the other young men that accompanied him on the hunt returned healthy. They only drank from fresh water sources." Lark silently pleaded with River to consider the thought, aware that what she was suggesting was a foreign concept to him. "Stone began to improve after he stopped drinking water gathered from the stream that runs just outside of our village."

"Lark, you've given him water from the wooden bowl by the fire," River looked at his son, willing him to rest and sleep so that he could regain his full strength.

"Yes, but he didn't display any symptoms of illness after drinking the water heated by the fire." Lark rubbed her forehead. "I think that it's the water from the stream that causes the illness."

"Impossible." Orchid entered the lodge without asking permission, drawing River and Lark's gaze at her intrusion. "If that was true, I would have to tell everyone in our village not to drink from the stream. It would be a disaster."

"Orchid," Lark lifted her chin. "Did you happen to overhear the reason why everyone needs to stop drinking the stream water?"

"I came to see about my nephew's welfare." Orchid inclined her head toward Stone. "I didn't realize that an invitation was necessary."

Lark sighed, "Orchid–"

"In answer to your question, the reason doesn't matter." Orchid tilted her head imperially. "It would cause a hardship to the women of the village if they should have to travel further into the jungle in search of water."

"Death would be a far worse punishment." River said.

Orchid inhaled sharply. "Death?"

"Your sister has valid concerns that I would think you would listen to before dismissing."

"I didn't know–"

"You act like a spoiled child at times, Orchid." River's patience had been worn thin by the young woman's inability to grasp the seriousness facing them. "You are the leader of this village. The lives of others depend upon your decisions."

Orchid's eyes flashed angrily. "I know exactly who I am."

"Then act like it." River stood abruptly, but not before turning to his wife and tenderly stroking her cheek. "I'll leave you to explain things to your sister."

"River." Lark met her husband's gaze with quite resolve. "Please see Ha'ini's mother, and tell her not to feed her daughter anymore of the stream water."

"Of course." River left without glancing toward Orchid, effectively telling her that he was finished speaking with her.

"He hates me." Orchid complained, before turning to her sister expectantly.

Lark's face was a mask of calm as she steadfastly refused to acknowledge her sister's petulant expression and uncooperative behavior.

Orchid's eyes widened as Lark stared at her without blinking. "Lark?"

"Listen closely if you would like to know how to help the people of our village."

Unsa was surprised by Suyan's strength. She walked behind him without faltering as they traversed the jungle, often stooping to travel under hanging limbs or rotting vines. He also had to stop many times to assess their trail, often pausing to remove evidence of their presence before continuing on.

Suyan was patient and quiet. The bleak shadows in her eyes told him that she didn't believe he could help her, but Unsa wasn't dissuaded from doing all he could for the young woman. He remembered her not as she was, but as she had been in their childhood – happy, carefree, and brimming with life.

Once, he took her hand to guide her up a steep incline and his fingers tingled at the contact. Her hand fit against his as if cast from a smaller mold and heat radiated from her hand to his, forcing him to release her. He was distracted by his unexpected attraction to her, having no basis for such things except that they were male and female, alone in the jungle. Protectiveness surged through him as she stumbled, and he reached for her instinctively, cradling her against his side as she regained her footing.

He wanted to tell her that it wasn't much further, but that would be a lie. His home was far above the jungle in the mystical cloud forest. It was the only place where he felt welcome, and it would be a safe haven for Suyan. She couldn't heal in the Saika Village, not when their people mistakenly blamed her for the illness plaguing their loved ones.

Even Lark, with all of her skill as a healer, would be of very little use to someone like Suyan. The thing that ailed her wasn't an injury of the body, but of the spirit, and he reasoned that in this, he was Suyan's only hope. He knew the spirit.

His desire to see her well surprised him. It had been a long time since he had cared about anyone but himself. It was true that River and Lark had tried to make him feel welcome by constantly reminding him that he was a member of their village, but Unsa didn't see it that way. He didn't belong to anyone or anything except the jungle.

He found it difficult to explain to others how the jungle had a spirit, a life force all its own and for some reason the Great Forest had chosen him.

Suyan's sharp inhalation of breath alerted him to the fact that they had been standing in one place for too long while he stood dreaming of things past and present.

"This way," Unsa guided her forward, using his body as a shield when thorny vines thwarted their progress or intrusive palm fronds blocked their way. Again, he glanced at her, and he noticed that the haunted expression in her eyes was the only sign of the anguish that lived inside of her. He was humbled by her courage and unearned trust, which made him want to protect her all the more. Unbidden, a solemn promise fell from his lips.

"I will help you."

Without another word, Unsa took her hand, leading the way to his lair hidden high above in the swirling mists and clouds.

CHAPTER TWELVE

The Agali Village

The celebration taking place within the Agali Village was one that Anyan would have enjoyed thoroughly, if not for the adoration heaped upon Carrum over his successful kill of a black caiman. Anyan scowled as he took in the festivities taking place all around him. With his wounds nearly healed, he was in fine form, sitting upon a raised platform high above the villagers.

Ayusha sat to his left, and he found it fitting that he was on her right side. She wore an elaborate headdress upon her head, made from the breast feathers of the king vulture. The soft white covering created an arch above the black swath of her waist length hair, drawing attention to her face. Her breasts were bare, standing at attention as she swung in rhythm to the singing and dancing. Her hips were circled by an intricately woven belt dyed red with annatto seeds, drawing his eye to her colorful skirt of woven palm fibers. She sat in full awareness of the impact that she had on everyone present. Her husband had perished, but her son was still present and he was their leader, undeniably securing her position within the village.

"I see that our people are merry." Anyan said.

"Yes," Ayusha agreed, accepting a platter of food from the serving women.

Carrum had washed in the very same river from which he had taken the caiman, cleaning his body of the blood from the kill. But first he had taken one of the chosen young women to his lodge under the watchful eyes of his mother. Several young girls vied for his attention, but he chose only the most beautiful to accompany him. With the losses that they had suffered many seasons ago, their mating practices had changed. No longer did they choose one mate for themselves. Men and women were known to have more than one mate, even allowing their spouses to join with their sons or daughters when they came into their season of maturity.

"Will you partake of the feast, Anyan?"

Ayusha's question tested him. She knew that there was a variety of food, but the platter that she held contained the meat from various monkeys killed and butchered by their hunters. Anyan's first band and subsequent villages refrained from killing the treetop dwellers, holding them as above the other animals of the jungle. Now that he dwelled within the Agali Village as their shaman, she wanted to see evidence of his loyalty, even if it was by partaking of their food.

"I will eat anything that has been prepared."

"Good." Ayusha said, but she watched him as he lifted a piece of raw meat to his mouth and chewed. "That is the caiman that my son brought in this morning."

"And you are a proud woman, aren't you?"

"Not every hunter is capable of bringing down such a predator." Ayusha crowed, pleasure washing over her face as she urged Anyan to drink some of the fermented brew that had been prepared, a blend of ripe manioc and whatever tuber was in season. "My son is a man that stands above other men."

Anyan remained quiet, content to let Ayusha think that she held the upper hand for the moment. They had a symbiotic relationship that benefitted both of them, but he knew his purpose, and he wouldn't allow Ayusha to dissuade him from moving forward with his plan.

"Anyan, why aren't you participating in the festivities?" Ayusha asked.

"I have other matters to attend to this evening, and I am certain that my presence here isn't required."

"Ah, but it is." She swayed to the music wrought by the drums and singing of the villagers. Her skin glistened attractively in the stifling heat, and she leaned forward, displaying ripe, round breasts that captured his attention. "You are our shaman. What would we do without you?"

Ignoring the question, Anyan fired back with one of his own. "What are you doing to bring about the downfall of the Saika Village?"

Ayusha grimaced, sitting silently as her son leaned forward to speak to Anyan in an angry whisper. "You have no need to worry about matters that no longer concern you."

"It is easy for you to sit in judgment. You have your choice of the available young women." Anyan was a master of sensing weakness within a person, and he knew without a doubt that their lack of women was an undeniable weak point. Men gained status and honor by the women that they claimed for themselves, but within the Agali Village there was a disproportion gap between the amount of men and the number of women. He knew that ten seasons from now their numbers might increase, but what were the men to do until then? "You swore that we would bring about the downfall of our enemies. Yet, nothing has been done! They continue to grow in number while we wither away in the jungle."

"You are a forest dweller." Carrum reminded Anyan in a cold voice. "You know nothing of our ways."

"I am your shaman!"

Carrum smiled, locking eyes with Anyan. "Your role within our village is a farce. You give our people someone to go to when their children are ill or the omens are dark. You reside amongst us because my mother believes in keeping to the old ways." Carrum leaned closer. "You are the face of hope for them, but need I remind you to remember your place?"

"My place?" Anyan seethed, angry that Ayusha would allow her son to speak to him with such overt disrespect.

"You are here at our whim and nothing more."

Anyan's vision dimmed, but he took a deep breath, unwilling to allow Carrum to get the best of him. "I want you to kill the Saika shaman."

Carrum laughed outright, dismissing Anyan with a malicious grin.

"Why?" Ayusha asked.

"Because he has taken something that belongs to me."

Carrum's gaze sharpened with interest. "What has he taken?"

Unwilling to reveal his secret to either Carrum or his mother, Anyan remained silent.

"Don't worry Anyan, the Saika Village will be ours far sooner than you think." Ayusha's voice was soothing as she dismissed his concerns, effortlessly turning her son's attention back to the festivities that were being held in his honor.

The Cloud Forest

Through the gathering darkness, Suyan observed Unsa closely, watching his natural use of stealth and cunning as he led the way forward. Despite her misgivings, his complete oneness with the natural world around them rang true, unlike the hollow feeling that had been with her from the moment that she was given into Anyan's care.

The way forward had become increasingly steep and they climbed until her legs burned with fatigue, and her breath rasped in and out from the exertion. As the sun began to set, she looked over her shoulder, stunned by the beauty of the immense jungle. Spread out behind her were trees too numerous to name, along with bracken and bramble, mosses, lichens, and small streams. The jungle gurgled, hummed, and sang if she cared to listen.

Drawn back to the task at hand, she realized that her limbs fairly vibrated with the intensity of their efforts, and she noticed a growing sense of exhilaration filled her with each step. She looked back once again, watching as the jungle faded away into a sea of living green.

"We are in the cloud forest."

There were scatterings of grassland and clusters of trees unlike anything that Suyan had ever seen before. She was born of the lower jungle, and entering the place where Unsa dwelled was like entering a foreign world.

She bit her lip in hesitation as Unsa turned to her and extended his hand. The fog and mist confused her, making it appear as if he would disappear at any moment.

"It might take some time for you to adjust to the higher elevation." Unsa's voice echoed and suddenly frightened, Suyan reached out for him, grabbing on to his carrying sack with both hands. "Don't worry, I know my way."

Suyan wasn't worried. She could feel the heat emanating from Unsa's back, warming her hands even through the woven carrying sack. She ducked her head, afraid that he would see the path of her thoughts, but she had nothing to fear. His attention was riveted on the trail that he forged by memory alone.

"Watch your footing."

Unsa was tempted to carry her, he knew that her legs had to be weak from the steep climb, but her unwillingness to complain kept her from admitting weakness. She had refused his hand, but clung to his carrying sack, further confusing him. Either she trusted him or she didn't, but he would need her trust if she wanted his help.

He realized in an instant that he *wanted* to help her, more than anything. She slipped, and he turned, bracing her weight with ease. "I'm right here, Suyan. I won't let you go."

Her breath feathered against his chest, and he felt her nod. Perhaps it would have been best to stop for the night, but they were so close to his home that he had pushed her farther than he should have. The unmistakable sound of a waterfall caught her attention, and he urged her forward, aware that she inhaled sharply at the sight of the water streaming from the mountain while thick fog and mist almost shrouded it from view.

"We're almost home."

Home. The word brought tears to Suyan's eyes. She hadn't had a home since she was a young girl and her father and mother had been her safety and security. Relieved that Unsa couldn't see the wet trails that traveled over her cheeks, she kept step with him, allowing her tears to fall freely. If ever there had been hope in her heart, it was for a place where she belonged. The knowledge that such a gift would remain forever outside of her reach opened up the well of deep sorrow surmounted only by the gathering darkness.

Aware that Suyan wept, but unaware of the reason for her tears, Unsa pretended not to notice. His heart ached for the young woman that clung to his carrying sack with such raw trust. He could have led her anywhere, and he had the feeling that she would have followed blindly, just as she did now.

The familiar craggy walls of the mountain appeared barely visible against the fading light. He reached out a hand, touching the smooth stone in welcome, and the mountain embraced him in return. A few more steps led him to an overhang that at first appeared to lead nowhere, but he walked forward confidently. High above, the majestic black crags reached toward the sky, but they were lost in a cloak of fog. Unsa continued around the overhang until he reached a crack in the mountain, which led to a shallow cavern that he had claimed for himself.

Inside, there wasn't a rock or stone that was unfamiliar to Unsa, and he bent at the entrance, quickly gathering the fire making materials that he had left for just that purpose. The cave was dim with the fading light, but he used the spindle in his hand with evident familiarity, and after a time, the first tendrils of smoke drifted into the air as he sighed with relief.

Fire would make Suyan feel safe and secure. He took the fire bundle and walked to the fire circle placed midway between the entrance and the back of the cavern. The fire caught and blazed as he added a few pieces of wood from his carrying sack, gathered from the forest below.

He heard Suyan inhale sharply, and he looked up, aware of the reason that she was startled. The cavern had a natural opening at the top, allowing smoke to escape and also allowing them to see the swirling fog above.

"When the sky clears you can even see the stars shining from above." Unsa cleared his throat, "You can see the starlight."

"My name means starlight."

"I know."

Turning away from her, he set down his carrying pack and weapons, waiting for her to settle in for the night. She stood beside the fire staring up for a long time, and he pretended not to see the twin trails of tears that she no longer bothered to hide.

"Why have you brought me here, Unsa?" Suyan asked the question that had bothered her since their arrival. She had slept peacefully upon a woven leaf pallet, covered by a thinly stitched blanket. Unsa's presence had been a comfort, surprising her as nothing else had.

"You needed a safe place to heal."

She lowered her head as she thought about the bleeding that had followed childbirth. It was a difficult thing to hear a man speak so openly about such things, but as she looked up at him, she realized that he wasn't referring to physical healing.

"I have a bad spirit, there is no healing that is there?"

Unsa grimaced, he didn't know how deeply entrenched Suyan's beliefs were, but from everything that he had seen, she wasn't afflicted by a curse or a bad spirit. "Who told you such a thing?"

"Chota," Suyan supplied. "And Anyan confirmed it."

"And Chota is an authority on all things mystical just like Anyan?"

The improbability of that thought finally penetrated, and Suyan's eyes narrowed as she shook her head. "But my son died."

"Children die." He knew that his words were harsh, but he held up a staying hand. "Women die in childbirth. Men die by trauma, battle, or the effects of time. No one accuses them of such dark wonderings."

Suyan shook her head in disbelief. "But my mother and the people of Chota's band convinced me that I was cursed. I had to leave my mother behind!"

"You were forced to bend to their will, Suyan."

"No."

Unsa remained silent. He had come to learn that with Suyan it was best to allow her to reason on a matter by herself. "Tell me, how was your life after you were taken by the Agali warriors to become daughters of the sun?"

"My life?" Suyan shrugged. "I *lived.*"

"And was that enough?" he asked. "I remember a girl with shining black hair and bright eyes. At the time, you were eager to learn new things, and you even took an interest in healing before your mother left to marry Chota."

"I am not the same girl that you remember."

"I know," Unsa took a few steps away from Suyan, drawing her from the cave as effectively as an invitation to follow him. He held out his hand, but this time he wasn't reaching for her, this time his hand was outstretched over the scenic expanse. Suyan gasped.

In the clear light of day, she could see the immense jungle stretched out before them and the vast Mother River running like a ribbon below. A crystal clear waterfall fell from the heights of the cloud forest into the depths of the jungle, flowing into the distance. A colorful pair of blue macaws flew above the treetops soaring in acknowledgement of their unabashed freedom.

"You still have that girl's spirit. I only wish to see if the woman that you have become can find herself again." Unsa left her standing alone, braced by the mountain at her back and the world falling away before her.

CHAPTER THIRTEEN

Several days passed peacefully between Suyan and Unsa. He left her to her own devices, walking into the jungle each day to hunt or fish. One day, he led her down a steep incline, waiting patiently as she gathered ripe fruit, berries, and moss. Her quick hands couldn't hide the moss, and he realized that she still bled from childbirth.

Each time she turned to look his way, he appeared to be studying their surroundings, but he was already certain that they were alone. He simply didn't want Suyan to see how attuned he was to her every breath, her every movement.

His efforts to keep Suyan safe and to give her time to heal had brought about an unexpected attraction that tightened his chest even as he looked at her. She was lovely, it was true, but he was drawn to her by the depth of sadness that he sensed within her spirit, as well as the rare glimpses of the young woman that she used to be.

Suyan moved to stand beside him, meeting his eyes with uncharacteristic boldness. "I've been meaning to ask you something."

"Yes?"

"Are you able to remove the curse that caused me to do such terrible things?"

Unsa didn't respond immediately. He hadn't realized that she had any reservations as to his ability to help her, let alone that she still believed she was cursed by a bad spirit.

A slight wind blew and he watched as she moved her hands in the way of those that hoped to ward off evil. Realizing then that she wouldn't believe him if he merely assured her that she was free from evil, he sighed. "Do you believe that Anyan is a true shaman?"

Suyan stared, afraid to answer truthfully, but also unwilling to lie. "He professes to be a mystic, a man that communes with nature, but now I know for certain that he wasn't what he claimed to be." She stared at Unsa as if he would scold her for her admission. "He made my mother's band believe that he could help me, but I think that he only wanted…"

Unsa waited, afraid that she wouldn't finish her thought, while equally afraid that she would.

"Me."

"He wanted you for himself?" Unsa watched as her eyes lowered, but not before he saw her shiver with remembered fear.

She nodded. "Before giving birth, I had a feeling that I was being watched, but whenever I looked over my shoulder, there was no one there. In the end, I went with Anyan because my mother's husband gave me to him." Suyan's eyes filled with tears. "In the jungle, he wanted to mate with me, but I became sick with a fever, and he brought me to the Saika Village." She shrugged, wrenching his heart with the helplessness apparent in the gesture. "I was with him because I had no other choice."

Unsa found a large boulder warmed by the sun and he sat down, gesturing for her to do the same. When her shoulders relaxed, and her breathing became steady, he turned to face her. "Tell me about the ways of Chota's band. Are they very different from the people of the Saika Village?"

Suyan hesitated, but she quickly found herself eager to talk about the differences between Chota's band and the Saika Village. "I would have chosen to stay with the Saika Village after my mother remarried, but that was not my choice. The people in Chota's band are closely related, many intermarry between close relatives. I found myself drawn to the other young women who welcomed me openly. I wanted to be like them. I wanted to belong."

"In what ways were they different from the village of our birth?"

Suyan lowered her head. "Chota believed in omens, signs, and portents. The people belonging to his band believed the same. I learned to observe their rituals and way of life." She stared into the lush green jungle that encircled them. "It was a small thing to ask of me and my mother."

"Was it?"

For the first time, Suyan probed the validity of Chota's teachings.

"I learned to ward off evil." She demonstrated by moving her hands in front of her chest in a circular pattern.

"Tell me how they welcome their young girls into the blessings of womanhood."

"We were treated kindly," Suyan responded. "My mother and I weren't abused by Chota or his people. It wasn't until I failed to bring new life into their band that things began to change."

Unsa remained silent, recognizing the far away expression in Suyan's eyes.

"I was only thirteen seasons the first time that I underwent the first fruits ceremony." She glanced at Unsa. "All of the young women have a choice to give themselves back to their people during the first fruits ceremony. Chota urged me to participate, even though I was uncertain." She clasped her hands together, rubbing her palms against each other, until Unsa took her right hand in his much larger one.

"Tell me."

"I don't remember much about the first ceremony that I participated in." She bit her lip, lowering shadowed eyes to her lap. "I know that we bathed in the river, cleansing ourselves in preparation for what was to come. The other girls were so excited, and I shared their excitement. We didn't know what to expect other than the understanding that if we did as they asked us, we would be blessed with a child."

Suyan was quiet for so long that Unsa didn't know if she would continue speaking. He kept his silence, but anger brimmed just beneath the surface at the thought of Suyan at thirteen seasons, young, vulnerable, and desperate to belong.

"The girls of Chota's band aren't allowed to take a mate until after they have their first child. I wanted someone for myself, especially after realizing that my mother wasn't the same as she had been while married to my father." Suyan lifted her eyes to meet Unsa's gaze. "I went eagerly into the first fruits ceremony the first time, but I wasn't blessed with new life, not then."

"What happened?"

"I was ridiculed when many of the other girls became new mothers. They were honored as any new mother should be, but I was left with nightmares that wouldn't cease. My dreams caused me to awaken with fragmented memories of…"

Unsa waited. He didn't pressure her to continue, but it took all of his willpower to remain silent.

"Hands touching me in places where no one had ever touched me before, someone…perhaps more than one person hurting me deep inside." Suyan turned pleading eyes upon Unsa. "We were given a fermented drink with a bittersweet taste, and the other girls made a game of it. We laughed as we sputtered and puckered our lips, but we shared the entire vessel together as instructed."

Suyan remembered the singing and dancing that took place, and she told Unsa about it, but when it came to the actual ceremony, she remembered very little from that first occasion.

"I underwent another first fruits ceremony last season, even though I had resisted for four seasons, despite pressure from Chota and pleading from my mother. I knew that it was time for me to take a mate. I was a burden to Chota, a worry for my mother, and even by then the nightmares had begun to fade."

"Was the second ceremony any different from the first?"

Suyan nodded, causing the tears that filled her vision to overflow. She started to wipe away her tears, but Unsa was there, brushing his hands over her face as she looked into his eyes. Even seated, he was powerful and strong, a warm and steady presence, and she felt as if she could tell him anything.

"I followed the same ritual, washing in the river, drinking the bittersweet drink given to all the girls. I was the oldest amongst them, and perhaps more scared than I realized, because I only swallowed a tiny amount before passing the vessel on. I remember the laughter and excitement from the girls, the sights and sounds of the men dancing and singing as the girls were sent to recline upon woven pallets resting around the fire."

Suyan remembered the trepidation that had filled her chest, causing her to hesitate. She could see herself looking over at the girls to her right and her left, but their eyes were glazed and it was easy to see that they were lost in the visions the drink induced. "The next thing I remember were the hands that held me down. The men wore ceremonial masks, I never knew which man mated with me and to this day, I don't know who fathered my child."

Anger on her behalf pierced his heart. "Your father never would've allowed–"

"My father is dead." Suyan interrupted, seeing at once that she had surprised Unsa with the vehemence in her tone. He stared at her for another moment; his eyes were bright with a fire that she couldn't name. She softened her tone of voice, "Speaking of him won't bring him back. It won't make me any less guilty of causing the death of my child."

"You were taken against your will, violated by men that you trusted."

"It doesn't matter." Suyan dismissed the attack that still haunted her dreams. "My son is dead, and I am responsible for his death.

"Then you admit that you wanted to kill your son." It was a statement, not a question, but she suddenly retreated, furiously shaking her head.

"Never!" she rasped. "Not once did I wish the death of my child. From the moment that I realized life filled my womb, I was glad."

"Then how can you say that you killed him?" Unsa asked, "Or are you simply repeating what they told you?"

Unsa didn't wait for her to respond. He handed her the carrying basket that held the things she had gathered, and then he turned away.

"Follow me." He left her no choice except to follow or risk being left behind.

"I don't understand what you want to teach me." Suyan grumbled, angry with Unsa for dangling hope in front of her eyes. She felt as if a festering wound had been scraped raw by their earlier discussion, and even though she knew she was safe high up in the cloud forest, she felt exposed and vulnerable. "I can never forget my son. I will never forget the child born of my body."

"I wouldn't ask that of you." Unsa said. "A child that was a part of your body was also a part of your spirit. He should never be forgotten."

She wanted to cry in frustration, but she couldn't find any tears. Her eyes were as dry as her spirit. "Then what do you expect from me?"

He didn't answer her as he went about the ritual of cleaning away the food that he had prepared for them and banking the fire. Shame filled her, for these were the tasks that women often oversaw, but Unsa didn't seem to expect anything from her.

She was surprised when he left the cavern without a word, returning with a bundle wrapped by a skin covering. She had barely had enough time to use the water from the pool in the cavern to wash and cleanse her body, packing softened moss between her legs to stem the light flow of blood. A reminder of everything that she had lost.

"The girl that I remembered could weave a basket from a handful of fresh picked leaves. Isn't that so?"

Unable to speak over the lump in her throat, Suyan nodded.

Unsa stood, covering the cavern in ground breaking strides, and Suyan flinched, aware of how utterly vulnerable she was with this man that she remembered, but barely knew. She held up her hand as if to ward off a blow and shuddered as the bundle he had been holding landed on her lap. She blinked, breathing shallowly as her eyes finally focused.

"Leaves."

Unsa nodded, his spirit aching over the fear that had initially filled her eyes. "Make a basket."

He turned away, leaving her to ponder his request.

"A basket." She repeated in the silence as the urge to laugh bubbled up from her chest. She wiped both hands over her face, smothering her bout of hysteria and then she turned to the task of weaving a basket from the lush leaves of the Great Forest.

As the days passed, Unsa found various tasks to keep Suyan's hands busy, observing her behavior indifferently as she completed one task after another. She had taken it upon herself to prepare anything that he brought from the forest whether it was fresh meat or fish from one of the nearby streams. He provided the firewood that kept them warm at night, but she saw to the fire and to the cleanliness of the cavern.

He found it difficult to become accustomed to the sight of a woman waiting in his cavern whenever he returned. She still startled him with her loveliness, but the shadows under her eyes weren't as dark and her movements were no longer listless.

"Unsa, what are the strange markings on the wall?"

He looked over to see her standing near the cave entrance and he grimaced. He already knew that Suyan shied away from anything that she didn't understand, including the mystical and spiritual aspects that made up his way of life. Would she understand his need to keep a count of the days and changing seasons? He didn't know, but he walked to stand beside her, momentarily distracted by her closeness.

"I live here alone," Unsa explained. "You are the first person that I have ever allowed inside my home."

Overwhelming shyness caused Suyan to stumble over her response. "Thank you."

Turning his attention to the natural rock walls, he pointed out the thumbnail moon sign that he had carved just last night. "The seasons of the jungle are either wet or dry. The children of the jungle keep track of time by watching for the first ripe berries, the peach palm fruit, or even the appearance of certain flowers. I have found that keeping track of the passage of the moon helps me best."

He tried to make his explanation as simple as possible, but Suyan raised her hands in the familiar sign to ward off evil, and frustration mounted, causing him to reach for her hands. "Are the people that taught you these hand signs to ward off evil the same people that handed you over to Anyan?"

"Yes," Suyan whispered, shocked by his display of anger.

"Are they the same people that gave you twice into the first fruits ceremony?"

Suyan struggled with him momentarily, but then she reasoned that if he had intended to hurt her, he could have done so well before now. "You know that they are."

His jaw clenched as he nodded. "I would never give my child into such a ceremony, but I wonder, would you?"

Unsa let her go, leaving her with that question lingering between them. Suyan's startled gasp of dismay let him know that he might have finally reached her in some small way.

After their confrontation, Suyan made amends by leaving him a colorfully made basket that was large enough to hold the blue tipped arrows that he worked on during the evenings. Unsa accepted the offering with words of appreciation and their daily lives began to take on a comfortable routine, and each new day filled Suyan with a sense of harmony and renewed strength.

As the days passed, Unsa became aware of the ephemeral way in which he was drawn to her, even when she was sleeping. However, he refused to satisfy the hunger that grew inside of him. Yet, the sight of her resting peacefully on her side of the cave, gave him a sense of peace that he hadn't realized was missing from his life.

He came to learn that she was capable of fashioning small animal traps, which she proudly displayed for him one day, and he put them to immediate use. Each night they rested upon their woven leaf pallets and stared up at the star shine shimmering overhead. His hopes of helping Suyan overcome the terrible adversity that had almost broken her spirit began to strengthen, until the night that he dreamed.

The moment Unsa's head rested upon his forearm, he was lost in a world of dreams. Images came to him, one after another, and he trembled inside as he forced himself to look closer.

He reminded himself of his purpose, given to him in his boyhood, but accepted by him as he grew into a man that others could respect. River's teachings had gone a long way toward helping him acknowledge the fear that always stalked him. Fear of the future. Fear of knowledge.

The deep sense of knowing that overcame him caused him to quake, and he was distantly aware of his body arching and his limbs flailing, but powerless to stop himself from thrashing uncontrollably.

He saw the Saika Village, and it was clear to him that a great celebration was underway. Sappa and his friends were secluded in a special lodge built just for him, and he purified himself in preparation for the upcoming ceremony. A cup was passed between the young men, and each person drank deeply, accepting the contents stoically.

All was well, until Sappa clutched his belly, writhing in agony as he fell over, convulsing even as he vomited. Blood mingled with the contents of his belly spewed forth, and Unsa knew in that moment that the future leader of the Saika Village had been poisoned.

A terrible moan worked its way from his throat and in the stygian darkness of the cave, he opened his eyes.

Suyan wept into her hands as Unsa convulsed and his eyes rolled back in his head. She had been alerted by his terrible thrashing and when she scrambled to his side, nothing that she tried seemed capable of rousing him.

"Unsa." She whispered fearfully, aware that his thrashing had ceased. She couldn't see him in the darkness, but there was just enough light to see that his eyes were no longer white. She ran to the low burning fire and stirred it, rushing back to his side to see that the round orbs of his eyes were unfocused. "Unsa, please…"

She wasn't certain if her tearful pleas helped draw him back to her or if he returned on his own, she only knew that he blinked several times and then he struggled to a sitting position. It was the weakness that she sensed within the limbs of a man that had appeared to be as strong as the Great Mountain that caused her breath to hitch in panic.

"I need to go back."

Unsa's voice was urgent as Suyan urged him to settle and drink from the waterskin that she held up to his lips.

"Back where?"

"I need to go back to the Saika Village." Unsa swallowed convulsively, aware that he grabbed Suyan's arms to steady himself, and she didn't back away from him.

"Why?" Suyan asked. "Is it something that I've done? I promise I won't cause you anymore trouble. Please, just please let me stay here."

"I can't." He shook his head. "You wouldn't be safe here alone. We need to leave at first light."

"Why?"

"The dream was the reason that I went down to the Saika Village to begin with, but at the time, I woke up before I could see everything." Unsa wiped a hand over his face, staring into the distance with an expression of disbelief. "This time, I saw the dream in its entirety."

"What is it?" As she looked into his shadowed gaze Suyan was almost too terrified to hear the answer.

"Someone plans to poison Sappa." He stood up, swaying in place until she braced him with her body. "I might already be too late."

CHAPTER FOURTEEN

The Agali Village

Having been summoned by one of his mother's serving women, Carrum swiftly entered his mother's lodge. He moved to her side, sending the women that attended her scattering. The stench of overwhelming sickness hung in the air, stifling in the heat. He leaned over his mother's prone form, but he wasn't prepared for the sight that awaited him.

Ayusha's normally bright brown eyes were dull and dry. Her round cheeks were sunken and her lips were cracked, completely devoid of moisture. The scent of vomit clung to her sleeping pallet, and when he clasped her hand it was to find that she could barely return his grasp.

"Mother," Carrum's throat worked as he took in her frail appearance. His mind spun as he wondered how she had become so ill in such a short amount of time. It was true that a few of the villagers had complained of various ailments, but that was always the case. Anyan had performed many shamanistic rituals that had appeased those that were ill, if only for the time being.

Ayusha wet her lips, "My son."

Her expression was vague, almost as if she wasn't aware that he was truly kneeling beside her.

"I'm here, Mother."

"Agali is displeased with me."

Carrum kept silent. They both knew that any instance of misfortune was a direct result of Agali's displeasure. However, he couldn't imagine what his mother might have done to displease their god.

"You must make the sacrifice sooner than we planned."

Hanuq's granddaughter. The little girl had been kept away from the festivities in preparation for the sacrificial ceremony that would gather her to their ancestors.

Ayusha's face crumbled as she grabbed at her stomach, stricken by a wave of pain that shattered Carrum.

"I will do just as you have asked."

Ayusha moaned, whether in response to his words or from the pain, he didn't know. He left quickly, allowing the serving women to return to his mother's side where they would see to her needs. His burden was a heavy one, and he felt the weight of the task set before him as he breathed deeply of the fresh air, filling his lungs as he hadn't been able to within the confines of his mother's dwelling. He would keep his vow to his mother, and he would honor Agali with the sacrifice of Hanuq's granddaughter before sunrise.

All was in place, and Carrum waited in anticipation as the Agali people knelt below the raised platform where he had recently dined with his mother and Anyan. The shaman was standing at the bottom of the platform, ready to assist him, just as he had been commanded.

Dressed in a ceremonial tunic, woven with strips of rattan, dyed red, Carrum marked the occasion as the leader of their village. Platters of food were laid out in front of a large fire, circled by stones brought from the nearby river. The women of the village had taken the time to paint their faces and everywhere he looked their features were adorned with the esoteric and mystical signs common to their village.

The men stood on one side of the fire, and the women on the other, leaving a space between them as Hanuq's granddaughter, Ne'pa, was brought forward. The girl was resplendent in a sun bleached woven tunic that fell to just above her knees. A jade necklace adorned her neck, and her wrists were similarly ensconced. Her bright smile let him know that she awaited his summons with pleasure, but her unfocused gaze told him that she had been given enough of the fermented brew to keep her malleable. Ne'pa's long hair had been shorn at the waist and forehead and then braided with painstaking care. Her tawny skin fairly shone with cleanliness, and her eyes sparkled as the men and women smiled down upon her, touching her reverently.

"Blessed daughter." Carrum held out his hands, urging Ne'pa to come to him of her own free will. She walked forward without hesitation, taking his hand as she stared up at him out of shining eyes. She was the epitome of innocence and perfection.

Agali would be pleased.

Carrum knew that his mother would have given anything to see him stand in his father's place and invoke the name of their god before his people. She would have lifted her chin with pride as he touched the sacred knife that his own father had used for rituals and ceremonies in the past. He felt the power of his lineage stir within his blood as Ne'pa climbed onto the sunstone that had been put in place to mark this ancient ritual.

Peering down at the little girl, he whispered, "Don't be afraid."

She nodded trustingly, watching him with interest as he raised his glittering knife high overhead, and his people cheered, echoing his fierce cry in one strong voice. "For the honor and glory of Agali!"

The Saika Village

The drums were played by several of the village elders, and the song was both familiar and compelling. Sappa was drawn forward by Orchid, a smile dancing upon her lips as she held her brother's hand, openly acknowledging the proud young man that would soon become their new leader.

A lodge had been built by the men, one that had never been lived in before and would be used by Sappa after he took his place as their leader. Tonight, he and the young men that were closest to him would enter the lodge and undergo a purification ritual of immense importance. High overhead the moon was almost full, signaling the time of the leadership ceremony.

Sappa was unarmed, wearing only a loincloth and the colorful yellow and green rattan strips tied at his elbows and knees. His long black hair gleamed in the firelight, drawn back from his face by a narrow band tied behind his head. Lark and River stood off to the side, watching the procession with their son standing between them. Yama's eyes brimmed with tears as she acknowledged her son with a mother's quiet smile. Ransa leaned close to his wife, sheltering her with one arm as he watched Sappa make the symbolic walk to his lodge. The walk itself symbolized his passage into manhood and in his case, the path to leadership.

He stood proudly, waiting for Orchid to acknowledge him before their entire village. All eyes were upon them as brother and sister stood side by side. Orchid's smile was stunning as she turned to face their people.

"Long ago, my father led our village by right of blood. His legacy lives on in the form of his children. In the past, my brother was too young to lead and it fell to me to stand in the place of leader." Orchid's features were lit by the village fires, and her braided hair hung free to her waist. She was adorned in a finely woven skirt, dyed yellow and bright orange. Her breasts were bare, and around her neck hung a necklace of jade stone. She touched their father's stone necklace with one graceful hand, before returning her attention to Sappa. "You will enter the lodge and undergo the purification ritual, and when you emerge, you will be ready to become our new leader."

She extended her hands, accepting the ceremonial vessel from Tupin who looked on with a curious expression upon his face. Orchid sipped from the cup, smiling boldly as she extended the vessel to her brother.

"Thank you, Orchid." Sappa said, "I'll never forget you or Lark for everything that you've done." He looked at his mother and Ransa, the man that had been like a father to him. "I hope that I will always make you both proud of me."

Yama smiled through tears as Ransa nodded. Sappa took a swallow of the fermented brew that signified Orchid's willingness to pass leadership over to him. The tears in his sister's eyes made his chest tighten as he was ushered into the lodge along with his closest companions.

The Agali Village

Anyan sat upon the raised platform where the sunstone gleamed in the dappled sunlight. He was surrounded by clay vessels containing the organs of the girl chosen by Agali. The Agali women had come forward to see to the girl's remains while he chanted in a low voice.

One woman's voice captured his attention, breaking through the trancelike state that he had entered. "The Great Sun has spoken."

Bristling due to the respect that he heard in the voices of the Agali villagers as they spoke of Carrum, he kept his eyes closed, shifting from side to side. They called Carrum the Great Sun, named as his father had been named. It was a sacred honor reserved for the leader of the Agali Village, but he also knew that they watched him with new reverence. Last night, under Carrum's watchful eyes, he had performed his tasks as shaman in a manner befitting a holy man of the Agali. Even with his eyes tightly closed, he sensed their reverence and fear. Fear of him.

A dark shadow fell across his face and without opening his eyes, Anyan spoke. "I have had a vision. It is a dark dream of death and mourning."

Carrum stood still, watching their shaman through eyes narrowed into angry slits. When Anyan opened his eyes, he drew back, surprised to see only the whites of his eyes showing.

"What have you dreamed?" Carrum barely recognized his voice as the hair on his arms stood on end.

"Ayusha," Anyan's entire body shivered as he forced the words forth. "Your mother will die unless you do something to save her."

Carrum swept forward, bending to clasp Anyan by the throat. "Do not speak my mother's death aloud. She is still living. She will yet live!"

Anyan struggled to break free as he twisted and bucked under Carrum's hands. When Carrum finally released him, Anyan blinked furiously, returning to himself as he placed both hands over his bruised throat.

"You know nothing of the future!" Carrum charged.

"I don't know what you mean."

"You said that my mother would die unless I acted."

"Ah," Anyan nodded. "A spirit induced dream inspired by Agali."

Carrum flashed a warning glance toward Anyan as the serving women backed away, leaving the men alone on the platform. "If there is a way to save my mother, tell me now."

Anyan's eyes flashed with a calculating gleam, noticed by Carrum. "There is always a way."

"What do you want?" Carrum growled, speaking low so that they would not be overheard.

"There is a woman that belongs to me. She dwells within the village of our enemies."

"Why would I give you anything?"

"Because in doing so, you will save your mother's life." Anyan's expression shifted as Carrum watched him steadily while reaching for his weapon. "Will you do what I ask?"

With a nod of his head, Carrum agreed.

"Betray me and you will find yourself holding your mother's lifeless body." Anyan spoke before Carrum could lash out at him with the knife that he held in his hands. "A similar sickness has fallen upon our enemies, and yet they have survived. Their healer knows how to bring life back to your mother's dying body. Bring her here, and you will save Ayusha's life."

CHAPTER FIFTEEN

The Saika Village

Sappa sat with the ten young men that would stand with him when he became their leader. Pago was with him, and he knew his friend was angry to find that Tupin had also been chosen. Tupin's family was one that had a close friendship with his mother's husband and also River. It would have been a slight beyond measure if he hadn't invited the ambitious young man into the purification ceremony.

Steam filled the lodge as Pago poured water over several stones, and the young men began to show the first signs of the heat. The air inside the lodge was stifling, but it was the drink being passed from hand to hand that held Sappa's attention. He wasn't familiar with the sacred brew known as Ayahuasca, but he knew enough about it to be wary. The men of his village had warned him that the visions that came from the drink were stunning and bold. They also told him that he should do his best to hold the liquid inside his body for as long as possible, even when every instinct would urge him to spew the contents of his belly upon the ground.

All of the young men were in fine humor, and Tupin smiled boldly as he slapped Sappa on the back and spoke, "We are glad to be with you during this pivotal time in the history of our people. Tonight we will drink with you and share our dreams and visions with one another."

Pago's low growl was barely audible and Sappa glared at his friend. He knew that it was Pago's right to give the speech that would begin the purification ceremony, but such small things didn't matter. Whether or not Tupin meant to take the honor from

Pago no longer mattered. Sappa felt the rightness of the moment, he felt the legacy left to him by his father shifting and settling upon his shoulders. Nothing and no one would ruin the moment that he had dreamed about for so long.

Tupin handed him the horned cup that rested near the fire. "Drink and we will follow."

Sappa nodded, accepting the cup with two hands as he inhaled deeply. This was his moment. He lifted the cup to his lips and swallowed before handing the vessel back to Tupin. As he watched, each of the young men drank their fill.

Unsa moved with an urgency unlike anything that he had felt since his boyhood. It was as if the jungle itself had turned against him, betraying him when he needed it most. Suyan followed behind, but even her sturdy legs couldn't keep up with the pace that he set. He stopped and faced her, holding out his hand to her as she slid to a stop.

"I must hurry." Unsa said, staring into warm brown eyes filled with worry.

"Then you should leave me." Suyan gasped as she tried to keep her breath. "I know that I'm only slowing you down."

"I can't leave you, Suyan."

"Yes, you can." Suyan stood to her full height and only then did the top of her head reach Unsa's chin. She locked eyes with him, unwilling to back down. "We're more than halfway there and you said that there was still a chance to stop what will take place."

"There is always hope."

"Then go." Suyan didn't know where her brave words came from. She wanted nothing more than to keep Unsa with her. He was the one that made her feel protected and safe. He was the one that made her feel brave.

She finally understood why he had given her task after task within the safety of his cave, hidden high in the cloud forest. With each task, he had given her back small pieces of herself, pieces that she didn't even know had been stolen away. Once, long ago, she had been a timid girl, but a young woman with spirit and heart. Living amongst Chota's band had stolen her spirit and heart from her, and it was this that Unsa sought to return. While Lark was a healer that aided the body, she had come to realize that Unsa was a man that healed the spirit.

The unfounded fears and irrational notions that had kept her prisoner slid to the wayside as she looked into Unsa's expressive eyes.

"Go." She urged.

Unsa hesitated. He couldn't tell her that he might already be too late, not when he could see in her eyes that she had hope that he might be able to intervene in events that were spiraling out of control. She needed him to succeed, he saw that as well.

Giving in to the desire that had been with him from the moment that he had first taken Suyan into his arms, he pulled her close.

Suyan gasped, but she didn't draw away.

"We're almost halfway there." Unsa said, holding her loosely. "I'll leave a trail that you can follow as it gets light." He inhaled slowly, his voice deep and compelling. "Tell me if I'm frightening you."

She shook her head, surprised by the intense swell of emotion that she felt as he held her close. The heat from his body was entrancing, making her wonder what it would be like to be even closer to him. Although she had shared in the mating ritual, it had never been by choice or without the mind altering affects of the ritualistic drink imbibed by everyone. Unsa made her wonder how it would feel to give herself to one man and one man only.

"Suyan," Unsa didn't know what more he wanted to say, the feel of her body pressed willingly against him left him wanting more. He leaned toward her, giving her more than enough time to draw away and when she merely closed her eyes, he brushed her lips lightly, keeping the hunger that he felt for her under control.

She gasped, inadvertently opening her mouth for his possession, but he kept the pressure upon her mouth gentle, tasting her essence, inhaling her scent. The innocence in her kiss told him that she had no experience with the pleasures that men and women were capable of giving to one another. His blood rushed through his veins as he thought about being the one to show her just exactly how much pleasure there was to be found, but the urgency of the situation made him end their kiss, albeit reluctantly.

"Suyan." He touched his forehead to hers, too winded to talk. It was she that surprised him as she pulled back to stare into his face.

"I gave that kiss to you." Suyan said. "It was my first."

Unsa nodded, "I know."

She wanted to draw him to her again, but if he wanted to help Sappa, he would need every moment. "He mustn't die. Go."

Unsa handed her his hunting knife and spear. Her face tensed, and he knew that she was afraid that she would somehow taint the power in his weapons, but he shook his head. "We make our own power."

Suyan nodded, accepting the protection that he offered.

He stroked one hand over her head, tugging the ends of her hair, just as he had in their childhood before saying, "We will see each other again." And then he was gone.

CHAPTER SIXTEEN

Unsa ran through the jungle with a strength and power that would have stunned even the most skilled hunter. The fate of an entire village rested upon his ability to traverse his surroundings with an agility and dexterity born of a lifetime spent within the jungle. He resisted the defeating thought that the jungle itself conspired against him. Instead, he drew upon the birthright given to him by his ancestors. He reminded himself that his blood flowed green; his father was born of this jungle, as well as his grandfather and on and on, since time before memory. He was a part of the bold, intense, ever changing world around him.

He had to believe that he wouldn't have been given the gift of visions and dreams unless he was also given the ability to do something about them.

It seemed incomprehensible to him that Sappa would be allowed to die. The young man was fully prepared and perfectly capable of being the leader that his people needed to ensure their survival.

"He mustn't die."

Suyan's words reverberated through his thoughts, and he could almost feel her avid desire to see him safely ensconced within the company of the young Saika leader. He couldn't help but admire her bravery and courage, along with her willingness to learn a new way. He even found himself admiring the way that she handled her grief over the loss of her son. He ran away from the one woman that he wanted tucked safely against his side. But no matter how much distance he put between himself and Suyan, he realized that while he had been focused upon helping her, she had stolen a large portion of his spirit while he remained unaware.

Releasing his breath, Unsa gave in to the downward sweeping landscape, working with it as it pulled him forward. When palm fronds, vines, and the thorny arms of branches touched his skin, he felt as if they were brothers of the flesh, urging him onward. Every step, every heartbeat was focused upon a single purpose: he needed to reach Sappa in time to save his life.

Lark and River remained with the other villagers as the festivities continued. Their son's face was bright with excitement, but the worst of his illness was past even though Lark watched him with a mother's watchful eye.

"He's fine, Lark." River noticed his wife's distracted stare, and he almost laughed when she looked at him guiltily.

"I know, but just a few days ago, he was so ill."

"That time has passed." Yama added. "I know what it's like to worry over your child, before long he will be a man fully grown, and you will have to contend with the same feelings that you have now."

Ransa exchanged a look with River. Both men grinned, thinking the same thought. *If it were left to women, boys would be coddled to death before they ever reached manhood.*

The easy camaraderie between the men faded as a commotion from the crowd drew their attention. River was instantly alert, drawing his wife and son to stand behind him.

"What is it?" Yama asked, "What's wrong?"

"I don't know."

River heard Lark answer her mother, but he kept a tight hold on her hand. As the village healer, she was often the one called forth whenever someone was sick or injured. He was more protective of her now in her delicate state, and as always, he was abundantly cautious.

He moved forward with his wife's hand upon his back, but the crowd shifted and River's eyes widened over what he saw. At his side, his wife silently handed her son over to her mother, and

Yama clasped the boy by the shoulders, holding him back protectively.

Lark's entire body stiffened as they caught sight of Sappa. He had been carried from the lodge by the other young men, but his normally ruddy complexion was devoid of color, and the pain on his face was a terrible thing to behold.

"Lark," River ran forward as his wife fell to her knees beside Sappa. "Is it the same sickness as before?"

Lark's hands flew over Sappa's body, checking for injury, observing the contents that he spewed until his body shook in dry heaves. Blood mingled with the last dregs from his belly stained the ground.

Lark locked eyes with River and tears blurred her vision, startling her husband.

"Tell me," River touched his wife's arm, while all around him the villagers wept and screamed in panic.

"It's not the same sickness at all." Lark answered. "I fear that Sappa was poisoned."

Unsa entered the Saika Village without receiving an acknowledging answer to his birdcall. His stomach dropped as he realized that the younger boys that should have been on guard for intruders were nowhere to be found. There were several fires burning in and around the village, but Unsa didn't stop as he ran directly to the center of the village, the same place that he had seen in his dream. The newly constructed lodge was there, and all around him people stood in a semi-circle looking down upon something on the ground.

Unwilling to believe that he was too late, Unsa pushed his way through the crowd. Once the villagers realized who had touched them, they began to back away. Grief stricken moans came from the inner circle and Unsa's heart fell. *It couldn't be.*

He stood in silence, looking down upon a scene of utter heartbreak as he saw Sappa's prone body with his sister Orchid weeping into her hands. Lark and River knelt on Sappa's other side, and he could tell that something terrible had befallen the young man by the frantic way that Lark touched Sappa.

"Lark," Unsa's voice was hoarse with dread.

Orchid looked up and there was fury in her eyes. She jumped to her feet and hurled herself at Unsa.

"You knew that he was in danger, and you left!" Orchid's grief induced attack barely registered as Yama and Ransa pulled the young woman away.

"Tell me what happened."

Lark's face was streaked with tears as she looked up, meeting Unsa's eyes for the first time.

"Someone poisoned my brother."

"Can you do anything to help him?" Unsa asked.

"I would have given him something to induce vomiting, but he has vomited until there is nothing but clear fluid left in his stomach." Lark gasped, unable to continue.

River stepped forward, placing one hand on his wife's shoulder in silent comfort. "Sappa and ten other young men entered the purification lodge. They were to drink a fermented brew made by our elders. But somehow the drink itself made Sappa ill."

"No, River." Lark wiped at her face, stubbornly refusing to give in to anymore tears. "This was a deliberate act of poison. The elders made a drink of Ayahuasca and fermented tubers, but nothing within the contents would have caused this type of response."

"Lark?" Orchid's eyes were swollen and red. "Will my brother live?"

An unaccustomed fury filled Lark's face. "He is *our* brother, Orchid. He belongs to no one but himself, but he is our brother."

"I know," Orchid's eyes welled with tears. "Please don't be angry with me, not now. I only wish to know if Sappa will recover."

Yama stepped between her daughters, but her hands trembled as she clasped them together. "Will he live?"

Her question echoed in Lark's ears, and she wanted nothing more than to weep out her sorrow. "I have done everything that I know," her voice broke and she swallowed. "We will see that he is made comfortable."

As one, Unsa and River lifted Sappa into their arms, carrying him toward Yama's lodge as the people of their village followed along. Orchid wept openly, while Lark's son guided his mother. The swell of grief that had come to the Saika Village was an intense eddying wave, unspeakable in its destructive power.

Unsa sat within Yama's lodge, surrounded by Sappa's closest family members. They were silent, sitting in wait as they all watched the young man for signs of life. Orchid's quiet weeping tore at their hearts, but they didn't urge her not to cry. Some of them wept with her, if only on the inside.

"I have done everything that I can." Lark's soft voice echoed her earlier assertion, but it was as if she was searching for something, anything that she might have missed.

"There must be something else that you can do." Orchid's outraged cry had all eyes turning toward her. "You can't abandon him."

"Enough!" River's strong voice nullified anything that Lark would have said in response to her sister's vicious accusation. "Speak one more word and I will see that you are thrown out of this lodge."

"Mother," Orchid fell into another fit of weeping as Yama stroked her hair and looked up with a stricken expression upon her face. "Lark, of course you know best in matters of healing."

Lark nodded once, locking eyes with Unsa as she left her mother's lodge. River and Unsa followed.

"Lark," River stroked his wife's hair, drawing her into his embrace. "Is there anything I can do to help you?"

"Yes," Lark nodded. "Stay with my brother while I see to those that are still recovering from the sickness that plagued our village.

It will give me comfort to know that you are here watching over him."

Unsa looked away, unable to watch the grief stricken couple as they spoke privately to one another. He would have remained inside if not for the imploring look that Lark sent to him. Just as he started to turn away, he looked to the village entrance and saw Suyan walk forward, carrying his spear and hunting knife. Her hair was windblown and her cheeks were high in color, but she appeared to be unharmed.

"Unsa." Suyan hurried over to his side, handing his weapons over with unsteady hands. "Is he…"

"He's alive." Unsa answered as Suyan faltered. "He was poisoned."

"No." Suyan covered her mouth as she turned wide, frightened eyes upon Lark and River. "I'm so sorry. We tried to reach you in time."

"You tried…" River looked between them in confusion. "How did you know?"

Suyan turned a startled glance toward Unsa. "You didn't tell them?"

"No, I didn't have a chance." Unsa rubbed her arms soothingly, "I wasn't able to stop it, no matter how fast I ran to get here."

River growled, breaking into their conversation with a slashing motion of his hand. "Unsa, tell us how you knew what would happen here."

"I dreamed it." Unsa answered.

CHAPTER SEVENTEEN

"If you dreamed that Sappa would be poisoned, I know in my heart that you did everything you could to reach our village in time." Lark's words offered comfort, humbling Unsa simply because as Sappa's sister, she was the one that he should have been comforting.

"I thought perhaps I would reach the village in time to stop it from happening, but I was wrong." The thought of Sappa's too still form brought shards of pain forth, and he closed his eyes, momentarily speechless.

"No." Lark stepped forward. "I refuse to believe that you were warned, but unable to help Sappa. He's still alive. That in itself shows that his will is strong. I only know of a few poisons that could have acted so quickly."

"You and I both know which poisonous plants grow in the jungle. I can think of three that are relatively easy to find." Lark twisted her hands together. "Nightshade, hemlock, and white snakeroot are all nearby, but who besides the two of us would know that?"

Unsa's eyes darkened to onyx, and his gaze hardened.

Suyan stepped forward, placing one hand upon his shoulder. "Unsa, if you know anything you have to tell them."

"Unsa?" Lark's tone was fearful, her brows furrowed in concern.

"I believe that Orchid poisoned Sappa."

Suyan and Lark reared back as if he had shouted the words instead of speaking in a clear, firm voice.

"No!" The cry came from the entrance of the lodge. Orchid stared at them out of eyes that brimmed with tears, and her face was a mask of anger and outrage. "How dare you accuse me of poisoning Sappa? If you had been here, you would know that I drank from the same cup as my brother."

"It's true, Unsa." River inserted. "We saw Orchid drink from the ceremonial cup before Sappa entered the lodge with the other young men."

"Lark!" Orchid called to her sister as she collapsed in her arms. "Everyone is against me."

Lark glanced helplessly at River, aware that he was concerned not only for her and Orchid, but for the young man that he had watched over since Sappa's boyhood. "We will find whoever did this, but we can't accuse anyone without proof."

River silently held Unsa's gaze and then Lark stepped forward, but not before giving Orchid into the care of their mother.

"Can you do anything for him, Unsa?"

It was the same question that River had asked him regarding his son, and coming from Lark it struck him like a blow. "You are the healer. Anything that I learned about healing, I learned from you."

"I heal the body when possible." Lark acknowledged. "But you touch the spirit." She looked at Suyan as if giving him proof. "If Sappa's spirit is strong, he will survive, but if he gives in to the weakness caused by the poison…"

Unsa heard the unspoken words. *He will almost certainly die.*

He was aware of Suyan's startled inhalation of breath, and he knew that all of her past fears had returned in an instant. However, he focused inward, sensing within himself the answer to Lark's request. "I will do what I can to sing back his soul."

"Tell me what I can do to help you." Lark turned to face Unsa, aware that he was at his most powerful and his most fragile whenever his eyes darkened until they were almost obsidian in color.

Unsa didn't speak. Instead, he motioned for River to bring Sappa and lay him on the matting of large leaves that he had prepared.

They were near a river with fresh flowing water, but it wasn't the river itself that drew them. It was the clay.

"Cover him from head to toe."

Lark's startled face was trumped only by Suyan's confused expression. River stood by protectively as the women scrambled down to the water's edge, gathering the gray tinged clay by the handful. Lark placed two large handfuls of wet, moist clay over Sappa's abdomen, looking once at Unsa only to find that his eyes were closed.

Suyan followed, but she hesitated, and in her uncertainty she lost much of the wet clay. The events of the day had taken their toll upon her, and she lifted a weary gaze toward Lark. "I'm sorry."

Lark didn't scold her, but when Suyan came to stand beside her, she tugged at her hand. "I need you to go."

Suyan stared at her uncomprehendingly. "Lark, he is my cousin."

And he is my brother. The unspoken words didn't need to be said.

Lark's brown eyes sparkled. "If you believed as I believe, then you would know that your doubt and fear is as much a poison to my brother as the toxin that threatens his life."

Suyan's eyes widened. "Oh, Lark, I would never purposely harm Sappa."

"Yes, but he needs those who believe surrounding him now."

"You're right." Suyan stepped away. "I wish that I could be different."

"Suyan." Lark watched as her cousin turned with a hopeful expression on her face. "Thank you for caring so much."

Confusion clouded her face, but Suyan nodded in uneasy acceptance. As she left, she stared at Unsa, waiting for him to acknowledge her departure, but he kept his eyes closed and there was a frown line between his dark winged brows, as if he was in deep concentration.

With River's steady presence at her side, Lark returned again and again to paint Sappa's body with clay.

Unsa wasn't aware of Lark and River backing away from him as he leaned over Sappa's prone form. While the women were busy gathering clay, he had searched the edges of the water for a particular frog, bright green and orange in color. Its purposes were known only to a few, and it wasn't long before Unsa had the frog stretched between two long sticks. He scraped the back of the frog with the stem of a plant, drawing out the viscous, sticky fluid that would aid him on his journey. He let the frog go unharmed, placing the dregs upon the insides of his wrists and a small amount under his tongue.

Sappa remained unresponsive, lying as still as death, but there was an irregular heartbeat that drummed out a rhythm against his palms. Unsa could feel the heat of life under his palms and he sensed Sappa's spirit clinging to the shell of his body.

He tilted his head at an angle, concentrating on the spark of life that made Sappa unique from any other creation. All around him, the jungle waited in breathless anticipation, but Unsa hesitated, uncertain whether or not to proceed.

Working from instinct and self-training alone would only take him so far. He didn't know if he could help Sappa; he only knew that he had to try. Lark's healing abilities had gone as far as they could and now their only hope rested with him.

He remembered how Yama had touched her son's face, holding back tears as River carried him from her lodge. The thought of Yama's grief should she lose her son, threatened to pull Unsa away from the tendril of power that flowed through him. He reached out with his spirit, drawing from the jungle, feeding off of its rich bounty.

Placing both hands over Sappa's stomach, he focused his attention upon the coldness that radiated up from his palms. The jungle was hot, burning in places, but Sappa's skin was clammy to the touch and the coldness that he sensed was one that radiated through the young man's spirit, threatening to burn out the life that flowed through him.

In this safe place of contentment and safety, he felt the connection of every living thing and it humbled and nurtured his spirit. He could see the vibrant hues that made up the Great Forest and everything within it. The colors were so bright that they blinded him, coalescing into a display of brilliant sunlight.

With his mind focused on the vociferous life around him, Unsa fought back against the cold draining Sappa's life force with the unending power of the jungle.

Captivated by the leashed power in Unsa's movements Suyan watched in quiet fascination as he left Yama's lodge without making a sound. She had slept fitfully throughout the night even after Unsa returned with Sappa prone form bound to a litter. River and the members of Sappa's family had looked on silently as they helped settle Sappa on the sleeping pallet inside the lodge.

Not a word had been spoken, and it was clear to see that Sappa's condition was unchanged.

To her shock and dismay, she was almost relieved. A part of her didn't want to believe that Unsa was capable of singing back Sappa's soul. The thought itself caused a frisson of unwavering fear to travel over her backbone. She asked herself what it would mean for their future if Unsa had been capable of saving Sappa's life. But almost immediately her selfish thoughts shamed her.

The kiss that she had given Unsa on their descent from the cloud forest had been rich with meaning. It had signified her first step toward the future, toward the mending of her broken heart and fractured spirit.

She stood, suddenly unable to remain within Yama's lodge when her conscience plagued her. It wasn't that she wanted Sappa to die, she would have given anything to see that he lived, but she didn't want Unsa to be the mystical, spiritual man that others believed him to be.

Perhaps his vision was only a fevered dream. Perhaps he wasn't a shaman at all, but a man like any other.

Suyan looked around as she realized that she had left the village behind without telling anyone where she was going. It seemed a natural thing to follow Unsa, but if she hoped to catch up with him, she would have to hurry.

Standing in one place while she contemplated her future wouldn't do her any good. Not too long ago, every sound, every snap of a twig or call of a bird had made her think that Anyan had found her. Somewhere along the way, she had come to believe that Unsa would protect her from Anyan and anything else that threatened her wellbeing.

She searched her surroundings for any sign of his whereabouts.

Her knowledge of the jungle was equivalent to any other woman her age, and she stared hard at the ground in the early morning light as she picked up his trail.

She moved cautiously through the forest, aware that Unsa might have sought a moment of privacy, and she had no reason to follow him. Would he be shocked to learn that the only comfort she had found since the death of her son was from him? His presence seemed to nullify whatever bad spirit had overtaken her at the birth of her child, and she needed him now more than ever.

It didn't take her long to find him, but when her eyes finally registered the scene in front of her, she clapped one hand over her mouth to keep from screaming.

Unsa sat upon the ground with his legs crossed and his back braced by the roots of a tall strangler fig. Something about his absolute stillness made her instantly wary. It was only as she raised her eyes to look past Unsa that she was glad that her hand covered any sound that she might make.

Her eyes widened as she picked out the details from the surrounding forest. A powerfully built jaguar crouched just ahead of Unsa, ready to spring at the first provocation. Its muscles bunched and quivered as Unsa sat unmoving, staring at the magnificent beast without any sign of fear.

Suyan took in the sight of the jaguar, noticing its fiercely lit eyes and stunning golden coat, dotted by solid black circlets of varying size. The animal's entire body rippled as it stretched once, flicking its tail as if in silent acknowledgement. Suyan was aware of the sounds from the jungle, which were normal and uninterrupted. She could hear birds singing from the treetops and upon the ground smaller animals scurried from place to place.

She was aware that Unsa was unarmed, and she tensed as the jaguar took a cautious step forward, flicking its tail in a hypnotic cadence that drew the eye. He walked past Unsa, leaving him unharmed, and it was only as he disappeared into the dense jungle foliage that Suyan allowed herself to exhale. The majesty, the sheer beauty of the moment overwhelmed her.

"You were right to be cautious." Unsa turned his head toward her, allowing her to see that he had been aware of her presence from the first. "But you shouldn't have followed me."

Suyan took a fearful step away from him, frantically making the sign to ward off evil, and then she turned and fled.

CHAPTER EIGHTEEN

Unsa sighed heavily as he watched Suyan flee. Disappointment surged through him, even as he recognized that he shouldn't have expected her to understand his affinity for the jaguar, but he also hadn't expected her to seek him out. She knew the jungle as well as anyone else, and she had every reason to fear the jaguar. The crushing power of the animal's jaws was unparalleled, coupled with its ability to kill prey in one lethal bite, marked the animal as one to be feared.

He followed her trail back to the village, and he wasn't surprised to find her sitting silently outside of Yama's lodge. The expression on her face was one of abject fear and utter disbelief.

When he reached out to touch her shoulder, she recoiled.

"Suyan," he kept his voice calm and evenly pitched. "You could have been injured."

"And you?" she asked with a caustic edge to her voice. "Shouldn't you have been cautious of the jaguar?" She pronounced the word in the ancient way. *Yaguar.* Coming from her, the sound of the elusive animal's name was unique and lyrical. Before he could answer, she shook her head, holding up one hand to forestall him. "You don't have to explain. I don't want to know."

She wouldn't look at him, and he walked to her side, standing silently until she finally met his gaze.

"I'm sorry that you were frightened."

She exhaled softly, her eyes wide as she met his gaze. "You truly are a shaman."

"Suyan?" Lark stepped out of Yama's lodge, but she stopped as soon as she saw Unsa.

The tense silence between the pair spoke volumes, and she was surprised when Suyan stood, hurrying to her side.

"Yes."

Lark tore her gaze from Unsa's face, unable to miss the way that his jaw ticked and clenched. "I wanted to know if you would like to gather a few plants that might help Sappa."

"Of course." Suyan grabbed the extra basket that Lark carried and held it in front of her like a warrior's shield. Lark couldn't help but notice that she wouldn't meet Unsa's gaze.

"Unsa," Lark captured his attention. "Thank you for everything."

His expression turned hopeful. "Has there been any change?"

"Not yet," Lark answered as she followed behind Suyan.

"How was your time spent with Unsa in the cloud forest?" Lark asked, keeping a watchful eye on Suyan.

Her cousin shrugged, but her eyes held a sadness that touched Lark's heart. "Speaking of what troubles you might help."

Suyan's eyes widened. "I know that you're worried about your brother, I didn't mean to upset you earlier."

"You didn't upset me." Lark answered. "I realize that many people have a difficult time believing in things that are unseen. My husband is one of them, but he can also see that there are some things that simply exist, with no explanation or reason."

"You mean Unsa's ability as a shaman."

"Amongst other things."

"Is it wrong that I see him as a man?" Suyan asked. "He's so strong, Lark. He's so powerful and protective. In the cloud forest, it's as if the rest of the world doesn't exist. He taught me so much." Suyan shook her head helplessly, unable to explain everything that she had learned.

"Try." Lark prodded, although she quickly explained, "Whenever my emotions are jumbled, it takes more effort to put my thoughts into words. In this way, you and I are very much alike."

Suyan nodded, thinking of the things that she wanted to express. "At first, I was afraid of everything." She shook her head. "I was even afraid of myself. In my mother's village, they believed that I had a bad spirit, that I killed my son."

"Oh, Suyan." Lark touched her shoulder, looking into her eyes as they welled with tears.

"I would never have hurt my child." Suyan spoke through her tears. "Never."

"I know," Lark soothed. "Remember, I knew you when you were a young girl ready to learn the ways of healing. You're naturally empathetic with others, and that is a part of your spirit that you can never change."

"I barely remembered the girl that I was in the past. After so many seasons of trying to fit into Chota's band, I didn't want to remember my past."

"Why don't you accept Unsa as he is?" Lark asked. "You were the first to reveal that he was a dreamer."

Suyan remembered seeing Unsa again for the first time in far too long. Gone was the boy with the frightened eyes and thin, lithe frame. Unsa had become a man that walked in full confidence, accepting himself fully and unwilling to bend for anyone. A part of her respected him, but another part feared his inherent use of the natural world around them.

"Chota's band was very superstitious, Lark. I was taught that there are omens everywhere, if one takes the time to look. I learned to heed the call of a bird, the flight of an owl, or a snake lying in wait. All of these things were signs to watch out for and they spoke of good or evil." She thought of the way that Unsa had worked to ease her worries about such things. He had helped see the beauty in nature, which remained at odds with the overwhelming fear that had haunted her for so long. "I was told that I killed my child, draining his spirit before he ever took his first breath."

Lark shook her head. "I don't know why anyone would believe that a woman as sweet and kind as you are could have ever harmed her child. Tell me that you don't believe that, Suyan."

"I don't," Suyan assured her. "At least not anymore."

"Suyan."

"At first, I blamed myself." Suyan replied. "How could I not? I used to believe that everything mystical must be evil."

"Suyan, I shouldn't have to tell you this because surely you know it in your heart, but I will say it and not speak of it again. Unsa is not evil. He is the opposite of anything vile or wicked."

Suyan bowed her head, startled by the vehemence in Lark's tone and suddenly ashamed that it had taken Lark to tell her something that she already knew in her soul. She couldn't bring herself to speak about Unsa and the jaguar. It seemed entirely too private to reveal, and she suddenly felt the burden of her rejection and how much it must have hurt Unsa.

Lark bent to grab the stem of a plant, and Suyan joined her. "Tell me, Suyan, you said that you used to be like the people of Chota's band, but what changed?"

Suyan was silent for a time as she considered the question, remembering the way that she had discovered herself in the cloud forest. Unsa had given her a rare gift by reminding her of the free spirited young girl that she used to be. In small ways, he had given her back pieces of herself, and she had also gained a sense of worth and confidence that swelled within her now. "I changed."

Lark smiled at her, even as she cast one lingering glance over her shoulder. She saw a familiar head peek out at them from the tall grass, and she almost laughed. Her son was becoming adept at stalking prey, and he enjoyed practicing with his companions within the safety of their village. She knew that wherever Stone was, his father wouldn't be far behind.

"We should return and find out how Sappa is faring."

A sound from the forest captured Lark's attention and she turned, expecting to see her husband. Something struck her jaw, and the last thing she heard as darkness enfolded her was Suyan's muffled scream.

Anyan howled with glee as Carrum and his warriors returned, carrying one woman between them while holding Suyan by her bound hands. He stalked forward, anxious to see how delighted she would be at the sight of him. The stark fear in her eyes as she gazed upon his face for the first time caused anger to burn within his stomach.

Suyan took in the sight of the Agali Village with its odd conical lodges scattered about the handmade clearing and she could barely still the trembling in her limbs. The sight of Anyan walking toward her threatened to buckle her knees. If not for the warriors holding her up by her arms, she would have fallen. Even still, she recoiled from Anyan's touch as if he were a viper preparing to strike.

"The woman is yours," Carrum spoke angrily, shoving Suyan toward him as his voice lowered threateningly. "If the Saika healer cannot save my mother, you should know that I will have your heart."

Fascinated by the way that Suyan's body had changed since he last saw her, Anyan leaned forward, entirely captivated by the pleasant handful she provided. He stroked one hand over her ripe breasts as Carrum's threat registered. Returning his attention to the others, he stared at Lark's unconscious body. "You fools! What have you done to her?"

"We needed to ensure her silence."

"If you've killed her, she won't be able to help your mother." Anyan stepped forward, grabbing Carrum's waterskin only to fill his cupped palm with water before throwing the entire handful into Lark's face. She coughed and sputtered, moaning as she opened her eyes and looked around. Anyan loomed over her with a careless smile gracing his lips. "You and I both knew that we would meet again one day, but this time, I am in the position of power."

Lark struggled against her captors, but Carrum stopped Anyan before he could cause her any harm.

"Leave her be." He turned to face Lark as his men held her up. "You are here to see to my mother's wellbeing. If you cannot help her, then you will die. If you try to escape, you will die. No one knows where you are. No one is coming to save you."

Lark remained silent, casting a concerned glance toward Suyan. Her cousin appeared to be utterly terrified, held as she was by Anyan. Taking full advantage of his control over her, Anyan rubbed suggestively against Suyan and then he whispered something that made the color drain from her cousin's face.

"Be strong, Suyan."

Carrum grabbed her chin with bruising strength, peering into her eyes with an evil smile. "Do you remember me, by chance?"

He walked in a circle around her, finally standing with his back to her as his people gathered around. He turned to face her, his eyes as dark as a thundercloud, his lips twisted into a sneer. "Your people attacked my village and destroyed what was once a powerful stronghold." When she remained silent, he shook his head, whispering between clenched teeth, "Perhaps so much time has passed that you have forgotten who we are." He leaned closer, his voice low and threatening. "You are in the possession of the blessed Agali Village, and you belong to us now."

"Father!"

River turned at the sound of his son's voice, immediately focused upon the distress that he heard. A few men tried to stop Stone, but he dodged their reach, running frantically toward his father.

River fell to one knee, placing a calming hand on his son's shoulder as the boy struggled to catch his breath. "What is it Stone?"

"Bad men took my mother."

River stood swiftly, lifting Stone into his arms as he turned to find Ransa already standing behind him. Ransa nodded, it was all River needed as he transferred the boy into the older man's arms. Unsa stepped forward with a look of concern and River beckoned him.

"Where is Suyan?"

His son answered. "They took her, too."

Unsa stopped in place, staring at River, though his question was directed toward River's son. "Who took her?"

"I saw them take Suyan." Stone said with an angry scowl on his tear streaked face. "And they hit Mother."

Orchid came out of Yama's lodge, her expression sharp and searching. She sent a scathing glance toward Unsa, unwilling to forget his accusation. "What's wrong?"

"Someone has taken Suyan and Lark." Unsa informed her.

"No, it can't be! Who would do such a thing?"

River's jaw clenched and unclenched as his hands fisted. "We have only to look toward our enemies for an answer."

The cry of attack went up throughout the Saika Village as the men gathered together and scouts were sent out to check the surrounding area. River bristled over the delay as he thought of his pregnant wife in the hands of the very same people that had once abducted and defiled her. He glanced over at Unsa who seemed just as anxious to set out and find both women. However, wisdom and planning were needed. They couldn't run into danger without knowing what was waiting for them. Lark and Suyan needed their clear thinking and their cold detachment.

Unsa stepped forward, and all eyes turned his way. "I know who has taken the women, and I will be the first to kill any man that tries to stop us from reclaiming them."

CHAPTER NINETEEN

Carrum led Lark to his mother's dwelling, urging her ahead of him when she hesitated. He wanted to vent his fury on the Saika healer, but he held himself steady, aware that she was his only hope of seeing his mother restored to her former self.

"Hurry," he pushed her, taking pleasure in the way that she tripped over her feet.

Lark righted herself and forced her trembling legs to walk. She didn't know if there was actually an injured or ill person within the lodge and even though the attack by Carrum's uncle had happened many seasons ago, she couldn't help but remember the violent assault that she had suffered at Jacali's hands. Fear that Carrum meant to violate her, caused her to hesitate and this time he hauled her forward by the back of her neck.

"Walk or suffer," he said. "It is your choice."

Lark forced herself to walk, and she was almost relieved when she inhaled the putrid scent that hovered within the lodge.

"My mother needs your help."

She could tell that Carrum hated to speak in her language. He spat the words out as if they tasted vile, but she didn't care. Her eyes roamed the lodge, taking in the sight of the many animal skins hanging on the hastily constructed lodge wall.

Several young women surrounded a prone form, but it was the sight of the woman covered in furs and resting upon bedding that was fouled by excrement and waste that captured her full attention. *Ayusha.*

Lark recognized her instantly, but she admitted to herself that she had hoped never to see the woman again.

"What happened to her?"

The women sitting at her side scattered away as Carrum made a slashing motion with his hands. "Enough!"

Lark gathered her courage, turning to peer at Carrum. Her face showed the contempt and anger that she felt as she spoke. "If you want me to help your mother, I need to know what ails her."

Lark never saw the blow coming. He hit her with just enough force to drive her to her knees.

She tasted blood as she protectively covered her stomach.

Carrum bent toward her, watching her the way a predator watches prey. "You will see that she is made well or you will die."

Lark watched as he stared at her for a time and then turned away, leaving her with the cowering women and his deathly ill mother.

Unsa led the men with River and Ransa by his side. He knew that their thoughts were divided. They were deeply concerned about Lark and Suyan, but they were also aware that in their absence, Sappa might perish. Most of their warriors had accompanied them, leaving only a few young men behind to watch over the village. The older men and the injured would keep watch as well, but they were few against the many dangers of the jungle.

He understood that it was risky to take so many men with him from the Saika Village, but what choice did they have? It was possible that their enemies wouldn't expect an attack. After all, they hadn't killed River's son, and any warrior that wanted to abduct someone wouldn't have left anyone alive to point the way to their location.

After carefully questioning his son, River had gained enough details from Stone to convince him that it was the Agali warriors that had taken Lark and Suyan. Yama and had watched them leave, along with the other women and children, fully aware that the men left on a journey from which they might not return.

One glance behind him told him that River and the other men were just as certain that they were exactly where they needed to be. Unsa recognized the risks, but he couldn't turn away. If anyone was capable of sneaking up on the Agali Village, it was him. He knew that they couldn't attack blindly, and he had volunteered to be the one to scout out the village.

"See to the safety of the women and then give the signal." River kept his voice pitched low, causing Unsa to strain over each word.

Silence was a warrior's closest companion, and it went hand in hand with stealth. They wouldn't speak again from this point forward.

His skin prickled with unease as he listened to the jungle around him. Something was wrong.

Holding up one hand in warning, he waited for the other men to see his hand sign; his ears were attuned to the slightest sounds while his eyes searched the darkness. He could feel the wrongness of the night even before the first arrow whipped past his ear.

Suyan fought Anyan as he dragged her toward the shelter that was camouflaged by the natural formations of the jungle. He seemed surprised that she wouldn't go with him of her own free will, and she noticed that his expression was almost one of confusion.

"Let me go!"

Anyan glanced at her in amusement, "You belong to me. Why would I ever let you go?"

His question stunned her, and she stopped walking as her knees threatened to buckle. "Anyan, I don't belong to you."

"That isn't true." His eyes narrowed as he looked at her as if seeing her for the first time. "Your mother's husband gave you to me."

"Chota had no right to give me to anyone."

"He had every right," Anyan sighed, watching her as if she had lost her senses. "You are mine, Suyan. You will become the mother of my children." He frowned, tilting his head oddly. "My brother says that you planned to betray me by remaining in the Saika Village. He says that you never intended to return to me."

Suyan watched as he held his hunting knife in his palm, balancing the weight of the weapon with a steady hand. She sensed that whatever she said next would either cause him to end her life or allow her to live.

"What do you want?"

Anyan leaned close, holding her by her bound hands as he pressed his forehead against hers. She struggled in his grasp, but he held her steady, looking directly into her eyes as she inhaled the scent of sweat mingled with her rising fear. "I want what I have always wanted." He stroked her face, brushing his lips over her forehead as he grasped her neck with one hand and squeezed just enough to gain her attention.

"What do you want?" she asked again, panting slightly as his hand twitched, cutting off her supply of air.

"It has always been about my need of you." Anyan laughed, but his eyes were hard as he pulled her into the crudely constructed shelter.

Suyan tried to twist away as Anyan ran his hands over her body, enjoying the way that she fought him. Her eyes seeped tears as she struggled against him.

"Don't fight me, Suyan."

"I won't let you do this!" she cried, looking for any way to escape. He hadn't bound her ankles, but her hands were almost useless. Anyan had stripped her naked, and he looked his fill as he removed his loincloth and squatted next to her.

"You are a delight to my eyes." He placed one hand upon her belly and she shuddered as he pressed almost gently against her. "I will teach you to dance for me. You will accept my seed, and I will have what I have always wanted."

Suyan closed her eyes, silently hoping that someone, anyone would save her. The cold press of his fingers upon her naked flesh forced her to realize that she was her only hope. There was no one that would step in and stop Anyan from brutalizing her.

She made herself look at him, surprised to see that his male member remained flaccid. Hope surged in her heart as she tried to think past the debilitating fear that thrummed through her spirit.

"Anyan, you aren't capable of fathering a child."

He reared back as if she had struck him, and she pressed the advantage that he had unknowingly given her. "Long ago, the Saika Village sent you into the forest as an outcast." She stared openly at his scars, which would have been marks of bravery on another man, recognizing that on Anyan they were signs of treachery. He wiped his brow with his damaged hand, displaying three missing fingers. "No matter what you do to me, I will never grow round with your child."

"Quiet!" Anyan's roar of fury shattered the silence as his face twisted into a mask of rage. He straddled her chest, but his attention was riveted on the entrance of the shelter. "She lies!"

Distracted by his rambling, Suyan barely saw the blow coming as he hit her with a closed fist. "Liar!"

Another glancing blow struck her chin, even though she tried to turn away. With her hands tied and her body pinned under Anyan's weight, there was no escape.

"I will see that you carry a child within your belly before the first fruit blooms." He placed both hands over her throat and squeezed, bending to place a kiss upon her lips as she fought him in growing desperation.

Despite her struggles, he pinned her legs down easily, subduing her with the full weight of his body as she frantically gasped for air. Suyan saw gray stars at the edges of her vision, and she renewed her efforts to break free, but Anyan's hands closed around her neck like an inescapable vise. The last thing she saw was his face as darkness filled her vision and the world fell away.

Unsa recognized the trap that had been set for them by the Agali warriors, as did the rest of the Saika men, but it was too late. The instant enemy arrows flew through the air, Unsa knelt, making himself a smaller target. He notched an arrow into place, and searched for their attackers. They had no choice but to fight against an enemy that had taken to the trees, hiding themselves almost completely in the upper canopy.

"Surrender or die!" One of the Agali warriors shouted in a compelling voice.

Arrows were abandoned for spears as the Agali warriors moved in to finish what they had started. It was an ambush, and their only choice was to fight or die.

Unwilling to admit defeat, the Saika warriors fought standing back to back, protecting the man that they had been paired with from the beginning.

Unsa dodged a spear thrust from a shadowed warrior, seeing only the whites of his eyes in the darkness. He was aware of River at his back, fighting for his life, and he whirled, frantically trying to turn the tide of the battle. The Agali warriors had chosen the perfect spot for their surprise attack, and they were fully prepared for the force of Saika warriors.

He knew that some of their men were wounded, lying upon the ground, having fallen as the first wave of arrows flew through the night. The cries of their men sounded all around them, and he turned to River, silently acknowledging what they had realized almost from the first.

There was no escape.

They were outnumbered and outmatched, fighting a losing battle. For the sake of the men still alive, Unsa knew that they had to surrender and hope for mercy.

A blow to his torso came from the warrior facing his way catching him off guard, and he fell to his knees, scrambling to rise again before the man could strike a deathblow. He stumbled as River slid to his knees beside him, trying to help him to his feet.

Unsa shouted once in defeat, and time seemed to slow as silence descended, overtaking the shouting, fighting men. "We surrender!"

A dark shape emerged from the shrouded jungle, and he looked into the face of the man that had risen to power despite the fall of his village and the death of his father. *Carrum.*

"Agali has placed his blessing upon us!" Carrum shouted orders at his men, urging them to round up the Saika warriors. "Remove their weapons and tie them to a long pole." He leaned close to Unsa with a triumphant smile upon his face. "Our village will delight in the bringing of captives. After all, you and each of the warriors with you will become a fitting sacrifice for Agali."

CHAPTER TWENTY

Unsa bent low in defeat as he and the remaining Saika warriors were bound and tied, urged through the forest at the prodding tips of many spears. Even the injured were forced to walk or die by the spear of an Agali warrior. As they moved forward, Unsa realized that the numbers belonging to the Agali Village were surprising, and he acknowledged to himself that they had foolishly allowed emotion to rule their thoughts.

He clung to the hope that they were still alive, that River and several of the men had suffered minor injuries in battle, but they were able to persevere. His wrists were almost raw from the strain of holding a long pole over his head as they were forced to march toward the Agali Village.

"Unsa, what are our chances?" He couldn't tell which of the men had spoken, but the whisper had been hushed and full of urgency.

His entire body vibrated with anger and the need to escape. "They will kill us one by one until their god is satisfied."

"There must be something that we can do."

This time, he recognized River's voice, and he lifted his chin proudly. There was honor to be found in a proud death. If they died trying to save the women that had been taken from their village, their lives would have meaning. This was an intrinsic part of the warrior's way. He remained silent as they were urged forward and before long, they entered a clearing.

Light filtered over the Agali Village, displaying conical lodges that were misshapen and oddly built. It was as if the Agali people had no intention of making a permanent home in the jungle. His eyes were drawn to a high platform situated at the rear of the village, and he caught sight of a heavy flat stone sitting in place as if waiting for unwilling victims.

"I will not die as a sacrifice to their sun god." Unsa spoke through clenched teeth as he strained to see the bound man standing behind him.

"Nor will I."

In this they were in agreement. They would rather die fighting than give their lives as victims brought forward for the slaughter.

Lark worked to help Ayusha drink and swallow some of the broth that had been brought in at her request. She didn't have her supply of herbs and roots with her, and she had to rely upon the things that the village women had gathered. She had instructed Ayusha's serving women to clean the lodge, and the smoldering fire purified the air, leaving behind the scent of sage. However, the fever that burned through Ayusha's thin body concerned her the most.

It appeared to be the same sickness that had affected their village for a time. Lark and River had circumvented the illness by urging their people to only drink from water sources where the river otter could be found. Lark's grandmother, Agama, had once spoken of the instinctual knowledge held by the creatures of the jungle, and the river otter had led the way to safe drinking water for the Saika Village. Wherever the river otter swam, the water appeared to be safe to drink. Lark believed that their former water source had become polluted, while others said that it was cursed.

She looked at Ayusha and saw a woman that could have been beautiful on the inside where beauty mattered if only she wasn't driven by the desire for power and vengeance.

"Leave me," Ayusha moaned, fighting Lark as she tried to urge more of the broth upon her.

"I'm only trying to help you, Ayusha."

The woman's eyes opened, and Lark had to force herself not to pull away from her. The darkness in Ayusha's eyes came from more than just their dark color; there was a raw coldness within her spirit that Lark saw, causing her to shiver. "Don't address me by my name. You are unworthy of standing in my presence."

"Very well." Lark responded, "But at one time, you and your people thought that we would make a fitting sacrifice to your god."

"Don't speak disparagingly of Agali."

Lark tensed, aware of another presence in the lodge, and as she turned, she saw Ayusha's son standing silently behind them.

Carrum's voice held the threat of implicit violence. "If your presence upsets my mother, I will have to remove you."

Lark shifted uncomfortably, recognizing that he had just threatened to kill her without any inflection in tone or change of expression. Her blood ran cold as she struggled to speak.

"Your mother is responding to my methods of healing, but I need my supplies."

He stared at her impersonally before turning to leave and when he returned, he carried the basket of roots that she and Suyan had gathered only this morning. She couldn't bring herself to tell him that there wasn't anything in the basket that would cure his mother. Ayusha was wasting away, and there wasn't a remedy known to Lark that would save the bitter, cruel woman that he called Mother.

Carrum knelt beside his mother's prone form, aware that her color had improved and her eyes no longer burned with an overpowering fever. "How are you feeling?"

Ayusha watched him steadily, smiling with approval as he leaned toward her. "I am proud that my son has managed to honor his father's memory." She licked her dry lips. "Tell me about the captives that you have taken."

"The Saika men were caught unaware." Carrum smiled. "They meant to reclaim their women, but I gathered our men together and we attacked them in the jungle. They had no choice but to surrender."

Ayusha's eyes gleamed with pride. "You will gather the men together and see that each one is given to Agali three days from now."

Carrum hesitated, it was his desire to sacrifice the men now, but his mother's gaze was focused, insistent. "Why should we wait?"

"The moon will be full in three days time," Ayusha struggled to sit up, but Carrum held her in place. "You will give the sun power by making the sacrifice at that time, and I will be there to watch the proceedings."

He nodded, glad that his mother appeared determined to regain her former health and attend the ceremony in person.

"Has the Saika healer been of help to you?"

Ayusha grimaced. "I would have recovered on my own." Despite the anger in her voice, her eyes gleamed as she looked at her son. "You have always been a devoted son."

Carrum sat patiently by his mother's side as she began to drift off to sleep. His eyes roved over her as she blinked and then clasped his hand. "See to it that you make them suffer before they die, Carrum. Make them bleed for their attack up us, and then secure your position as leader by reclaiming the high places that were once ours."

"The high places will belong to us once more," Carrum soothed. "Sleep now and I will send the healer in to sit with you."

"Whether she heals me or not, you must promise that she will never leave our village alive."

Carrum didn't hesitate as he offered his mother the words that she waited to hear. "I promise."

Ayusha's lips moved, but she said nothing more, and Carrum reluctantly left her side. His mother had given her express permission to increase the suffering of the captives before death, and he knew exactly how he would accomplish the deed. One of the captive men was the husband of the Saika healer, River. He was the very same man that had murdered his father in cold blood.

His expression darkened as he left his mother's lodge with a clear purpose in mind.

"River!" Lark shouted her husband's name, stunned to see him tied with several of the Saika warriors. She had been ensconced within Ayusha's lodge for two days, only leaving to relieve herself under the watchful eyes of an Agali warrior. The humiliating treatment wore upon her, but she had remained hopeful of rescue, until now.

Carrum had sent her from the lodge so that he could speak privately with his mother, but Lark had never expected to find her husband tied and led as a captive through the Agali Village.

River wouldn't look at her. She could see Unsa, Pago, and several of the other men tied in front of him, but her husband wouldn't look her way. She clapped a hand over her mouth as she realized that she had almost revealed to the Agali Village that they held her husband captive.

Carrum stepped from his mother's lodge, and she swung to face him, realizing that surely he was aware that River was the very same man responsible for killing his father in battle.

"Carrum…" Lark struggled to say something that would sway him, but the words died in her throat as she looked into his glittering black eyes. She saw bloodlust reflected in his gaze, and she unconsciously touched her belly.

"You carry new life."

Lark's eyes widened as she realized that she had given much away with the revealing gesture. She remained silent, unwilling to answer him.

"Your husband is my captive." Carrum stepped closer. "I wonder what you would do to see him set free."

Lark took a step away from him, but the warrior at her back kept her from fleeing.

"You have the look of your sister."

Swallowing, Lark dared to glance toward the captive men. "What will you do with them?" She already knew that he wouldn't let them go.

"They fought well." Carrum mused, content to make her wait for an answer. "They will be honored as gifts of Agali, our sun god."

"No." Lark recoiled. "No, please, you can't mean to sacrifice them."

"I can and I will."

"No!" She flew at him, but the warrior behind her grabbed her and shook her roughly.

"Don't harm her." His tone was almost dismissive. "She is needed to see to my mother's wellbeing."

Lark struggled to be set free, but the warrior didn't release his hold until he received a nod from Carrum. "If you kill those men, I won't help your mother."

Carrum laughed. "You will help my mother no matter what I do." He placed one hand over her stomach, stepping closer when she flinched and tried to turn away. "You will do whatever I ask, or I will cut your child from your belly while you watch."

Sappa opened his eyes, blinking again and again until his gaze cleared. He was inside of his mother's lodge, but other than her quiet breathing, he heard nothing. The familiar sound of children playing, and the voices of men and women talking were absent. He struggled to sit up, surprised by the weakness in his limbs and the sour taste in his mouth.

"How long have I been sick?" Sappa spoke each word slowly, unsurprised when his mother sat up with a gasp and came to kneel at his side.

"My son."

"Water."

His mother quickly gave him water to drink even as tears filled her eyes. He looked down at his body, only to find that it was coated in gray clay that was caked and dried. "Why am I covered in clay?" Sappa asked.

"You were poisoned." Yama said. "We didn't know if you would live or die."

"Poisoned?" Sappa struggled to remember. "The last thing I remember was drinking from the ceremonial horned cup inside of the lodge of purification."

"Unsa performed a sacred ceremony. He sang back your soul. But even though he said that he had done everything he could, you have remained asleep for three days."

"Three days." Sappa could barely comprehend the passage of time. He felt weak, depleted of his usual strength and vitality. "Mother, where is everyone? Why is our village so quiet?"

"Lark and Suyan were taken, and the men went to retrieve them." Yama replied, holding up her hands as he began to rise. She quickly told him that the older men, including any man that had been injured, remained behind. "Wait, Sappa. You need to regain your strength."

Despite her words, Sappa struggled to rise, forcing his knees to hold his weight as the room spun. "How long have they been gone?"

"Three days."

Sappa stared at her in silent disbelief. Three days. Three days was much too long. They should have returned by now or at least sent one of the younger men back to them with word of their wellbeing.

"Sappa, you can't get up yet."

Unwilling to be swayed, Sappa forced his legs under him, reaching for the spear that lay on the ground beside him. Yama knew better than to protest. She bit her tongue, watching as Sappa leaned heavily upon his spear.

"Mother, where is Orchid?" His sister should be here. In truth, he was surprised that she wasn't clinging to his arm, shedding tears over his recovery.

"Sappa, you have to understand that we thought you might die," Yama began to explain. "Your illness crushed your sister, and Orchid hasn't been herself these past three days. She went into the forest, but she hasn't returned."

He nodded, taking a bracing breath as he left his mother's lodge and stood in the sunlight. "What aren't you telling me?"

"Unsa asked any able bodied man to join them." Yama swallowed, forcing herself to speak even though she knew that her words would cause harm. "Tupin and Pago were the first to volunteer."

CHAPTER TWENTY-ONE

Standing on legs that threatened to buckle beneath him, Sappa reached the top of the hill where Ajaya had given him his father's blessing. Several of the village boys followed him with armloads of dry wood and large leaves from the sago palm. He watched silently as they built a large fire, and then he directed one of the older boys to lay the sago palm leaves upon the blaze.

The thick, acrid black smoke that began to billow into the clear blue sky clogged his nostrils and made his eyes burn. At a gesture from him, the boys retreated, racing down the hill to their waiting mothers.

Flanked by the older men, the women and children watched from the bottom of the hill as Sappa stood with his feet braced apart and his spear held at his side. From such a distance, they couldn't see that the moisture on his face came from tears that he hadn't been able to shed within his village. He kept his posture firm, his back straight and proud as he burned away the last remnants of his childhood.

At fifteen seasons of age, he was ready to take his place as the leader of what remained of the Saika Village. But first, he would have to deal with the person that had betrayed his trust, desecrating the sanctity of their bond by poisoning him with the expectation that he would die.

"On the blood of my ancestors, I seek a blessing from the heavens, from the Giver of Life." Sappa looked high above, searching the vast domain of the endless sky where he could see the distant peaks of the Great Mountain. The wind changed, and the black smoke swirled around his body, almost hiding him from view as he turned his face up to the sun. "Hear my plea! My strength has failed me, and my power is nothing without your help. I am Sappa, the son of Umbra, the future leader of the Saika Village, and I have been betrayed. My people have been devastated by the loss of our warriors and we are now few in number. As one, our spirit weeps."

Sappa's legs trembled with strain, but he raised his voice in a familiar song, taught to him by Ajaya at the behest of his father. It was a song of power, supplication, and sacred vows to be upheld no matter the outcome of their fate. Sappa sang as the smoke billowed high into the heavens, he lifted his voice and sang until the tears dried upon his face, and his jaw hardened with resolve.

Down below, Yama waited with her grandson and the others of their village.

The eerie, keening song that drifted to their ears caused her to shiver, and she had no doubt that the others stood in silent witness to her son's communion with the spirit world.

She knew, just as Sappa had known the moment that he opened his eyes, that something terrible had befallen the proud warriors of their village.

Three days. If their warriors had been successful, surely they would have returned by now.

Her heart filled with pride as she watched her son, battling with the same frantic worry and fear that she felt for her loved ones.

High above, Sappa stood with his father's proud bearing, legs splayed and shoulders drawn back. The anger, hurt, and disbelief that swam in his eyes upon realizing which one of their people had poisoned him would remain a secret between mother and son.

As she watched, Sappa raised his arms high over head, lifting his voice in a wail of ardent entreaty, and Yama knew one thing for certain: Sappa was his father's son, and like his father, he would not rest until the wrongs committed against him were avenged.

The remaining villagers waited with baited breath as Sappa prepared for battle. He stood naked in the village center as several women came forward and painted his face, chest, and back. With fingers dipped in achiote, a paste made from the blood red seeds of the annatto plant, the women drew the designs that protected their warriors in battle.

The older men sat together, watching the proceedings with eyes that burned with the same fire that raged within Sappa. Darkness had fallen, but the central fire provided warmth as well as light to see by.

A loud murmur overcame the Saika villagers as one of the village boys ran up to Sappa and whispered something that only he was able to hear. He turned, drawing all eyes his way as he looked into the distance, toward the towering peaks of the Great Mountain.

Everyone quieted, listening intently as they hoped to see the return of their men. Perhaps their warriors had been successful after all. Perhaps their situation wasn't as dire as they had begun to believe.

The silence lengthened and the stygian darkness outside of the fire circle seemed to hold ominous intent.

The darkness that had prevented the people from seeing at any distance, seemed to heave and shift, breaking into multiple pieces. One woman's muffled scream brought all eyes her way, but Sappa's gaze never wavered from the village entrance.

The shadows shifted again, taking form, and as the clouds overhead parted, they saw that the shadows had become men.

One figure stepped out, separating himself from the others.

"I saw your signal fire, and I gathered the men belonging to Sipán." Ajaya spoke, his voice a booming call in the dark. "Why have you called us forth?"

Before Sappa could answer, another man stepped forward, amidst the surprised gasps of the Saika Village. "Sipán."

Stepping forward to meet him halfway, Sappa quickly explained all that had befallen their village and then he turned to Sipán. "I didn't expect you to come."

"Then you haven't come to know me." Sipán said. "I wouldn't have missed it."

Sappa fell in line with the shadows of the forest to hide his presence as he crept toward the Agali Village. He had circled through the jungle at a great distance from the village, until he was able to enter the Agali boundaries from the river that they used as their source of water.

There were two warriors settled in to wait, but their lack in numbers told him that they didn't expect an attack. He dispatched both men quickly, using his obsidian hunting knife to slit their throats from ear to ear. His stomach immediately rebelled, and he bent over, vomiting the contents of his belly as he struggled for control. He told himself that the bloody task wasn't one that he relished, but he also knew that if he had any hope of helping his warrior brothers, he would have to act quickly and decisively.

There was no room for hesitation in battle. Nor did he waste time with remorse over the men's deaths. The fallen Agali warriors had purposely laid in wait, hiding within the confines of the jungle, and they would have slaughtered him without warning if given half a chance.

He moved quickly, soundlessly, just as River and Unsa had taught him. Distractedly, he struggled to push thoughts of both men aside. He would need his complete focus if he hoped to ascertain the danger that they were in without being captured or killed.

The forest shifted as he walked, welcoming him as he drew strength from the life teeming within. He could hear the calls of the monkeys that inhabited the treetops, and the night birds of prey that stalked the unwary. An owl hooted in the distance, and he heard an answer much further away.

Sappa took painfully slow footsteps as he approached the Agali Village. He walked as if stepping over a nest of vipers, and the Agali Village was no less dangerous.

He saw several torches flickering in the distance, recognizing instinctively that they appeared to be closer than they actually were. Inhaling sharply, he forced himself to exhale slowly, silently urging his heartbeat to slow its thunderous pounding. He needed to hear, and he wasn't able to hear anything at the moment other than the frantic drumming of his own heart.

Suddenly, from within the Agali Village men began to shout in the Saika tongue and he drew closer, his eyes widening in disbelief as he stared in abject horror at the scene unfolding before him.

Carrum walked the length of the bound captives. Deciding that he would choose one man that would set the precedent for what was to come. He eyed River and the Saika shaman, letting them know by his cold glare that they would die before sunrise. But he walked past them, certain that they were unafraid to meet their fate.

He wanted to make them scream in rage and fear.

Inside his mother's lodge, he knew that she fought for her life. He blamed them for the sickness that had weakened her, stealing her vitality, just as he blamed them for his father's death and their fall from the sacred high places.

"Forest dwellers." Carrum cursed them even as his people cheered. "Tonight you will die at my hand, but not before you suffer for the wrongs that you have committed against my people!"

The Agali villagers cheered. They were entranced by the sight of Carrum, fully adorned in the regalia worn by their former leader, Talud. He stood proudly with his hands upon his hips, just above the ceremonial knives that would be used during the bloodletting sacrifice to come. His warriors stood just behind him, but he had no fear of the Saika captives. They were weak from hunger and thirst, tied by the hands to a pole that had been pounded into the ground.

They wouldn't be able to strike back, no matter what he did to them.

"River," Carrum called, drawing the man's attention. "I want you to know that I will keep your wife as my captive for as long as she is able to help my mother. Each night, I will bury myself between her thighs, and when your child begins to round her belly, I will rip it from her womb with my bare hands."

River roared, shocking the Agali villagers into silence, and only Carrum's laughter brought his people out of their stupor.

He leaned close to River, staring him in the eyes as he spoke, "If she pleases me, I will let her give birth to your child first before I kill her. Perhaps if you she has a son, I will raise him in the Agali way, and if she has a daughter, I will take the girl as a lesser wife."

Carrum taunted the other men, drawing laughter and cheers from his people. But other than River's outcry, he hadn't been able to gain a reaction from the captives. He quickly grew tired of their unmitigated silence and stony stares. He decided that it was best to share the fate that he had in store for them while he still had the undivided attention of his people.

"Each of you will be honored by giving your life upon the sunstone," Carrum announced. "By first light, Agali will rise to bestow his blessing and favor upon us."

The captive men remained silent, watching him coldly as he withdrew his father's ceremonial knives. He crouched in front of one young man, a few seasons younger than him. A few of the other captives shifted, and Carrum narrowed his eyes knowingly. It appeared that the men were protective of the youth that stared at him out of hate filled eyes and he grinned, suddenly certain that he had found a worthy target for his wrath.

"What is your name?" Emboldened by his silence, Carrum held his knife against the throat of the man to the youth's left.

"My name is Pago." The youth answered, staring at the knife until he pulled it away from his companion's neck.

"Pago, I will kill you first unless you chose another of the captives to die in your place." Carrum chuckled when the youth remained stubbornly silent. "Go ahead," he prompted. "Choose one of the other men to take your place, and I will spare you."

When the young man still didn't speak, Carrum cut him loose, sawing through the ropes that bound him with ease. As soon as he was free, the young man swung, catching him with a glancing blow to his face.

"Pago!" The captive warriors shouted his name, struggling against their bonds as Carrum grunted, surprised that he hadn't seen the blow coming. His warriors stepped forward, but he shook his head angrily and they stood back, protective and watchful.

"You shouldn't have struck the Great One of the Agali." Carrum's voice was low and threatening, but to his surprise the youth didn't cower. Stunned, Carrum stepped forward, closing the distance between them. "I will give you a second chance to choose one of the other captives to stand in your place. Choose another or die."

Pago sneered, "Today is the day that you die."

"Ah," Carrum said, whirling so fast that the young man had no time to react. He buried his knife in the captive's belly, twisting it with relish as he withdrew the knife. The other captives shouted as their voices coalesced into a frenzy, and he forcefully yanked his blade away, only to stab the youth again in three rapid, bone jarring movements.

CHAPTER TWENTY-TWO

"Carrum, no!" A woman ran forward, falling to her knees beside the fallen warrior, the long fall of her hair concealing her face. Blinded by the surge of power that flowed through him, Carrum barely saw the woman as she wept over the captive. He froze when she looked up at him, her face tear streaked and stricken.

"Orchid?" Carrum stepped forward. "I told you to remain within my lodge."

"What have you done?"

Carrum closed the distance between them, drawing her to her feet with a practiced movement. "Why do you question me in front of the people of my village?"

"You killed Pago." Orchid gasped. "He was an innocent young man, and you killed him in cold blood."

Carrum's white teeth flashed as he gripped Orchid's arm securely. "You're wrong. He wasn't innocent. None of them are innocent!" He turned her to face the captive Saika warriors, as he pointed at them. "Look and see, Orchid. These are the same men that attacked my village, forever changing our way of life."

"You said that we could move forward together." Orchid swallowed painfully, aware of the condemning eyes of the Saika warriors upon her, but especially unnerved by the dark stares of Unsa and River. "You said that together we could unite our two villages."

"I waited for you to act, and you hesitated until it was almost too late!" Carrum sneered. "You have a choice, Orchid. Stand aside and watch as I make a sacrifice that will never be forgotten or join the man that you weep over in death. It is for you to decide."

Orchid's eyes widened with stark fear as she realized that every word that Carrum had spoken had been meant to seduce her over to his way of thinking. "You lied to me."

Carrum jerked her close, claiming her mouth possessively. "I have given you a choice. Don't make me decide for you."

"Orchid!" Lark broke free of the warrior that held her by the arm, but another man stopped her by holding the pointed tip of his spear against her belly. "What have you done?"

Orchid swallowed, keeping her eyes turned away from her sister and the men of her village. She was unwilling to face them when she knew what they would think of her. Looking steadily at Carrum, she stepped closer to him. "I choose you, Carrum. I have always chosen you."

Satisfied, Carrum released his hold upon her. "Go stand with the other women."

"But, Carrum…"

He grabbed her throat, jerking her off her feet as he pulled her close. "Don't make me doubt your loyalty, Orchid." Releasing her, he pushed her toward the Agali women. "After this night, my people will welcome you as one of their own."

Sappa's blood ran cold as he saw Carrum strike his friend once, followed by three successive strikes. He knew that Pago couldn't have survived, but he wouldn't let himself think about whether or not his friend was alive.

A bird called again, this time it was the triumphant hoot of a winged animal that had captured its prey. Sappa ran forward, intent upon freeing the captive men, even if that meant fighting against the Agali warriors. It was as if the shadows of the forest left their assigned positions as all around him, men rose with their spears posed for battle.

He saw the strong men belonging to Sipán on his right and on his left, and he knew that he had only to reach his warrior brothers so that they would have a chance at standing against their enemies.

Sappa whooped in a loud war cry, shouting at the Maki warriors that had joined him from the various bands belonging to the Great Forest. Ajaya led his men, accompanied by his son, Sipán, who stood as tall and strong as his father.

Sappa's complete focus was on reaching the bound men, and his obsidian knife flashed in his hand with each stride that he took. The Agali people were stunned, frozen in a moment of inaction that cost them greatly as their enemies converged upon them from all sides. With the Maki warriors fighting on their behalf, it was as if each man could be measured as two instead of one.

"We are under attack!" One of the Agali warriors screamed, but his fearful cry was cut short as an arrow landed in his chest.

Sappa stretched his legs, but he felt the impact of something sharp against his left arm as he ran toward the men that waited for him to cut them free. He slid toward the first man, realizing almost at a distance that it was Unsa, the Saika shaman. His knife flashed out and he cut the rope binding Unsa's hands to the long pole, handing him another knife simultaneously. Unsa reacted quickly, slicing through River's bonds as he reached for the man next to him.

The warriors belonging to Sipán carried more than enough weapons to arm the Saika warriors.

The Agali women and children ran toward their men, seeking protection while all around them chaos reigned. Sappa caught sight of Orchid fleeing with the other women and he was momentarily blinded by rage and anger beyond comprehension.

Remain detached, and you will live through the fight that seeks to claim your life.

River was nowhere near him, and yet he heard his voice clearly, repeating the words that made up the warrior's way.

Sappa lifted his spear as an Agali warrior faced him, dancing back and forth with a short spear in his hands. He thrust with his spear, holding it firmly in his hand only to pull back at the last moment and twist, driving his knife into his opponent's chest. Behind him, Unsa fought like a man filled with thunder and lightning, moving with powerful strokes of his arms as he fought off an attacker and turned toward River.

"Find the women!" The concern in Unsa's voice rang out, rising above the shouts that came from the other men.

Sappa had no time to acknowledge his kill, or to sort out the riotous thoughts that ran through his mind as he heard Unsa's shout. He turned just in time to see River run toward a lodge in the distance. Chasing after him, Sappa watched River's back as he fought off one warrior and faced the next. Screams filled the night air, as all around him those loyal to the Saika Village fought for their lives.

River lengthened his stride, remembering that at first he hadn't acknowledged his wife when she screamed his name in the hopes that Carrum wouldn't recognize that Lark was his mate. But his silence had been in vain, it was evident that Carrum knew exactly who he was, even though the Agali leader had been a boy when River fought against his father in battle, ending his life. Carrum knew exactly who Lark was and he had made it abundantly clear what he planned to do to River's wife and unborn child.

He ran with frantic steps as he sought out Ayusha's lodge. He could only hope that he would find Lark and Suyan together. Unsa's unaccustomed silence told him that he was worried about Suyan's whereabouts.

Seeing his wife had been both a blessing and a curse. He had no doubt that Unsa had suffered along with him, and his concerns had mounted as their captivity lengthened and Suyan was kept hidden from sight.

River still couldn't comprehend Orchid's presence within the Agali Village, and he refused to contemplate what her betrayal would do to their people. Right now, his main focus was on reaching his wife who had been dragged away from the battle by one of the Agali warriors. He heard footsteps behind him, and he glanced over his shoulder, relieved to see that it was only Sappa.

River started to shout to him, but thought better of it as he turned with his spear and threw it with all the strength that he could muster.

Shocked by River's attack, Sappa ducked, but the movement was unnecessary as the spear arced over his head and landed center mass in the chest of the warrior directly behind him.

Sappa's steps never slowed as River acknowledged his quick nod of appreciation. He pulled River's spear free and tossed it to him as they both warily watched their surroundings. When River turned and ran toward Ayusha's lodge, Sappa was right behind him, but this time he cast quick glances over his shoulder in expectation of an attack.

Ayusha coughed and choked as laughter bubbled from her lips. "Your men will die at the hands of my son."

Lark was thrust forward by an Agali warrior, and she fell to her knees while shielding her stomach protectively. Her entire being was seized with a feeling of disbelief as she thought of her sister in Carrum's arms.

"I see that you have learned that your sister betrayed you and your people."

"No." Lark shook her head. "Orchid couldn't have...she wouldn't."

"It took too much time on her part, but I see that she finally acted against your brother."

"No." The word sounded more like a moan of stunned disbelief.

"Ah, yes." Ayusha laughed weakly. "Have you forgotten that she was chosen by my husband's men as a daughter of the sun? She recognized the honor that we hoped to bestow upon her. She never forgot that my son would have chosen her as his mate, had I allowed it."

Lark stared at the Agali leader's mother, angrier than she had ever been, closer to violence than she ever wanted to be. "Ayusha, you should know that there is a reason that I couldn't heal you.

You're dying. Your body will continue to weaken and then you will die."

"No!" Ayusha screamed, seeing the truth reflected in Lark's eyes.

The Agali warrior behind her grunted and Lark turned, expecting him to strike her for her insolence, but instead she saw him grip his chest as the bloodied tip of a spear protruded from between his clenched hands.

Behind him, River stood, his face ablaze with fury, his eyes sweeping the lodge for danger as Sappa rushed in behind him.

"Lark!" River crouched beside her, eyeing Ayusha with a look akin to hatred. "Where is Suyan?"

Sappa turned toward her expectantly, and she barely recognized her younger brother. His eyes held the same ferocity that she saw in her husband's gaze, and his expression was rigid and fierce. "I haven't seen Suyan or Anyan since the day we were taken."

Unsa swept under the lodge entrance, and it was apparent that he heard her words as he stood to his full height. "We will search the village for Suyan first, but I am almost certain that Anyan has taken her."

"Where?" Lark asked. "Where would he take her?"

Unsa urged River to take Lark to safety. He knew that River wanted to stay and finish the fight, but many of the Agali villagers had already fled, deeply frightened by the sight of the warriors belonging to Sipán. They were sworn enemies that had battled and lost against Sipán's people in the past.

"Our god has forsaken us!" The villagers cried, falling to the ground in fright as the attacking warriors threatened them with their spears.

Carrum stood with a small circle of warriors, and Unsa stalked forward, aware that he was backed by more than half as many men.

"Fight!" Carrum shouted, facing Unsa and the men with him. "What are you waiting for?"

Unsa lowered his spear, staring coldly at Carrum. "Many of your men have fled. Your women and children cower at our feet, but if we kill you, your people will seek revenge, just like you sought revenge for your father's death."

Carrum stared at him without comprehension and it was clear to see that death, fighting, and battle were all that he knew. "How does it feel to know that your sister chose me over her own people?"

Sappa watched him closely, but he didn't respond to Carrum's attempt to taunt him. "If we let you go, you could disappear into the jungle, never to be seen again. You could live to see your children and grandchildren. You wouldn't have the life that you wanted, but you would have life itself." He and Unsa took another step forward. "I wonder though if that would be enough for you."

Carrum met him step for step, his eyes alight with the thrill of battle, even though it had shifted in favor of the Saika warriors. "What are you offering?"

"We can strive for peace if you order your people to turn and walk away, but you must disappear into the forest and never show your face again." Sappa saw Ajaya come to stand at his right side. He knew that Ajaya had almost killed Carrum when the man was little more than a callow youth, and he wondered if he was making a mistake by letting him choose to live now. "If you seek peace, give me your vow, and I will order my men to turn back."

Carrum laughed harshly, clutching his belly as he glanced confidently at his men. Their expressions were fearful, distant, and uncertain. As a wraithlike figure walked forward, he turned, welcoming his mother into the protective circle offered by his warriors. "You must kill them, my son." Ayusha's voice was thin and weak. "You must keep your promise. Honor your father. Honor Agali."

Carrum wouldn't allow his mother to see his weakness. He had hesitated momentarily, afraid that his own men wouldn't back him. His mother's presence shamed him. He shouldn't have needed her to remind him of his duty. He silenced her with a glance and lowered his spear.

"We will walk away with our lives."

"No! You will kill them, Carrum! Destroy them!" Ayusha cried, shoving weakly at the warrior that held her upright.

Sappa nodded, lowering his spear as Carrum turned away. Out of the corner of his eye, he saw Carrum whirl toward him and he ducked, coming up with his knife in his hand as he plunged it into his chest, perfectly orchestrating the move that he had practiced with Pago, his fallen companion.

Ayusha's hoarse cries rang in his ears as Carrum's knife flew harmlessly through the air and her son's body slid to the ground.

"Carrum!"

The Agali warriors dragged Ayusha away as she screamed her son's name.

Sappa held up a hand, quietly telling the others to let them go. "His mother is dying, and the men are no longer a threat to us." The men cheered as he ordered the burning of the Agali Village. "May it never rise again!"

As controlled mayhem ensued, Sappa turned to face Unsa, thankful that their shaman had stood with them until the bitter end. "It is my hope that you will find Suyan." At a gesture from Sappa one of the men belonging to Sipán stepped forward and he explained, "I wanted you to have your obsidian knife, and we found your quiver of arrows, bow, and long spear. I wish nothing more than to join you in your search for Suyan, but I must see to the safety of our village."

"I understand." Unsa quickly replied as he thanked Sappa, and accepted the weapons along with a small sack taken from Lark's lodge. His movements were fluid and quick, but his gaze was already fastened upon the surrounding jungle.

"You're free to go."

The words had barely left Sappa's lips, and Unsa was in motion, running in long strides toward the dark heart of the jungle.

Suyan opened her eyes to blinding sunlight and motion. She twisted, remembering everything that had befallen her, and she looked up to see Anyan's back as he pulled her along on a travois.

"Anyan?" Suyan called, hoping that he would stop so that she could stand up. Silent tears trickled from her eyes as she saw that he had tied her tightly to the travois so that she couldn't move her arms or legs. "Anyan, please, you don't have to do this."

He kept walking, dragging her tirelessly through the jungle, and she began to realize that he couldn't hear her. He was in a world of his own, and the voice that he heard didn't belong to her.

Anyan turned to stare down at the woman that had been the cause of so much trouble. He told himself that it didn't matter if he couldn't mate with her. She would still become pregnant and carry a child after he was done with her.

"She seeks to escape you."

Anyan faced his brother who walked beside him. Challa had a curious smile upon his face, as if he knew a secret that he refused to share with his brother.

"She will become all that I want her to be." Anyan responded. "I will finally have the things that have been denied to me for far too long." He could almost see the son that she would give him, and he could hear the boy's childish laughter. "I will return to the Agali once my quest has come to an end, but not before."

"You weren't capable of taking her body and filling her with your seed. You're worthless!"

He didn't know when his brother had become vindictive, speaking to him unkindly when he had always respected him in the past. "Challa, you're not yourself."

"I am everything that you made me!" Challa responded in an accusing tone, shifting into a shadow as Anyan turned to glare at him.

The frantic fear that his brother would disappear spurred Anyan into motion, and he reached out for Challa with one hand. "Brother, forgive me. Don't go!"

Silence lengthened and then Challa laughed merrily as a soothing breeze touched Anyan's face and body. *"I'm right here, Anyan."*

He shuddered, utterly dismayed by his brother's playful antics. The loneliness that filled him whenever Challa disappeared was unspeakable. "You frightened me."

Challa's sheepish expression soothed him. Although he was caught in death's hold and forever a boy of sixteen seasons, Anyan knew that the maturity of season upon season of life lurked within his brother's eyes. "You mustn't frighten me again."

"I won't," Challa promised, *but there was laughter hidden in his voice.*

Suyan became aware of her surroundings in fading shadows and blurred images. She realized almost at once that the blows Anyan delivered to her face had caused one eye to swell shut and the other was barely open.

"Water," she croaked.

Anyan stopped walking and towered over her, peering down at her. She felt infinitesimally small and completely at his mercy. He knelt at her side, pressing his waterskin against her lips and she choked and sputtered, unable to swallow while tied down.

"Drink!" he ordered roughly.

Water clogged her throat and she inhaled, bringing the fluid down the wrong way. Forcefully turning her head to the side, she spewed the water out upon the jungle floor, choking, sucking in great gasps of air until she was certain that she could breathe freely.

"Anyan," Suyan didn't recognize the raspy sound of her own voice. "Untie me."

He stared at her, judging whether or not she would try to flee. "My brother says that you will run at the first opportunity."

Suyan trembled uncontrollably as she saw that his pupils were tiny awl points, and his fists were clenched angrily.

"I won't run."

"Liar!"

"No, Anyan …" she hesitated. "I don't know where we are, and I wouldn't know where to go. I will follow you."

"Will you behave like a wife or will you continue to fight me?"

"I'll behave." Suyan was ready to promise him anything if he would just untie her.

Anyan withdrew his hunting knife, and she froze.

He leaned closer, tapping the knife against her cheek as he whispered, "I would hate to scar this face of yours, but I might remove that pesky mole to teach you a lesson in obedience." He tapped her mole with the serrated knife's edge. "Should I remove it first, as a warning, or will you obey?"

"I will obey."

The knife moved to her mouth, hovering over her mole as tears coursed unchecked from the corners of her eyes.

Suyan didn't breathe, not at all. She waited.

"I trust you, but Challa doesn't." He made a sound of disapproval, and then he moved his knife lower, over her throat, in between the swell of her breasts and over her abdomen. A scream built in Suyan's throat as he made the first cut.

CHAPTER TWENTY-THREE

Darkness came early in the jungle, and as dusk approached, Unsa's footsteps flew over the ground with a strength born of fear. He didn't know how long Suyan had been with Anyan or what he might have done to her by now. His ribs ached from a blow that he had sustained in battle, and he stopped long enough to mix some of the powder from the small sack given to him by Sappa with water. He cupped his hands, swallowing the contents without hesitation. He tasted the root powder of maca, mixed with something green, leaving a sweet aftertaste. He could only guess at the contents, but it reminded him of the guayusa leaves that he had gathered at the base of the Great Mountain, during one of his journeys to the Saika Village. The mixture was one made by Lark, known to enhance a warrior's power before battle, and he realized that Sappa had been wise beyond his seasons to offer it to him.

Within a few moments, he felt the return of his strength and renewed focus. His injured ribs still pained him, but it was as if the pain was held at a distance. He knew that the root powder of maca wouldn't harm him, but the sharply bitter leafy green was known to him in shamanistic rituals. It would bring about a series of truths known by his inner self. Unsa didn't fear the revelations to come, however, he would have preferred to run without distraction, but he couldn't reach Suyan with his own strength. He needed help from the jungle.

He swallowed convulsively, shuddering once against an onslaught of raw power surging through his body. The jungle bent outward, allowing him to run unfettered with his spear held in one hand and his bow slung over his back. He dipped and lunged, avoiding low hanging vines, thorny bushes, and debris scattered amidst the underbrush. The rhythm of his pace was set by the jungle, but Unsa delved into the true source of his shamanistic power, aligning himself with a much greater force as he focused all of his will on finding the one woman that he had promised to protect. *Suyan.*

Suyan struggled against the need to scream as Anyan sawed through the ropes binding her to the travois. She had been certain that he meant to kill her based solely upon the advice of his long dead brother.

When he simply cut her free, it took several moments for her to realize that she wasn't bleeding from any stab wounds. Her arms and legs were numb from having been tied too tightly, but it wasn't long before pain seared her limbs as if fire burned from the inside out.

"Ah!" Suyan couldn't muffle her distressed cry, not even when Anyan turned his cold eyes upon her again.

"Challa says that if you would have danced for me, I would've been able to give you my seed." He looked her over as if contemplating whether or not he would force her to dance, but Suyan knew what type of dancing he was referring to and she shuddered, forcing her limp arms into circulation. "You danced for the men of your village, didn't you?"

She looked away, a mistake that she regretted almost at once. Anyan pounced, moving so quickly that she had barely turned back toward him when he grabbed her and lifted her to stand upon shaking limbs that barely held her.

"Walk!" he shouted.

Suyan cringed, she wanted to be brave and stand up to him. She wanted to raise her hand and strike him with a closed fist, but he had the advantage of strength and cunning on his side.

"If you run from me, I will find you." The whispered words were all the more chilling because she hadn't realized that he was standing so close.

Even as she nodded in understanding, it occurred to her that if she hoped to escape Anyan, she would have to bide her time and look for the right opportunity. She took several faltering steps forward, peering at her surroundings while her entire body throbbed painfully.

Managing to hide her gasp of recognition cost her, but she held the startled expression inside with an abundance of self control.

They were within the outward boundaries of Chota's band, the husband of her mother, but a man that had never been a father to her. Not truly.

"You will dance again, Suyan." Anyan spoke from just behind her in a voice filled with conviction and certainty. "During the first fruits ceremony, you will dance upon your back, and then you will become my wife."

With no choice but to walk or risk another beating, Suyan forced herself to follow Anyan. The jungle foliage was so thick and close that at times, she considered running a few steps to the left or right so that she might hide. With darkness settling upon them, she hoped to free herself from the rope that Anyan had looped around her neck. It occurred to her that if she was free she could lose Anyan in the jungle.

She told herself that she only needed an instant.

Having learned from Unsa to watch her surroundings at all times, she took the time to surreptitiously observe Anyan. What had always appeared to be shamanistic power emanating from the man, now appeared to be caused by something that he had imbibed. His eyes darted furiously around, and he appeared to keenly hear sounds that were distant to her ears. Her observations were confirmed when Anyan stopped walking as an owl flew past, its wings flapping almost soundlessly as it sought worthy prey. Suyan had barely registered the sound of the owl's flight when Anyan stood still and listened intently.

It was then that she realized he had taken something into his body that enhanced his senses, perhaps strengthening his sense of sight and hearing.

If you run from me, I will find you. That was his promise, given in a chilling whisper that resounded inside her mind.

Suyan didn't know what she would do if they reached Chota's band and Anyan tried to force her into another first fruits ceremony. She only knew that she couldn't allow herself to be given to the men of her village; she wouldn't willingly suffer degradation ever again. But as Anyan's pace increased, her worries coalesced, and she knew that her chances at escape had come and gone. There was nothing to do but face Chota's band and throw herself upon their mercy.

As the light slowly faded, aided by the tall trees that shrouded out the sunlight, Suyan realized that she had learned something from Unsa that made sense only as she faced her torturous future. For so long, she had fallen under the spell of Chota's band, seeking to belong, accepting their rigid beliefs about the spirit world and the ways of good and evil. Even when she was surrounded by people who cared for her, she had believed that she was cursed.

No matter what Unsa said, no matter how Lark reasoned with her, she stubbornly held on to her beliefs and ignored their wise words. Until now.

As if waking from a dream, she remembered Unsa showing her the great Mother River, twisting like a colorful ribbon through the jungle. The power and majesty of the wide flowing river was unmistakable, and yet she hadn't understood what he wanted her to see.

It flowed with unmatched supremacy, brimming with life. For her and the people that called the jungle their home, it was the source of all things. Unsa had told her that nothing evil could surmount the maker of something so powerful.

She had shied away from the one man that had always been kind to her, treating her with respect and compassion. How many times had she caught Unsa looking at her, even when they were children, as if she was something beautiful and rare? The last time that they were together, she had run from him, fleeing the sight of Unsa sitting in kinship with the sacred jaguar.

Suyan almost wept with sorrow and remorse as she thought about the hurt that she had caused Unsa. *I'm sorry.*

The words were silent, spoken only in her heart. She looked up and saw shimmering lights just ahead. Firelight.

She inhaled and her nostrils flared over the familiar scent of torches burning brightly.

"They will welcome me."

Anyan confirmed that they had reached their destination as a hard hand of fear fisted in Suyan's belly. Reaching for the rope around her neck, Anyan dragged her forward, and he pitched his voice low as he spoke near her ear, filling the gathering darkness with sound. "Behold my triumphant return."

Anyan stepped out of the confines of the jungle, glad to be free of the darkness and dense foliage that had scraped, bruised, and burdened him throughout most of their journey. Suyan twisted away as if seeking escape, and he absently jerked on the rope that was fashioned to tighten around her neck upon contact. She gasped, reaching up with bound hands to touch the rope at her throat, and he pulled harder, satisfied when she fell to her knees.

"I was right to tell you that she couldn't flee if you tied her just so." Challa's whisper thin voice was full of mirth. *"You and I both know that she would have left you as soon as you allowed her a small amount of freedom."*

"No." Anyan didn't want to listen to Challa, but he knew that he would become angry with him if he turned away. "You're wrong. She is the one that I have chosen. She will become my wife."

"You made a mistake bringing her back here." Challa said, laughing harshly. *"They will keep her for themselves now that you have made her well."*

"No! I won't allow it." Anyan turned to face Challa, seeing his brother standing in the glow of the shimmering firelight that beckoned just behind him. Challa appeared completely unconcerned, his youthful face was set in a mask of calm, his eyes hard and focused. "You promised that you would help me."

"I never break my promises." Challa responded. *"I led you here for a purpose. See to it that you remind them that she is cursed, but you have determined that the only way to ensure the curse doesn't affect their village is to offer her in another first fruits ceremony. If she becomes pregnant, only then can you confirm that she is no longer cursed."* He waited for Anyan to step closer and then he whispered, *"Other men will take her body, but you will have the child of their union, and you will have a son, this I promise."*

"A son." Anyan's eyes swept the faces of the people that had come out of their lodges as the first sounds of alarm swept through the village, announcing his presence. He turned to speak to his brother, but Challa was no longer there. "It will be just as you said, Challa. I will see it done."

Suyan heard every word of Anyan's one sided conversation, recognizing that the people of her mother's band would believe that he spoke to the spirit world. For the first time since he had taken her from her village, she knew better. Whatever conversation Anyan was having, it came from within, not external forces.

Determined to stand before her people and plead for their help, she waited for Chota to come forward as she struggled to her feet. He wasn't the first to leave his lodge, but she saw faces that she recognized, people that she had known for over six seasons, and she remembered sharing happiness and sadness together, sharing the things that made up everyday life, large and small.

Chota's large girth parted the growing crowd, and she saw that he was the same as she remembered. His eyes took in everything at once, sweeping over her dismissively before turning to Anyan with a look of fearful expectation upon his face. He wore a long loincloth that hung to his knees, and she saw that he had acquired several necklaces of jade and the small, shiny bones of a yellow and blue parrot. She knew the bones belonged to the parrot, because he wore its feathers on bracelets adorning both wrists.

Suyan opened her mouth to speak, but tears clogged her throat as she caught sight of her mother.

Esta ran past Chota, throwing her arms around Suyan as she hugged her tightly. Suyan openly sobbed, embraced by the very woman that she had longed for night and day.

"Mother!"

"Oh, Suyan." Esta cried as Suyan's knees buckled and she followed her to the ground. "I have longed for your return."

Suyan felt her mother run her hands over her face, stopping as she touched the rope tied around her throat. "What is this?"

"I had to tie her to ensure her compliance." Anyan stepped forward, towering over Esta where she knelt with Suyan. "Your daughter fought my attempts to help her."

"That isn't true!" Suyan struggled to stand, finding it almost impossible to do so with her hands tied and the tension on the rope cutting off her air supply.

"Let her go!" Esta pleaded, watching as Anyan loosened the rope enough to allow Suyan to breathe. She turned to Chota with her hands clasped in supplication. "Please Chota, you must tell him to release my daughter."

"If I release her, the curse that she carries will run rampant through this village." Anyan narrowed his eyes expectantly, and Chota leaned down to pull his wife away from Suyan. "You should tell your wife to be careful. The cursed one isn't the daughter that she knew before."

"Of course," Chota responded, glancing around at the worried faces of his band. "Why have you brought her back if she still carries a bad spirit?"

"I don't have a bad spirit!" Suyan struggled to stand. "He lies! I'm not cursed." She looked at her mother and the other women with pleading eyes, seeing Agada standing just outside the reach of the fire's light. "I didn't kill my son."

"The bad spirit speaks!" Anyan intoned, raising his hands over his head as he turned in a circle around Suyan.

"What can we do?" Chota made the familiar sign to ward off evil, and Suyan sobbed in disbelief. How many times had she made the same sign out of morbid fear?

"Please, Chota…" She reached out to him, but he backed away, looking to Anyan for guidance.

"You must test her out to see if she receives the seed of this band. If she undergoes another first fruits ceremony and becomes pregnant, you will know that she is no longer cursed." Anyan held up a sack, the same sack that he had carried during their journey. "I have brought bounty from the jungle to honor you, Chota."

Without waiting for further prompting, Chota stepped forward, accepting the sack with both hands.

"What is it, Chota?" A few of the people called, careful to stand at a distance.

Chota peered into the sack, lifting out objects of jade stone and gold that gleamed in the firelight, causing the others to gasp. They had never seen such items of rare and unmatched beauty. Even with only one eye barely open, Suyan recognized the items as jewelry belonging to the Agali Village, and Chota accepted the gifts with reverence and pleasure evident upon his face. In that moment, any hope that she had of protection and safety vanished like fog retreating from the sun.

CHAPTER TWENTY-FOUR

"There is no other way, Suyan." Esta pleaded with her to understand and comply with the requests of her husband. "You must do this one thing and then you will prove to everyone that you are no longer cursed."

Suyan had cried herself to a place beyond tears, having first fought the hands that held her, dragging her toward the river where she would wash in preparation for the evening ceremony. Something shattered within her the moment that her mother joined the other women as they forced her into the water. With barely enough light to see by, the women washed her body, scrubbing until her skin felt bruised and raw, and she realized that instead of breaking her spirit, her mother's betrayal had somehow freed her.

After her father's death, Suyan had done everything possible to be the shoulder that Esta could lean on whenever grief and unhappiness caused her to retreat into her own world. The chance to become a wife again, even at what was considered an advanced stage of life, had been the lure that Chota used to bring them here. Suyan had gone along so that she wouldn't be separated from the only parent that she had left. But now she realized that her mother wasn't the same woman that she had been when her father was alive.

Esta was a shell of the woman that she had been.

Suyan distantly wished that she could be a proud warrior like Unsa. With his many weapons, he was capable of defending himself against those that would take what he wouldn't willingly give. Suddenly, she realized that their morbid fear of the spirit world was the only weapon that might work for her instead of against her.

"Your husband and the other men will decide which one of them will take my unwilling body during the evening ceremony."

Her strong words caused the women to stop their hasty washing, and she smiled as several backed away. "One of your men will force me to submit to them. They will mate with me against my will and leave me with their seed in the hope that I will carry new life. This is your way, but it is not my way!"

The women backed away as if she had cursed them, and empowered by the new spirit that rose within her, Suyan stepped forward holding up her palms so that they could see her hands. *I am not evil, I am not cursed,* she silently reminded herself as she breathed in and out and spoke a promise that she knew would separate her from her mother forever. "You have forced my hand, and now I will offer the only defense that I have if it will make you stop your husbands, brothers, sons, and fathers from taking me by force tonight."

"Suyan…"

She ignored her mother's fearful moan of warning.

"I promise you this on my life and the life of this band, you will be cursed until your dying breath if you allow your men to mate their bodies with mine." Suyan's eyes hardened as she took several steps out of the water, standing naked before them as the women backed further away.

Agada stepped forward to stop her, and she hissed, a perfect imitation of the sacred jaguar, freezing the older woman in place.

"I will curse you and your children if you allow this to happen. I will curse the soul of this band," Suyan promised. "Unless you let me go."

Agada stood rigidly with the other women, but she didn't move forward to stop her again. Emboldened by the raw fear in their eyes, she searched the jungle longingly with the hope of escape.

"I will walk past you, and we will never see each other again." Boldly, Suyan stepped forward and when her mother reached out to her, she slapped her hands away. "Don't touch me. Don't ever touch me again!"

Esta retreated fearfully, and distantly Suyan mourned, because she knew that the woman cowering before her wasn't the mother that she had loved as a child. She walked past the women, daring any of them to stop her.

A noise from behind her was her only warning as a painful blow cracked against the back of her head. As she fell, she felt the jungle's dark heart beating wildly, and she knew in her spirit that all things were connected just as Unsa had said and then she knew nothing at all.

Suyan struggled to see as she barely managed to open one eye, remembering everything that had taken place before someone had hit her over the head. Her head ached fiercely, and she turned with a groan, suddenly alert as she realized that she was inside an empty lodge and completely naked.

She was alone, but that could only mean that someone waited for her outside. She searched for her clothing, but there was nothing there with which to cover herself. Distantly, she heard the drumbeats that were as familiar as her nightmares of this occasion.

She cautiously edged to the lodge entrance and looked down, startled to find that most of the village waited for her. There was no escape.

The only way out was to leave by way of the rope ladder. She even considered throwing herself from the lodge, but the height wouldn't be enough to kill her. She frantically searched the empty lodge, only to notice a clay bowl sitting in the center of the dwelling.

The sickeningly sweet smell told her that the contents would contain a brew that would render her almost senseless. She realized that she had a choice, she could swallow the contents whole and she wouldn't have to remember anything that took place tonight.

She wouldn't have to remember the hands that would hold her down or the voices that would whisper instructions in her ears. She wouldn't have to remember the violation of being filled by someone that she hadn't chosen, someone that had no right to touch and invade her body, filling her with their seed.

A broken sob lodged in her throat, and she convulsed violently as she pounded her hand upon the lodge floor.

"This is not my way!" The primal shout came from deep within, a rejection of everything that Chota's band stood for and everything that they had tried to force upon her. "Once! Twice! But no more! Never again!"

Each word was punctuated by her fist as she hit the lodge floor again and again.

Somewhere nearby she heard the sound of a wounded animal fighting against the overwhelming darkness of the night and the contents of the bowl flew across the lodge. As shadows filled the lodge entrance, Suyan distantly realized that the scream filling the lodge, drowning out all sound, came from her.

A sudden calmness filled Suyan's mind as she was dragged fighting and kicking into the light cast by the village fire. Ordinarily, there would have been several girls standing naked and uncertain before their band. The young women would be led in a circle around the fire so that the eyes of their people could fall upon them. But Suyan now realized that what had once seemed to be only a part of the ceremony was actually a selection process. While in the past, she and the other girls had been given a fermented brew that dimmed the pain and faded reality from dreams, this time she entered the first fruits ceremony with stark clarity.

She panted in mind numbing fear, but she looked around, forcing herself to see each of the women that watched from the shadows. This was a familiar occasion for them and many of them would have already partaken of the brew that morphed dreams with the present and the past. But Suyan's mind remained clear and for the first time, she realized that even though the men hid behind hideous masks of animalistic design, she was able to recognize several of them.

The grass skirts that the men wore were short, falling only to their knees. The flickering firelight made it difficult to determine who was who, but Suyan knew enough about each member of Chota's small band to determine their identities.

A sudden shiver overwhelmed her as she realized that Anyan stood amongst the men of Chota's band, and he would be waiting for a chance to defile her. It didn't matter if his male member wouldn't strengthen and rise, there were other ways that he could make her suffer, and as the women brought forth baskets laden with fruit, it settled within her mind that no one would stop him.

She didn't know which of the men had partaken of the ceremonial brew, but their wavering footsteps told her that some of them had certainly had their share. The drumbeat was furious, drawing the men into a shifting, dancing step that continued as they encircled her.

She told herself that she could endure the touching that would ensue, even though she had never suffered alone before. In the past, the other young women had been there to serve as a buffer, but tonight the men that participated in this ceremony were intent upon claiming her.

The men began to push and shove at each other, and again, Suyan knew what to expect. Those that wished to bow out would do so by returning to their wives to enjoy the ongoing festivities. The men that wanted to mate with her would continue to dance, expressing the power of the animal spirit that they believed inhabited their masks.

Suyan forced herself to watch, even as the ground shook beneath her feet. It took her a few moments to understand that it wasn't the ground that was shaking, but her entire body. The men were upon her then, touching her shoulders, arms, and breasts, pushing and shoving as they stroked their hands lower, seeking the hidden secrets of her body. One man held her from behind, pinning her in place when she tried to turn away from the others.

Despite the hands that held her, she turned toward the majority of the women who stood off to the side with their babies tied to their bodies and their little ones standing nearby.

Suyan shouted in a primal roar, "I curse you by the power of my spirit!"

She saw the women flinch and recoil as she was forced to her knees upon the ground, held steady by the hands of the men. The drumbeat filled her ears, and a masked man leaned close to say, "Now you will dance."

"Chota!" Suyan called out, fear lending strength to her voice. "Will you take your wife's daughter?"

She recognized the fat of his belly and the sweaty smell of his body as he twisted toward her. His face was covered by a mask that was shaped in the form of an eagle, painted and affixed to his face. "Isn't my mother enough for you?"

He reared away from her as if she had struck him, and Suyan lashed out, striking Anyan in the throat with her hand. She felt him pull away from the blow and then she was pushed forward, brought forcefully to her knees as a rough hand shoved her face against the ground.

Spitting out dirt and grass, Suyan struggled to turn her body away. She knew that they planned to take her like this as an example to the other women. She knew and yet there was no escape.

Suddenly, she laughed. Her laughter welled up from deep within as the man holding her recoiled and she rolled to her side.

"Chota! Anyan!" Suyan shouted, as her spirit lifted and floated above her body. "I see you, and I will never give myself to you!"

She heard the murmurs of the women as the drums ceased, and she thought for a moment that she had finally managed to reach them in a way that nothing else had.

A hand swept out and struck her face and she tasted her own blood.

Anyan.

She couldn't see his face, but she knew that he was the one bold enough to strike her. The first fruits ceremony had never been violent before, and even though she disagreed with their ways, she knew that it was simply their tradition. But Anyan had forced their hands with that first blow and now the drums took up a new beat at his signal.

The drumbeat increased until it flowed faster and stronger, drowning out all sound.

Panting, lying upon her back with no place else to go, Suyan focused on a distant star high overhead as the men fell upon her, and this time she knew that nothing she said or did would stop them.

CHAPTER TWENTY-FIVE

Suyan strained away from the man that fought for his place between her thighs as he drew back, fully engorged, ready to plunge into her body. His meaty hands greedily gripped her thighs and instead of focusing upon the bruising strength with which she was held, Suyan thought of the cloud forest and the abundant life that dwelled there.

She kept her thoughts centered upon the mystical fog, distant peaks, and mountains that were seared into her memory. As her spirit soared high up above, she saw the distant star shine and wished herself far away.

The masked man above her jerked and though she felt no pain, she knew that he must have pushed his way inside her body. Surely he was taking his pleasure even as the others held her down. His sudden, crushing weight upon her chest forced her mind back to the present, even as she struggled to remain in the distant place where pain and violation didn't exist.

Another man fell on top of him, and the women began to scream as chaos reigned.

Suyan couldn't breathe, she couldn't speak or scream as another man fell and then another.

It was only after blinking several times that she realized the men weren't ravaging her like a pack of violent creatures molded out of the depths of the jungle. The arrows protruding from their backs told her that someone had stepped forward to stop them in the midst of their assault.

But it was the blue feathers that tipped the arrows that caused her to focus upon reality with startling clarity.

Unsa.

Wherever the blue feathers were, so was he.

Suyan would have gained her feet and run toward the jungle, but she couldn't move. The weight of the man pinning her to the ground was crushing, and she couldn't gain a new breath after releasing the last.

"Unsa." There were at least ten men left alive, and he was one man against many. But despite everything, he had come for her. She spoke his name with her last breath, knowing that he fought a losing battle, and there was nothing she could do to help him.

Unsa moved unseen, blending with the shadows as he heard Suyan rage against the men that sought to defile her under the guise of a sacred ceremony. He forced himself to remain detached, even as he entered the milling group of villagers unnoticed.

He saw Suyan on her back with a man poised over her, his braided grass waist covering torn away to reveal his protruding manhood. The arrow left his fingertips with the first inhalation of breath, and three more quickly followed. His hands were a blur, his gaze penetrating and focused upon the moving scene unfolding before him.

The Wuyari men didn't seem to realize that the first man that had fallen upon Suyan wasn't caught up in lust induced frenzy, but captured in his death throes. Unsa used their confusion to his advantage, sending his next three arrows into the backs of the men closest to Suyan.

Several women began to scream, and Unsa fell to one knee, notching another arrow into place as he sent it flying toward the man whose face was covered by an eagle mask. Suyan had identified Anyan, and though his face was hidden by the parody of a black caiman, Unsa had known him upon first sight.

He ran forward as panic reigned and women grabbed their children, running toward the forest.

Suyan's body appeared pale in the searing darkness, and he recognized the emotion of crushing grief, barely succeeding at the need to keep his thoughts clear. He swiftly knelt beside her, pushing the dead warrior off her body as lightening flashed overhead. Her head lolled to the side when he attempted to lift her, but a cry from one of the men caused him to turn.

Anyan rushed toward him with his spear raised to strike and Unsa fell back, crushing Suyan beneath him as he blocked Anyan's spear thrust. He held his own spear horizontally across his body and pushed upward, almost managing to knock Anyan's spear from his grasp.

"It's over Anyan!" Unsa held his position, unwilling to back away. "The Agali Village has fallen, and your treachery has been laid bare."

"No!" Anyan shouted in disbelief, running forward with his spear raised. "Suyan is mine!"

Unsa roared.

Time slowed, as it often did in battle, but he moved in a blur of motion, rolling away as he gained his feet. Out of the corner of his eye, he saw Suyan lying naked and still as rain began to splatter upon the ground.

There was no time for words or threats, and he couldn't have spoken even if he wanted to. Without warning, without making another sound, Unsa pounced.

He struck Anyan on the side of the head with his fist closed around one of the fire stones. Anyan's spear fell aside and Unsa spun, bringing his spear around with the full weight of his body behind it.

Anyan realized his intent, and he dodged left, holding his head with one hand while keeping his spear pointed at Unsa with the other. Both men stumbled away from Suyan, and Unsa gave chase, crashing into one of the poles that held a lodge high above the ground. He stood to his full height, ready to die if need be, but not before he took Anyan with him.

Anyan circled to the right and then to the left, his eyes glittering madly as the clouds parted and moonlight lit their surroundings. Anyan fought with renewed vigor, and Unsa feinted to the right, kicking the swaying pole with both feet as Anyan stumbled and fell. A crashing sound overhead brought Unsa's attention up to the towering lodge, and he rolled out of the way, just as the lodge crashed to the ground, covering Anyan completely.

Unsa struggled to his feet, distracted by an unlikely sound, and his heart missed a beat as he heard the sound again. A cough came from the ground nearby, followed by another.

Suyan.

Suyan blinked as rain wet her face and a cough erupted from her lungs. She gasped, choking on rainwater as she tried to swallow mouthfuls of air. Rolling to her side, she looked up to see a man standing over her with his spear poised to strike.

A scream filled her lungs, but as moonlight graced his face, her heart sped up in rhythm.

Unsa.

Suddenly, she remembered the blue tipped feathers, and she looked at the men that had fallen on her right and on her left. Unsa had come for her.

"Suyan, can you stand?" Unsa struggled against the need to gather her into his arms, uncertain whether or not he would frighten her. He didn't realize that he had already made a choice until he felt the cold wetness of Suyan's body pressed against his chest.

"I can stand."

"Good, because I need you to be strong." Unsa said.

He twisted around shielding Suyan with his body as he watched the men that had gathered their weapons and encircled them.

"Hear me!" Unsa shouted. "I am Unsa, shaman of the Great Forest, and this woman is under my protection."

"She's a witch!" An older woman screamed. "She cursed our children along with the men that sought to help her, and the people of our band. She betrayed her mother!"

Suyan's trembling only increased as Agada railed against her.

"Give me a weapon." Suyan said, unsurprised when Unsa handed her his obsidian knife.

A terrible anger seized hold of Unsa as he heard the older woman refer to the attack upon Suyan as an attempt to help her. Raising his chin defiantly, he stared at the people gathered close with cold eyes that dared them to stand against him. "Collect your dead and help those that are injured, but I will tell you this only once..." He waited, watching the shadows for trouble, unaware that they stood wreathed in moonlight. He was injured and bloodied from battle, but fully capable of standing against them if they made one move toward him. "The Agali shaman was a deceiver, a trickster that shouldn't have been trusted. If you refuse to let us pass, I promise you that your blood will flow like the Mother River."

He didn't wait for the crowd to disperse.

Grabbing Suyan's hand, he led her from their midst, watching their backs as he handed his spear to her and notched another arrow into place. She took the weapon without hesitation, searching her surroundings as thoroughly as he did, and it was only after they plunged into the welcoming darkness of the jungle that she released the spear from her numb fingers and threw herself into his arms.

CHAPTER TWENTY-SIX

Unsa held Suyan against his chest as she sobbed. He couldn't resist the primal need to hold her close and assure himself that she was alive. Edging deeper into the jungle was instinctive. Ensuring that they weren't followed was second nature. He carried her as far as his legs would travel and then he collapsed, still holding her in his arms.

Somewhere along the way rain began to fall again, sheathing the jungle in relentless torrents while coating their skin and mingling with Suyan's tears. Unsa choked once as the band that had tightened around his chest at the sight of Suyan standing against so many threatened to unman him. He buried his face against her wet hair, inherently thankful that she was capable of clinging to him with such strength.

In this way, he began to assess her injuries.

In the darkness, he couldn't see her, so he ran his hands over her skin, touching her possessively when she didn't pull away. Satisfied that she was at least capable of walking without help, he urged her to her feet.

She held his hand trustingly, and he led her onward, aware that they needed to keep moving until they found shelter.

Before long, the severity of the rain forced them to take cover under a low hanging tree. He urged Suyan to stand behind him with the tree at her back, and he could feel the small puffs of air from her lips as she struggled to catch her breath.

The rainfall stopped just as suddenly as it had begun, taking away the thunderous noise of raindrops falling upon countless leaves. He could hear the trickling sound made by the rivulets of water streaming down the tall trees to the forest floor, and he turned to face Suyan.

"Unsa," she touched his face, looking into his eyes. "You saved me."

"No." He shook his head, "I saw you, Suyan. You saved yourself."

When the sun rose it took away the chill in the air, and the warm sunlight filtering through the upper canopy caused the temperature to rise drastically. Unsa was glad that Suyan no longer shivered with every breath. Although the sight of the bruises on her face, breast, and thighs made something inside of him burn as if seared by an internal fire. He quickly related the details of their fight with the Agali Village, and her eyes widened as she listened to the retelling of events.

"I only wish that I had reached you sooner."

She stopped walking to look at him. Her left eye was open, but the other was still swollen closed and mottled in purple hues. "You couldn't have known what Anyan would do once he had me."

Unsa recounted the details of all that had befallen him since her capture, and she was stunned to hear that the Saika warriors had mounted an attack against the Agali Village. It was with great relief that Suyan learned that the people belonging to Sipán had responded to Sappa's smoke signal, freeing the Saika warriors before they could be put to death.

It was clear to see that Unsa was injured, but he refused to treat his injuries, telling her that they needed to hurry. Suyan wanted nothing more than to stand within the safety of the Saika Village once again. She watched him as he scaled a nearby tree with an agility that never failed to surprise her.

Returning to the ground, he used his knife to slice through the ripe star fruit to reveal the unique shape inside for which it was aptly named. She accepted half of the lemon sized offering, admiring the red tinged flesh inside before sinking her teeth into the fruit.

"Unsa, why did you say that I saved myself?"

"You spoke out against them," Unsa answered almost immediately. "You wouldn't allow the men of Chota's band to simply continue their depravity."

"If I was brave enough to stand against them, it was because of something you once told me." She continued speaking when he raised his eyebrows in question, "You said that we make our own power."

"You were brave enough to stand against them."

"I had no choice." Suyan amended. "I stood against them even though I knew that the ceremonies and customs they practice aren't wrong in their eyes."

"They were wrong because they forced you to participate against your will." Unsa clenched his teeth as he glanced at her, taking stock of each injury.

Her right eye was bruised purple and the other was swollen. There was a cut on the corner of her mouth, and he knew that someone, probably Anyan had struck her, perhaps more than once. Mottled bruises on her arms, breasts, and thighs had been visible in the early morning light. But she had fashioned a skirt from the leaves of a sago palm, her hands moving with a fluid rhythm known to the women of the jungle as she split the giant leaf along each bend and wrapped the skirt around her waist, leaving her breasts bare. She looked away under his inspection, and he touched her shoulder.

"You have nothing to be ashamed of, Suyan."

She ducked her head, but he knew that she heard him.

Unsa trailed his fingers along her arm, reaching down to touch her hand, content when she interlocked their fingers. He wanted to know how much she had been forced to endure before he reached her, and he wanted to know if the men had succeeded in their attempt to violate her, but he couldn't bring himself to ask.

Seeing the unspoken questions burning in his eyes, Suyan swallowed. "They tried to hurt me. Before he brought me to Chota's band Anyan tried to mate with me, but he didn't succeed." She bit her lower lip, gesturing with her free hand. "You stopped the others before they harmed me."

It took all of Unsa's willpower not to clench his hand while she held on to him so trustingly. She might not have been raped, but she had been brutalized, terrorized, and dishonored. "I wish that I had killed all of them."

The wild ferocity in Unsa's voice caused Suyan to turn toward him and lift her chin in acknowledgment. "You did more than enough. But you should know that I will never go back, Unsa. I won't ever see my mother again, and I have accepted it, but I also realize that even though she gave birth to me, she isn't the same woman that I loved as a child."

Unsa kept his silence.

He didn't tell Suyan that he had watched as her mother stood aside while the men pawed at her, forcing her to the ground. His fingers had twitched upon his bow as he considered ending Esta's life along with the men that sought to harm Suyan.

"Unsa, I want things to be different now." She tried to smile, but her lips wobbled as her eyes flooded with tears. She sobbed into her hands until she was able to gather herself together and continue speaking. "I don't want to keep everything bottled in, never telling anyone about the fear, the sense of helplessness, and unworthiness that almost swallowed me whole in the past."

"How can I help?"

His question rang with sincerity and she dipped her head, only to find that his fingers gently touched her chin until she had no choice but to look into his eyes.

"I need to tell you exactly what happened to me." Suyan said. "I need to tell you all of it."

Unsa inhaled, holding his breath for long moments before releasing it slowly. He knew that she was giving him something rare and precious. Her trust.

Anything she wanted to tell him, he decided in that instant, would be heard by him without judgment. He told himself that he would suppress his own emotions so that she could speak freely. He searched for the right words, and then simply settled upon the only words that would communicate his thoughts best.

"I'm listening."

Suyan began by telling Unsa about the terror that she had experienced when she and Lark were taken. Then she told him how scared she was after being separated from Lark and singled out by Anyan. "It was as if he knew that he held all the power and no one would stop him from taking whatever he wanted from me."

Unsa's steady presence was like a soothing shell; a place where nothing could come in and cause pain. With each word, she felt as if something broken inside of her was beginning to heal. He didn't interrupt her, and his posture told her that she could speak without censure. Although she knew that he had questions, he didn't ask, and it wasn't long before everything came pouring out.

"In the end, I think Anyan wanted what other men already have. A wife and child. Perhaps even more, I think he wanted to belong." Suyan suppressed a shudder as she thought of Anyan's cold eyes. "I cursed him and the others for what they tried to do to me, and I don't regret it. I would have cut out Anyan's heart with a dull stone if I could have found one."

Unsa's eyes gleamed in understanding. "Anyan will never touch you again."

"Do you think that he's dead?"

"He was buried under the weight of the lodge that collapsed. I doubt the people of Chota's band will lift a hand to remove even one log from the pile covering him."

"Chota," Suyan remembered that her mother's husband had been one of the first to fall under the barrage of arrows sent from Unsa's bow. "I think my mother's husband is dead."

"So be it." Unsa felt no remorse. "He sealed his fate the moment that he allowed Anyan to cause you harm."

"Unsa, I don't want the memory of what they did to me to remain the only knowledge that I have of what transpires between a man and woman." Suyan wet her lips as she struggled to find the right words. "The mating between a man and woman can bring pleasure. I've seen the joy in the eyes of Lark, and the other women of our village when they speak about their mates."

Heat pooled low in Unsa's belly, but he kept his voice even. "Yes, the mating act can bring pleasure. It doesn't have to be painful or shameful. But Suyan, you said that they didn't succeed in their attack upon you…"

"This time." Suyan's brown eyes dimmed. "But I endured two first fruits ceremonies, and I have those fragmented memories along with what happened last night." She gestured at her body, drawing his eyes to the bruises and scratches on her skin. "I don't want to remember pain and fear when I think of the mating act."

Unsa shifted, standing in place, but uncertain how he could help her, and then it dawned on him that she wasn't merely telling him her concerns; she was asking him for his help. "No. I can't."

Releasing his hand, she turned away as if he had struck her.

"Suyan, you misunderstood." He took her hand again, pulling her closer to him with gentle insistence. "If I take you, if we share pleasure together, I won't ever let you go." He sighed heavily, his lips a breath away from hers. "If we share our bodies with one another, you will be my wife forever into the horizon."

"Oh." Her startled response filled the silence. "That isn't the way of Chota's band."

"It is my way." Unsa stated with force. "I think that you seek to remove the stain of what happened from your mind and heart. You want to use me to do that, and I understand."

She felt startled by his insight. Perhaps it was wrong to think that Unsa could help her forget. "You kissed me before."

"I kissed you because I wanted to." He clarified, but then another thought occurred to him. "Suyan, after everything that you've experienced, aren't you afraid of me?"

"I was afraid." She nodded, holding his gaze. "But not of your touch. I was afraid of your power, afraid of the spirit world and everything that it stood for, but then I realized that you exist as the jungle exists." Her expression shifted as she pressed her hands against her heart. "I'm not afraid of you, Unsa. You would never hurt me. I'm asking you to take away the burden that they placed upon me."

"I would do so and also take you as my wife, if that was what I thought you truly wanted. But I think that you want to feel as if you have rid yourself of their touch, their possession."

"I do!" Angry tears shimmered in her eyes, trailing along solo paths over her cheeks. "Is that so wrong?"

Taken off guard by the flare of pain that her words caused him, he retreated slightly. It shouldn't have surprised him that she didn't feel the same strong, overwhelming tug on her soul that existed within him. She didn't know how he had nearly come undone when he mistakenly thought that she had perished. She didn't know that for him the thought of life without her meant that his world ceased to exist.

"Unsa is that wrong?" she repeated.

Finally finding his voice, he said, "No, it isn't wrong, but it won't help you in the way that you might hope." Unsa pulled her into his arms, holding her close. "Surely you remember that as a young boy, I ran away from things that were too painful for me. You know that it didn't prevent the inevitable from happening. No matter how far I ran, I still had to face my fears. I had to learn to stand under the weight and burden that was placed upon my shoulders. Tell me that you remember."

"I remember."

He sighed, drawing her close, sheltering her despite his pain as she leaned trustingly into his strength. "You are a treasure, Suyan.

You must give yourself time to heal, time to face your fears and recover from your injuries both seen and unseen."

"But I want you to take it away." Tears poured down her cheeks, and she pounded one fist against his chest.

"I can't take it away." Unsa responded. "We have caused the men that hurt you to suffer for their actions, now you must learn to let it go."

He brushed the hair away from her face, tucking it behind her ears the way she often wore it, unable to resist tugging the ends slightly, just as he had when they were children.

Holding her gaze, he said, "Just like any warrior that goes into battle, you will have scars, but you must learn to accept them and allow them to heal." He hesitated, realizing that he was inflamed by her desire for him, even though he knew that deep inside she felt lost and frightened. "I can't mate with you, but I can give you a memory that might ease the pain."

Suyan gasped as Unsa pulled her flush against his body and gently brushed her lips with one calloused thumb. He pulled back to look into her eyes, then lowered his head slowly, letting her see what he intended as he relaxed his hand upon her waist, allowing her to draw away if she chose.

She stood still, lips parted in anticipation as he dipped his head and kissed her, sending sparks like lightening shooting to her core. She closed her eyes and simply felt his presence as an extension of herself.

His scent mimicked the jungle around them, reminding Suyan that he possessed a leashed strength that spoke to her on a primal level. He tasted of the star fruit that they had eaten together, and as his tongue sought hers, she sighed, leaning into his entrancing heat. She didn't know how long they kissed or how long they stood lost in the passionate haze that surrounded them, but she knew one thing for certain after he pulled away.

She wanted him.

Her heart raced as if it would explode, and her body hummed with pleasure and even though she recognized that she wasn't ready to become his wife, she still wanted him as she had never before wanted any other man.

CHAPTER TWENTY-SEVEN

Unsa didn't regret kissing Suyan, far from it. Instead, he regretted the nearly overwhelming desire that their kiss engendered within him. Her kiss tasted like tears, and all of his protective instincts rose to the surface. She was like a fire in his blood, and he hungered for her, even though he knew that she needed rest, sleep, and the comfort that only the Saika Village could provide.

He was tense and on guard as they traveled through the remains of the Agali Village. If he didn't know better, he would have thought that the village itself hadn't been lived in for many seasons. Without the Agali villager's presence, the jungle was already working to reclaim the area that they had cleared. Lodges that had been burned were crumbled heaps where birds perched and small animals scurried past. Abandoned fire pits marked the charred remains of burned lodges, and their sacred platform had been destroyed. The sunstone that they venerated had been broken in two, dropped from its secure height by their enemies, allies of the Saika Village.

There was no sign of any other people in the jungle, but Unsa remained cautious, leading Suyan forward but keeping both hands on his weapons. They would walk for another day to reach the Saika Village, but Unsa was determined to pay close attention to their surroundings. Many of the Agali villagers had fled when the battle took a turn for the worse, and he couldn't say for certain whether they had traveled deep into the jungle.

He wouldn't risk Suyan's life on an assumption of safety, and he remained vigilant, his eyes in constant motion as the jungle enveloped them once more. Suyan's footsteps had begun to drag, and she hadn't spoken in awhile. He turned to glance at her, but her face was lost in shadows.

Unsa found a clearing near a stand of trees, and he built up a small fire, one that would take away the chill of the night, but also give Suyan a sense of safety. He urged her to eat and drink, but he kept his eyes turned toward the fringes of the jungle.

Long ago, he had learned not to ignore his instincts, and he heeded them now. After carefully selecting a tree that was free of crawling insects and biting ants, he rested his back against it and watched over Suyan, sleeping by the fire. He reasoned that it didn't matter if they built a fire or not, no matter how tired he was or how much his ribs still pained him, Unsa knew that tonight he wouldn't sleep.

They were up before the sun rose the next morning. Unsa was eager to reach the Saika Village before nightfall, and he urged Suyan to hurry. He didn't tell her that his ribs still pained him and that he would see her settled before returning to the cloud forest.

As a man of the jungle, he had suffered injuries before, and he thought that perhaps he had bruised a rib or two during the battle against the Agali warriors. The unrelenting pain kept him sharp, and he lengthened his strides as he thought about Sappa. The young man was forever changed by the death of Pago.

He had no doubt that the Saika Village was in mourning, but he would help them through the burial rites and rituals that would bring about a lasting sense of comfort. Unsa glanced over his shoulder to find Suyan watching him with a distant look in her eyes. He stopped and turned to face her, surprised when she stood close to him expectantly.

"Why did you stop?" She watched their surroundings warily.

"I wanted..." He almost told her that he wanted to touch her, to kiss her and assure himself that she was real, and not a figment of his imagination. "I almost lost you."

Suyan knew that he wasn't referring to the present, but the past. "Did you see the sunrise today?"

"Through the upper canopy." He nodded. "Yes, I saw the sunrise."

"Today is a new day, Unsa. The past is behind us."

He nodded, surprised by her insight. "We're alive today."

"Yes."

Her willingness to look to the future caused a kernel of hope to grow in his chest. He leaned close, and this time, she closed the distance between them by leaning toward him to gift him with her kiss. Unsa took full advantage, sweeping low to capture the sweet fruit of her lips. He sucked gently, entranced by the catlike pure that she made at the back of her throat.

"Unsa," Suyan whispered. "There is something else that I wanted to tell you." She waited until he opened his eyes and looked at her. "I'm sorry that I ran from you when I saw you with the jaguar. I didn't understand how you were able to make such a majestic creature heed your command, and I was afraid. But I'm not afraid anymore."

"The jaguar is my namesake." Unsa leaned back so that she could see his face. "But you should know that the jaguar doesn't heed my command. He merely tolerated my presence."

Suyan nodded in dawning realization. "What does your name mean?"

"The painted jaguar. The predator that kills with one pounce."

Startled, Suyan nodded, remembering her conversation with Lark. "For us and many others, the jaguar is sacred."

"My spirit recognizes the jaguar as a brother."

Silence lengthened between them as she digested his words. But when he reached for her hand, she responded without thinking, interlocking their fingers as he led her toward the waiting Saika Village.

Lark and River stood with their son while all eyes fastened upon Sappa. Ransa and Yama were nearby, standing together as Sappa walked into the village center. Orchid was brought forward, but she wasn't the proud young woman that they had always known. Her shoulders were slumped, her hands bound behind her back as she stared at them out of eyes devoid of any emotion.

Sappa wore a loincloth that fell to his knees, accentuated by colorful yellow rattan strips tied around his knees and ankles. He held their father's spear in one hand, and he stared at his sister with eyes that were as black and intense as a hawk's sharp gaze.

"Orchid," Sappa addressed her in a voice that carried. "You have committed treacherous acts against our people and for this you must be punished."

"I did nothing wrong!" Orchid strained against the young men holding her steady. "I am the rightful leader of the Saika Village. I am the one that should stand in your place."

Yama leaned into her husband's solid shoulder, angry and hurt that her daughter would act in such a deceitful manner, while showing no remorse or regret. Out of respect for Sappa's authority, she kept silent, but her heart burned within her chest, and if not for Ransa's steady support, she wouldn't be able to stand on her own.

Sappa made a slashing motion with his spear, "It is my right to command your death!"

The Saika villagers moved closer, many were overcome with anger and rage ignited by Orchid's blatant display of disloyalty.

"And it was my right to do as I saw fit for the Saika Village." Orchid stared at Sappa without flinching. "You have no right to judge me, Sappa. Until you have sat in my place and carried the burdens of this village, you have no right to judge."

Sappa's eyes hardened even further. "Unsa was the first to discover your betrayal, but the evidence of your treachery is plain for all to see."

Perhaps it was the chilling tone of his voice, or his half raised spear that finally reached Orchid. Lark nearly wept as her sister closed her mouth and waited.

"As a child, you treated me with care and concern, and I cannot reconcile the young woman that told me stories by the fire with the vile creature that stands before me now. You are a liar and a deceiver. You are a person deserving of death." Sappa's brow furrowed as he turned to address Lark and River. "Do you stand with me?"

Lark nodded immediately, though her heart broke as she gave her consent.

"We do." River answered.

He asked the same question of Yama and Ransa, aware that his mother's heart was laid bare.

"We stand with you." Ransa answered after Yama gave her consent.

"Your fate has been decided by the people that were closest to you, the very same people that you sought to betray." Sappa took a step away from Orchid, and then another. Each step was answered by the Saika villagers as they also backed away.

Orchid's expression was bewildered as the men holding her arms released her and stepped away. *They were setting her free*, she thought, *perhaps they had realized that she had every right to choose the best path for their village.*

Despite the defeat of the Agali Village, her heart still ached over the loss of Carrum. He had promised to make her his wife, and it had been her hope that they would lead their people together as one harmonious village. But Carrum was dead; he would never again hold her in his arms or mate with her. No one else had ever understood her needs the way that he had and now he was gone. She glared angrily at her people, unconcerned when they took another step away from her, leaving her standing by the village fire as they moved out of arm's reach.

She watched Sappa with a feeling close to triumph building within her chest. He might stand in the place of leader, but surely some of their people preferred her over her brother. It still surprised her that he had lived, when the poison that she placed in the ceremonial cup should have killed him.

Orchid's eyes narrowed as Sappa turned away from her, along with Lark, River, Yama, and Ransa. "What are you doing?" she asked. "Where are you going?"

The Saika villagers walked away without looking at her or responding to her words. It was as if they didn't hear her at all. She saw a few of the women cover their children's eyes and ears, and her heart began to beat furiously.

"Sappa?" she called out with rising panic, but her brother wouldn't look at her. "Lark, you have everything, a husband, a son, and another child in your womb, and what do I have? I have nothing! I have no one!" Orchid twisted to the side to see Lark walking away with River's arm encircling her shoulders. Her sister had always heeded her in the past, and it was inconceivable that she would abandon her now. Undaunted, she turned toward Yama. "Mother? Please…I need you now more than ever."

Yama paused, but she didn't turn around. She kept walking in slow steps that led away from her youngest daughter.

Orchid nearly wailed. Her mouth hung open in shock as she realized what Sappa must have meant when he asked their closest family members if they stood with him.

She had been banished from her village as an outcast. Renewed panic caused her to run toward her family, but she was blocked by several warriors that held their spears toward her menacingly. Their silence spoke for them. One more step and they would use their spears against her. One more step and she would have the death that she deserved.

Orchid's breath came in spurts as her eyes stung with tears born of fury and disbelief. "You can't do this!" She screamed as her family continued to walk away. "You can't force me into the jungle to die!"

They didn't have to tell her that after today if she showed her face again, her life would be forfeit. As the former leader of her village, she knew what would happen to an outcast. She caught another glimpse of Lark, one hand upon her belly, sheltering the new life within and the other placed upon her son's shoulder protectively. Her sister must have heard her frantic cries, but Lark refused to look at her or heed her voice at all.

"No!" Orchid screamed in fear as the Saika warriors held their spears up threateningly, chanting together as they would against an enemy in battle. There was no choice but to back away as they came toward her in a formation that brooked no argument. She realized then that she was being turned away without even the most basic provisions needed for survival. Disbelief choked her as she stumbled toward the waiting fringe of the jungle. "I'll die out there on my own!" she shrieked. "Lark, Mother, Sappa, do you hear me? I'll die!"

Her cries went unanswered as the warriors moved forward menacingly. She looked into their eyes, pleading with them as tears streamed down her face, but the men showed no emotion other than the antagonistic posturing that came right before they made a kill in battle. It was as if the jungle reached out and folded her into its quelling grasp as she was forced away from her village, her family, and the only way of life that she had ever known.

Outcast. Cursed One. Deceiver. This was what she had become.

Orchid wailed in grief over all that she had lost.

Throughout the day she tried to enter the boundaries of the Saika Village, unwilling to believe that her people would allow Sappa to banish her, unwilling to believe that her family would cast her from their midst. But on each attempt, she was turned away at the sharp edge of a warrior's spear.

CHAPTER TWENTY-EIGHT

"My heart weeps," Lark spoke through tears as she returned to her lodge with River and Stone. She had left her mother's lodge, after sitting with her until she fell asleep. Only a strong brew of herbs that induced sleep had given Yama any relief. "My mother's heart has been stricken by my sister's actions."

Never again would Orchid's name be spoken within their village. For all intents and purposes she was dead to the Saika people. Just as they would never call upon the dead, they wouldn't speak Orchid's name.

River placed a steady hand upon Lark's shoulder. He wouldn't admit to his wife how difficult it had been for him to stand and listen to Orchid's plaintive cries. She had called to them from the outskirts of the jungle, begging them to allow her to return. As darkness fell, her frenzied attempts to reenter the village had finally ceased.

They could all feel the strain that her banishment had caused. But River's heart ached for his wife more than anyone else, including Sappa and even Yama. Lark had always protected and sheltered Orchid, in keeping with a promise that she had made to her father long ago. She had suffered deprivation and harm, even surviving a brutal rape in an attempt to save her sister's life. River had no doubt that Orchid's betrayal pained Lark deeply, causing unseen harm to his wife.

After settling their son for the night, Lark came to sit beside her husband. "The pain that I feel goes beyond words, River." Lark turned in her husband's embrace, burying her face against his shoulder. "I have never known such grief."

"I know, Lark." River held her tightly, trying to shelter her from the turmoil that burned inside of her heart. "I know."

"Sappa was lenient." Lark blinked away her tears, allowing River to help her sit upon their sleeping pallet. "He could have ordered her death, but she still has her life." It was part of the reason that Lark had agreed to banishment. Sappa had been very clear; Orchid would receive banishment or death. He had left them with that terrible choice the night before, and in the light of day they had responded in kind. "Can she survive in the jungle without a village, without the security of warriors standing between her and great harm?"

"Who can say?"

"My heart aches, River." Lark pressed her hands against her chest, sobbing against her husband's shoulder as his arms closed around her.

River couldn't hide his concern. Orchid had always held a special place in his wife's heart, but he wouldn't allow her to weep inconsolably over a young woman that had been selfish and hardhearted where Lark's welfare was concerned. He couldn't help but wonder if the life of their unborn child was at risk because of the enormity of Lark's emotional pain. When her tears quieted, he gathered his thoughts together and spoke. "Lark, your sister had every opportunity to turn aside from the path that she set for herself."

"I know, but–"

River held up a staying hand. "Orchid poisoned Sappa with the intent to kill him. She was the reason that we were captured by the Agali Village." They had been over this before, but River felt the need to remind Lark of the reasons that her sister had become an outcast. "The Agali warriors sat in ambush for us, Lark. They killed Sappa's closest friend, leaving a gaping hole in his chest where his heart should be. They would have slaughtered us without remorse, spilling our blood for their sun god, and Orchid knew what they had planned. She might have even helped them plan their attack."

Lark shuddered, distraught at the very thought of losing the man that she loved beyond reason.

"She knows that you carry a child." River placed his hands over Lark's abdomen, touching her reverently, bringing a new flood of tears to her eyes. "She knew how much you wanted another child, but she didn't stop Carrum from taking you away by force." River allowed Lark to see the agony in his gaze, lit by the flickering fire as he glanced at their sleeping son. "I could have lost you and our unborn child. Stone could have lost his mother and father, all because of one vindictive, power-hungry woman."

"River..." Lark could feel her husband's pain, the roiling fear that swam through his eyes at the thought of losing her and the child that she carried.

"Grieve for her if you must," River spoke between clenched teeth, before taking a deep breath. "Because you loved her, and you would not be the woman I married if you denied your bond with your sister." He stroked his wife's hair, running one calloused thumb over her cheek as he followed the trail of tears to the top of her chin. "I will even hold you while you release the pain in your heart," he promised. "But you should know that I can't grieve over the woman that your sister has become. She made her choice, and she did so with cold purpose and jealousy driving every footstep. She would have destroyed us Lark, and my sympathy doesn't rest with her, it all belongs to you."

Overcome by emotion, Lark collapsed in River's arms, unable to respond as he crushed her against his chest. After the first storm of tears subsided, she listened to his steady heartbeat and his whispered words of love and reassurance.

Wrapped in the warmth of his arms and secure in the assured belief that he would be there when she opened her eyes, Lark finally drifted into a quiet, dreamless sleep.

Unsa's footsteps dragged as he entered the Saika Village. He noticed the vigilant eyes of the Saika warriors, and he wondered at their tired appearance. The battle with the Agali Village had taken place almost five days ago. To his knowledge, most if not all of the Agali warriors had been killed in battle, and the few remaining stragglers had disappeared into the jungle.

Suyan walked like a shadow at his side, sticking close to him, even though she had every reason to relax her guard. He had been hard pressed to reach the village before nightfall yesterday, but Suyan had begged him for another night in the jungle alone and to his surprise, she slept in his arms. He hadn't wanted to release her this morning, but knowing that she would find safety, warmth, and security within the Saika Village had spurred him onward.

He glanced at her now, aware that she was embarrassed by the bruising visible upon her face and body. "You have no reason for shame. Remember, we make our own power."

It surprised him when she straightened her shoulders and tilted her chin at a defiant angle. He hadn't seen such spirit in her since they were children. Even then, she had always been timid and reserved, but the special light that shone in her eyes drew him now just as it always had in the past.

"You're home now." Unsa led her forward by the hand, walking through the village center as he headed toward Lark's lodge. He had no doubt that Suyan's cousin would take her in, but he was loath to let her go. "Remember that you can put the past behind you."

"Unsa…" Suyan's hesitant use of his name drew his attention to her, but they were both interrupted as River came outside, followed by Lark.

"Oh, Suyan," Lark embraced her cousin, drawing her forward as she looked her over for injury. "Unsa brought you back to us."

"Yes," Suyan nodded, quietly assuring Lark that she was already healing from her injuries. Lark's eyes clouded with concern as she embraced her again.

"You must come with me," Lark said. "I'll take you to my mother's lodge. After everything that has happened, seeing you will lift her spirits."

Suyan glanced at Unsa, but he was embroiled in quiet conversation with River. She saw him watch her for an endless moment as Lark led her away. "I have something that will help with the swelling…"

Suyan barely heard Lark's words, but she realized that her cousin only meant to assure her of her welcome. Still, she had so much that she wanted to say to Unsa, and the stark expression in his eyes had looked too much like an unspoken farewell. Lark led her by the hand as Stone ran ahead of them, leading the way. "It's so good to have you home."

"Yes." Suyan answered, but she was beginning to think that she should have told Unsa about the feelings that grew stronger each time she looked his way. Relenting, she allowed Lark to lead her forward, certain that she would have time to speak to Unsa when they returned.

"I'm sorry to hear about Lark's sister." Unsa wondered where Orchid might have gone. She was nowhere to be found as they entered the Saika Village, and a shiver traveled over his neck when he thought of her wandering the jungle while he was unaware. "I wish that I had been wrong."

He watched Suyan until she disappeared from sight, and then he turned his gaze back to River who studied him with a quiet confidence that surprised him.

"I see that you have found your mate."

Unsa's jaw ticked, but he knew that River didn't mean any harm. "She isn't mine."

"Unsa, are you certain?" River glanced in the direction the women had taken. "With the way you looked at her, I thought you two might have decided that you wanted more than mere friendship."

"I did…" Unsa shrugged. "She isn't ready for more."

River grunted. "Maybe with time."

At this Unsa turned away and River stepped forward. "There is much to share with you, but first I should bind your ribs."

"Your wife is the healer, not you." Unsa almost chuckled, and might have done so if not for the pain of losing Suyan. "How did you know?"

"I'm a Maki warrior, just as you would have been if you hadn't been a dreamer and a shaman." River shrugged. "I've seen my fair share of bruised ribs."

Unsa raised his eyebrows in disbelief.

River grinned. "I was standing beside you in battle when you received the blow to your side."

Unsa winced over the reminder, but he followed River as the man led him into his lodge. He made quick work of binding his ribs with long strips of woven cloth, and the relief he felt was almost immediate.

"Lark would tell you to keep the ribs bound until the next full moon." River's mouth tilted up at one corner, but there was sadness in his voice that Unsa heard clearly.

"The ache that you and Lark feel will ease with time."

"But it will never fade completely," River responded. "My wife has lost her only sister, her mother has lost a daughter for the second time, and Sappa…"

"Sappa has lost his doting older sister and his best friend." Unsa replied.

"Yes."

"Where is he now?"

River pointed toward a distant hill and Unsa could see a lone figure sitting in silent vigil.

"Lark said that he will come back to us when he is ready."

"He grieves deeply over the loss of his companion." *Pago.* Unsa silently added as he considered leaving while Suyan was busy with Lark and her mother, but he knew that he needed to see her again, if only to say goodbye.

"We leave on a hunt today," River asked. "Will you join us?"

Unsa nodded, following River as easily as he had in his boyhood. He thought to himself that there were times to lead and times to follow. The tightening in his chest had nothing to do with the binding around his ribs. With every step that he took, he realized that he was putting up a barrier between himself and the one woman that had made the world vivid and meaningful. It was the way that he had always dealt with hurt in the past, and it was no different now than it had been for him as a child. Keeping to the ways of the past, he put distance between himself and the realization that Suyan wasn't his, she was just another dream.

CHAPTER TWENTY-NINE

Most of the bruising had faded, and her limbs no longer ached as Suyan sat with Lark and several other women, preparing long strips of meat for drying by the fire. The task was mindless and common, one that she could do with her eyes closed if needed, and she threw herself into the work, barely listening as the women talked in subdued tones with one another.

Unsa had led the village in several burial ceremonies, and Lark had worked tirelessly to heal those that had been injured in battle. During that time, she and Lark were able to secure their bond by mourning together over the loss of Orchid. Lark listened with rapt attention as Suyan recounted the tale of how Orchid had once saved her life, and the lives of many other young girls. Eventually, Lark spoke of their childhood together and they were both determined to remember Orchid the way she had been in the past, instead of dwelling upon the woman that she had become.

Despite her surroundings, discontent warred within her. No matter how much the other women included her in their conversations, or how hard Lark tried to make her feel at home, Suyan couldn't seem to let go of the hope for more. She had everything that she could ever need within the Saika Village: The promise of home. The lure of family. The welcoming smiles of friends and loved ones.

However, she had come to realize over the past few days that it all felt empty and meaningless without Unsa.

The men had left on the hunt almost immediately, returning triumphantly several days later with the evidence of their success. Over the past few days, she couldn't stop herself from peering into the deep folds of the jungle in search of Unsa. She couldn't count the instances where Lark looked at her in question when her thoughts wandered back to the jungle, and the kisses that she had shared with Unsa.

"Are you still afraid of Unsa?" Lark asked quietly.

"I feel foolish for ever being afraid of him." Suyan thought of all that she had endured and of the strength that was like a deep well inside of her, a strength that Unsa had helped her to reach. She felt a feeling of peace wash over her as she thought of her son, lost to her in this lifetime, but forever a part of the larger whole. Unsa had helped her find peace in the jungle, a place where all things were connected and alive.

Lark nodded, but she said, "You're too hard on yourself, Suyan. You couldn't help the natural fear that you developed."

"And now?" Suyan asked. "What about now?"

"Life is what you make of it." Lark shrugged. "If you have given your heart to Unsa, perhaps you should tell him before he leaves."

"He's leaving?"

Lark's nod startled her. She thought that she would have time to figure out what she wanted to say to him. She wondered where he was going, and then she realized that she already knew the answer. It was the same place that had captured her heart, drawing her gaze constantly as she studied the distant clouds drifting high overhead. "After Sappa accepts the position as leader of our village, Unsa will return to the cloud forest."

"Yes. It is his home."

The yearning that filled Suyan's heart didn't surprise her. She had recognized the truth of her feelings for Unsa some time ago, but fear and superstitious beliefs had clouded her judgment. He was also the only man that she had ever trusted with her mind and spirit. Suddenly, it occurred to Suyan that she had also given him her heart.

The drumbeat echoed the rushing sound in his ears as Sappa stood before the people of the Saika Village. In the past, whenever he imagined taking his father's place, he had envisioned his mother standing proudly to one side along with Ransa, the man that had raised him from boyhood. In his mind's eye, Pago would have stood to his right, eyes gleaming in unabashed mirth and mock seriousness, despite the solemn occasion. Both of his sisters would have been present, Lark with her husband and son, and Orchid would have bestowed their father's stone necklace upon him. A deep well of sadness filled his heart, threatening to consume him, but he looked at the people that he was destined to lead, and he saw the hope and unwavering loyalty reflected in their eyes as they watched him.

His hair hung past his bare shoulders, and his chest had been painted with a red paste by the women of his village. He wore a decorative waist covering, woven by his mother and sister, and his elbows, knees, and ankles were adorned with rattan strips dyed yellow. Upon his head was a circlet made from iridescent hummingbird feathers, gathered by his people with painstaking care in preparation for this very occasion.

Lark met him halfway, stopping only as he reached her, and she smiled tremulously as she gazed up at him with pride. "Welcome, Sappa, the leader of the Saika Village!"

"Hai, hai, hai!" Their people chanted, stamping their feet and clapping their hands as the drums resounded.

Lark lifted their father's stone necklace high, so that all could see as Sappa lowered his head, and she settled the necklace in place.

"Today, I have become your leader, but you should know that I am as much a part of this village as you are. My blood belongs to you, and it runs in your veins. You are my band and my family."

Unsa stepped forward, clasping Sappa at the elbows as he looked into the eyes of their new leader. His eyes, chest, and torso were painted red with achiote paste, signifying the importance of the ceremony. His voice was loud and firm, lifted to be heard by all. "Sappa, you will lead this village with the integrity of spirit that was seeded within you on the day of your birth. Never forget that you lead, not only by right of blood but by choice, because you were set on a path of special purpose by the very people that have chosen to follow you."

Cries of delight and agreement resounded as the villagers chanted, "Hai! Hai! Hai!"

Sappa held Unsa's gaze, nodding solemnly as he accepted his blessing while high above the jungle the Great Mountain rested like a silent sentinel, watching over the Saika Village below. Sappa knew that the people belonging to Sipán resided securely in the sacred high places, but he felt Ajaya's presence in his spirit, along with the full blessing of his father's approval. Long into the night, the people of the Saika Village joined together to honor their new leader by securing the familial bonds necessary and vital for their survival.

Seeing their solidarity, Sappa set his sorrows aside, recognizing the moment for what it was instead of wishing for what might have been. He was surrounded by his loved ones, those that he called friend and brother, and it was just as it should be.

Unsa walked along the steep path which led to an unseen trail that would take him home. His time spent with the Saika hunters had renewed the bond between the men, and he had even been able to draw Sappa out of the darkness that swamped him.

The hunt itself was a celebration of life, an acknowledgement of the need that drew men forth to search for food that would sustain them. Instead of the customary rituals that came before the hunt, Unsa called the men together to dance.

He led them in the ancient footsteps; the same steps walked by his father and his grandfather before him. Through his experience in the jungle, he was able to bring about a new spirit of empowerment to the emboldened hunters. Somehow his journey to bring Suyan home had translated itself through the hunting dance. He couldn't explain it, but he knew as he moved around the fire with the other men that he had tapped into a source of power that was immense, immeasurable, and as real as the air that moved through his lungs with each breath.

It had taken all of his willpower to finish the dance with the men and remain with them long into the night before they took part in the hunt the next morning. He was glad that he had stayed. River's watchful eyes told him that he understood the turmoil that existed within him, but he was also grateful that their shaman had done what his wife's healing of the body could not, soothed the spirits of their people.

Unsa had also spent time with the younger children, telling them the story of his boyhood and the fear that had been with him for as long as he could remember. He was no longer that frightened boy from the past, but the memories were clear. After completing one last task, he had taken his leave.

Standing above the jungle now, he could look back over the verdant sea of green and it was almost as if he looked into his past. He felt a sense of rightness and peace move through him, and he knew that he walked along a path set out for him by a power greater than his own. It was in moments like this that he sensed the abundant life-force that swirled through every living thing. From the smallest stone to the greatest boulder, from the crawling insects to the flying creatures, he drew upon the power of the jungle. Having lived through pain before, Unsa knew that he wouldn't forget Suyan or the future that they might have shared together, but he was determined to appreciate life, moment by moment. Therein lay the foundation of his shamanistic power.

He placed one foot before the other as he climbed higher and higher into the cloud forest that was his home.

Suyan drew to a stop, staring ahead at the man that stood ensconced by trees, surrounded by the lush green undergrowth. He was almost indistinguishable from the jungle, standing so still and silent, but she felt drawn to him as if by an invisible string.

Mal cun uk. Unsa chanted silently, calling upon the process that allowed him to orient himself within the dense jungle foliage. He instantly sensed home, aware of which path would lead him directly back to the heights of the cloud forest, but as in the past, he chose to follow another direction.

Mal cun uk. Led by his spirit, he turned back toward the Saika Village, unwilling to leave without finding a way to make Suyan understand that she held his heart even if she wasn't ready to give herself to him fully.

She might have been a young sapling, standing in his path, growing with shallow roots from the forest floor, except for the way that the long strands of her hair drifted in the light breeze, and her bright eyes watched him steadily.

He stared at her, surprised that she had been able to get so close while he remained lost in thought with his back turned.

His eyes swept over her body from head to toe, and he saw the beaded necklaces that she wore angled across her torso, necklaces that he had left as a gift for her. The richly colored beads sparkled in the dappled sunlight, beckoning him forward, even as he stood in rigid disbelief. She carried a waterskin slung over one shoulder, and a carrying sack hung next to it along with a newly formed basket that rested in her hands.

He stood in front of her without any memory of how he had come to be there. One moment, he had been standing at a distance from her and the next, his breath seized in his lungs as he grasped her arms, drawing her forward. "Suyan."

"You said that we make our own power, and I believe you." Her eyes glistened with unshed tears, but he also saw hope brimming in her gaze as she touched the necklaces that adorned her breasts. "I'm honored by your gift. One necklace would imply that a woman is favored, two or three might mean that she is highly favored, but this…" Her voice drifted away as she touched the many necklaces adorning her neck and torso, hanging in strands that made their own music as she shifted closer toward Unsa. She took a deep breath, meeting his eyes, "I am ready to be your wife in every way."

Unsa began to deny her claim by telling her that it was too soon, that she couldn't be ready to receive him. But the jungle spoke, and he listened to the soothing voice that told him to look at the things unseen and see clearly that which had been hidden from him.

Suyan saw Unsa tilt his head as if listening to a voice that she couldn't hear, but she didn't feel any fear. He was simply connected to the jungle in a way that was awe-inspiring and nearly tangible. He grabbed her hand as if she would make a sign to ward off evil, but she merely smiled and met his handhold, interlacing their fingers.

It was then that he saw the truth in her eyes.

She wasn't afraid. She wanted to become his mate.

He didn't know whether he leaned toward her or she rose up on the tips of her toes to reach him, but it seemed as if they met each other halfway. Their lips touched and they stood on an invisible path leading to the cloud forest, pressed chest to chest, captivated by the swirl of passion that caused them to cling to one another. Unsa held her firmly, unwilling to release her now that she had told him that she would become his woman, his wife.

The jungle had never stopped speaking, but Unsa refused to hear anything other than the rapid pounding of his heartbeat in his ears. He refused to see anything except for the smooth expanse of skin under his hands and the ebony eyelashes that fluttered in surrender as he kissed her again and again.

They could have returned to the Saika Village and taken their places beside one another under the watchful eyes of their people while they vowed to stand as husband and wife, however, that was not Unsa's way.

He stood with Suyan under the very same waterfall that had welcomed her to his home the very first day that he had brought her here to heal, to reclaim the spirit of the young woman that she had been in the past. They washed until their skin fairly squeaked with cleanliness, and Suyan's eyes sparkled with happiness as Unsa smoothed her hair with his fingers, tugging upon the ends just as he had in their childhood.

"Who will know of our joining?" Suyan asked, although he noticed that the timid light in her eyes was also touched by mirth. "We are alone."

Unsa drew her closer until they stood chest to chest, and water skimmed along their skin in rivulets. "The jungle will stand as our memory keeper."

Suyan felt the rightness of his answer and she shivered, but not with fear. Anticipation coursed up and down her spine, reminding her that Unsa would claim her body just as he had claimed her heart.

His lips brushed her forehead, feathering lightly over her skin, and she looked into his eyes, giving him her implicit trust. She welcomed the feel of his hands as he stroked her shoulders, urging her to stand even closer. There was nothing between them except the steamy heat of their skin, and she couldn't tell where she stopped and he began as she met him chest to chest, and thigh to thigh.

"Today, I will become your mate, your husband, and you will become my wife."

"Yes." The raspy response that came from Suyan surprised her, but the solemn moment resounded within her spirit, stripping away any lingering hesitation as she stared into Unsa's eyes.

"You should know that my heart belonged to you even when I was a scared boy, running from his own shadow."

Suyan gasped. She hadn't known. Season upon season of life flashed through her mind, and she realized that Unsa had been the only one to stand and watch as she and her mother disappeared into the jungle, leaving the Saika Village behind.

"You have given me back pieces of myself that I didn't even know I had lost." Suyan's lips trembled, but she shook her head, banishing the tears that threatened to stop her from speaking.

"When you found me, I no longer knew who I was or whether I wanted to keep living. But I know who I am now, Unsa. I am the woman that would lay down her life for you. I am the one that will bear your children and love you each day of my life."

"I am yours," Unsa said.

Her tears fell then, but she didn't release him to wipe them away. "And I am yours."

"Forever into the horizon." They said together.

Their first kiss as husband and wife was endless, broken only when they both gasped for lack of air. Unsa laughed, entranced by the wonder and surprise on Suyan's face when she realized that he had moved his hands along her back, touching her arms and shoulders, only to sweep low and capture the round softness of her bottom in his hands.

"Unsa?" she questioned, startled when he drew her against him even more firmly.

He stepped back, drawing her onto the lush softness of the grass and she followed, content to rest with her cheek pressed against his chest as she listened to his heartbeat. He stroked her body from the top of her head to mid thigh, enjoying the way that her stomach jumped as he ran his fingers lightly over her belly.

"My starlight."

Suyan trembled anew as he spoke.

Unsa watched her reaction, ready to pull back if she showed any signs of fear. When she leaned toward him, he acquiesced, running his lips over the fading bruises that touched her honeyed skin. He also saw that Suyan watched him with the eyes of a woman that was fascinated by the man in front of her. His desire for her grew until it was raw and primal, streaming through his blood like lightening, and he forced himself to remember that he would have to use great care during their mating.

"Unsa." She murmured, lifting toward him as he angled his head and suckled gently. His fingers trailed along her thighs, and trails of fire followed as he reached her core. Suyan kept her eyes open, watching as Unsa studied her face in return. With each touch, he lowered his head and kissed her, using his tongue to mimic the dance of his fingers. It wasn't long before she found herself reaching for him, her eyes squeezed closed as she welcomed the exquisite sensations that his touch evoked.

"You are my wife, Suyan."

She nodded, wanted to tell him that she was ready, but her voice wouldn't work, not when he spread her thighs and pulled her slowly toward him. The possessive light in his eyes would have been frightening if she didn't trust him so completely. He surprised her again by turning, rolling with her so that his back was upon the soft grass, and she rested on top of him.

She gasped at the exquisite sensations that rocketed through her when he lifted his hips and pressed against her core. "Unsa."

She found her voice, urging him to take her, waiting for him to finish what they had begun. Instead, he touched her chin, positioning her hands upon him so that she could make the first move. His tender care touched her deeply, but the need to feel him inside of her made her almost blind to anything else.

She lifted her hips, positioning herself over him as he watched her through half closed eyelids, a look of intense pleasure upon his face. He couldn't resist grabbing her hips firmly, though he kept the pressure light, ceding control to her in the way that he knew she needed. Finally, she leaned forward to kiss him, claiming him as her mate in a dance of passion that swept them both higher than the clouds above.

Over four seasons later…

From his perch on a large bolder, high above the jungle, Unsa looked out at the iridescent colors of the early morning. The sunlight filtered through the gossamer white clouds that rolled in from the morning's recent rainstorm. The fog hung high above the jungle, but it didn't obscure the immensity of the Great Forest below and the life protected therein. The world hummed with the familiar jungle sounds, alerting him to the living creatures that remained just out of sight. Far below there were animals large and small, rivers full of fish and trees that sheltered animals of all kinds. The cloud forest stood like a silent sentry over the jungle below and it left him with a feeling of complete peace and resolve.

A sound from behind had him turning toward the cavern that he and his wife called home. Suyan had adjusted to life in the cloud forest, and she was never as happy as when they were ensconced high above the jungle. Unsa smiled as his son ran toward him, his chubby arms and legs churning in a blur of constant motion. His wife ran behind the boy, laughing as Unsa leaned down and swept him into the air.

"Unsa, you know I don't want him running while we're up so high."

"He's like a young mountain goat, Suyan." Unsa kissed his wife, holding their squealing son upside down. "You don't have to worry that Sican will fall."

Their son was almost three seasons of age, but he was daring like his father, and he enjoyed running unfettered. They took him down to the Saika Village as often as possible, and they had spoken at length about remaining within the village for a time, so that Sican could spend time with his relatives, namely Lark and River's daughter, Raven, who was slightly older than their son.

Suyan narrowed her eyes at Unsa, waving her finger at him in a mock display of anger. "Your son is mischievous, and he learned his behavior from you."

Unsa blew upon his son's stomach, unsurprised by his shriek of laughter. "Have no fear, Suyan. I will teach him to listen to his mother or risk my wrath."

Suyan watched as Unsa walked away, holding their laughing son high over head as he tossed him into the air, mindless of the dizzying heights below. She shook her head, muffling her laughter as Sican threw out his arms, either unaware of the danger or uncaring. Recognition sang in her blood as she acknowledged the same brave spirit in her son as she saw in her husband.

She rested one hand over her belly, smiling a secret smile at the thought of the wonder of welcoming another child into their lives. She no longer feared childbirth after Unsa took her to Lark for the birthing of their son. The happiness that she had experienced when Sican was placed upon her chest remained with her even now. While she would never forget her firstborn child, she was at peace with the loss that she had suffered, and she no longer blamed herself.

Suyan knew that Unsa suspected that she was carrying new life, but it was a secret that she was determined to keep to herself until she was certain. Yet, last night after they fell into each other's arms in an attempt to quell the passionate fire that always burned between them, Unsa had pressed his lips against her belly, kissing her there several times before gathering her into his arms.

She thought perhaps he already knew for certain that she carried another child in her womb, or maybe he had dreamed it without divulging the details.

"Suyan," Unsa called. "Your son awaits his mother."

Smiling to herself, Suyan ran along the narrow pathway even though she had scolded her son for doing the same. She turned the corner to find Unsa waiting for her with Sican propped on one shoulder.

Her son smiled widely, imitating his father perfectly, his features a miniature of Unsa's, and her heart thumped in response. To others, Unsa was a hunter, a proud warrior, and a revered shaman, but with Suyan, he was simply her husband, and even a lifetime with him wouldn't be enough. The life that they shared was something that she had always wanted, but never dreamed would be hers. At times, she even feared that it would all be taken away, but she banished those thoughts quickly, hurrying to her husband's side as the sun finally broke through the fog overhead.

Standing in a pool of sunlight, Unsa opened his arms to her, somehow knowing that she had experienced more in a single moment than she could express.

"Remember what we know in our spirits, Suyan." Confidently holding their son upon his shoulder, he leaned down to kiss her lips, lingering for a moment in silent promise, before stroking one hand over her hair only to tug the ends affectionately. "We make our own power."

Author's Note:

I hope you enjoyed Unsa and Suyan's story, as well as a glimpse into the life of Lark and River. For those that enjoy reading about the vast and ancient Great Forest, you might also enjoy the other books in this series.

I would like to sincerely thank the readers that faithfully support the stories that I live and dream. I truly appreciate positive, encouraging reviews. With hundreds of new books published every month, it can be difficult to stand out from other authors, and every positive review helps.

If you enjoyed the story, please post a review on Amazon.com and share the things you enjoyed with other readers. I truly appreciate your kindness!

To join the mailing list and to receive **free** early release copies of future books, please email: Karah.quinney1@gmail.com

Thank you!

Karah Quinney

**KENNEDY PUBLISHING
TITLES BY KARAH QUINNEY:**

The Whale Hunter
Pillar of Fire (Book One)
Sacred Fire (Book Two)
Sacred Path (Book Three)

The Great Land
The Seeking Star (Book One)
Shadow of the Moon (Book Two)
Light of the Sun (Book Three)

Sundancer
Legend of the Sundancer (Book One)
The Last Sundancer (Book Two)

Warrior
The Warrior's Way
Daughters of the Sun
The Cloud Forest – New Release

Excerpt of Legend of the Sundancer (Book One) – Available
Now!

Thousands of years ago…

"What is the rest of the story, Mother?" Kaichen and Siada had
heard the story before, but they never tired of hearing their mother
retell the story from beginning to end.

Denoa smiled warmly at her young sons. Twins, boys that
resembled their father in word and deed. They carried the blood of
warriors in their veins, just like Shale.

"Listen to all that I will tell you, my sons, and you will grow
wise." Denoa felt a well of laughter fill her chest as both boys
leaned forward, eager to listen to all that she would reveal to them.

"This is the story of the legend of the Sundancer…" Denoa
released her mane of long black hair and invited her sons to imitate
her posture and bearing. With her legs crossed and her eyes
downcast, she turned her thoughts back through time to the birth of
her husband, Shale.

"A son has been born to the leader of our village. He is called
Shale, son of Sakyma and Idyra." The words were repeated until
each villager knew of the child's birth. All heads bowed over the
words and each man wished for a son to carry his name forward
into the future.

Shale was the firstborn son of Sakyma, their leader. His
grandfather proudly accepted the words of good health and happy
tidings that the people lent to him. In time, Idyra bore three sons,
one after another.

"I am a grandfather to three strong grandsons, Shale, Tonaka
and Ni'zin. Sakyma has made me proud." In truth, Ra'olt would

have wished for a female grandchild, but he had no doubt that his daughter, Idyra, would be overjoyed that she had given her husband another son.

Idyra sought only to please Sakyma. At times, he was troubled by his daughter's devotion to her husband, but their joining was still new and it was good for a wife to seek her husband's favor. Sakyma was a good leader, though he was never satisfied, always hungry for more power. Even now, as many grumbled over the conditions and hardships that they had been forced to endure, Sakyma made plans to travel into an unknown land.

He sent scouts ahead to ascertain the dangers that might befall their band as they traveled into unknown territory. The people were apprehensive, but they were malleable and ready for change. For his part, Ra'olt kept his silence. He was not a leader of men, nor would he ever choose such a responsibility for himself. He was a man past the time of hunting and fighting to become an able warrior. He had no need to prove himself to anyone, but the same couldn't be said of Sakyma.

Each day, the men fought in the village circle. It was well known that Sakyma took pleasure in causing pain, but there was no one to stand against him.

When his men fell under the superiority of his skill with weapons, Sakyma simply told them to fight harder. If he left a man unable to hunt or fight, then the man would either heal or starve, along with those that slept at his hearth fire.

Sakyma's features were masculine and burnished by the sun. His body was well sculpted and hardened from a life spent as a hunter and warrior.

The women were swayed by Sakyma's looks and the men were awed by his exemplary ability to defeat any enemy. There was no one to tell Sakyma that he should walk this way or take a different path. It was Sakyma's desire to make a great name for himself and the people followed wherever he led. Their band cared only for the sating of their hunger and the desperate search for water that plagued the many bands that roamed the desert sands.

If a person died as a result of an injury or the poisoning from a scorpion sting, the people looked to Sakyma for an answer. It was in this way that Sakyma quickly took power, seducing even the wisest amongst them from following the ways of their ancestors.

Ra'olt had lived his entire life in one place and he had no desire to leave the land of his birth, but it went without question that he would go where he was led. His place was with his daughter and the children of her womb. He cared for the strong sons that would look to him as their grandfather and though he had failed his daughter in many ways, he vowed that he would not fail his grandsons.

Many seasons came and went before the men that were sent out as scouts finally returned. They brought a message that put fear into Ra'olt's heart. There was a place far into face of the rising sun that had water for all and people that lived upon the land. It was said that the people were not skilled with the use of a spear, nor did they turn their bows and arrows against each other. The men that acted as scouts for their band said that these harvesters of the land did not display any interest in fighting for their place beside the river.

The day came when Sakyma stood with his sons, Shale and Tonaka. Both young men were constantly standing in his shadow and he smile down at his sons. By this time their mother had breathed her last breath, she was taken swiftly after the birth of her third son, Ni'zin.

Sakyma tolerated Ra'olt's presence simply because the elders of their village expected him to care for Ra'olt as the father of his last wife. He did not have a valid reason to keep Ra'olt at a distance, but Sakyma did not like Ra'olt's influence over his sons, particularly his firstborn son, Shale. In the eyes of their people, Ra'olt was his responsibility and he saw to it that the old man was fed and clothed simply because it was expected of him and a matter of status amongst his people.

By might and strength alone, he had taken on the role of leader of their band. If he did not provide for a member of his family, then what would the villagers say about his ability to lead them?

Sakyma had no reason to think that one of the men that he led would challenge his right to lead them but he was cautious and wary. He would often arrange for any man that challenged him to meet with an accident of some kind. Those that went with him to hunt for meat, returned wrapped in a burial garment and deeply mourned for their sacrifice.

Who was there to say that the men had not been gored by a wild animal or fallen to their death during the hunt? Sakyma would defeat any man that openly challenged him. Although such a thing had never occurred before, Sakyma was wary.

It was for this reason that he took foreign wives instead of choosing women from amongst the daughters of his people. He did not wish to join himself to any of the men that provided for their families while under the protection of his leadership.

In this way, Sakyma set himself apart from those around him, those that followed in the way that he walked. There was no man amongst him that could call him brother or claim a relationship by blood ties or the joining of lifemates, except for Ra'olt.

"We will journey to this new land and if the people stand in our way we will crush them under our feet like dust. This is the way of our people and it is the way of our ancestors. We do not fear the unknown." Sakyma's voice was decisive and firm. He met the eyes of each man, woman and child that watched him with rapt attention. "We are the Ma'leiki!"

This last shout was echoed in the way of a victory cry. Soon all raised their voices to match that of their leader.

Sakyma's brown skin fairly shimmered with the full onslaught of power. He wore his hair long and adorned with the various feathers from the birds of the land. His neck was adorned with the necklaces made from the bones and teeth of his more noteworthy kills. He lacked for nothing and his sons stood proudly beside him, imitating the bearing of their father.

His people were easily led and they would do anything that he asked. Slowly, overtime he eroded their sense of free will until it was worn away to nonexistence. Under his direction, girl children were considered almost valueless and easily given in trade. If a man had no sons and only daughters it was quietly suggested that his wife not fail him by giving birth to another girl child. If the wailing of women affected the men as they gave up their girl children to the desert sands, no man was foolish enough to show such emotion before the others.

The men understood that strong sons would secure their future. If the old ones lamented the death of the girl children, then so be it. Sakyma encouraged his men to make sons that would grow to be strong warriors.

Already Shale and Tonaka had made their first kill. Sakyma pushed his children to compete with one another, to stand head and shoulders above the other boys of their band.

He was a man of power and glory and through his sons, he would live on for generations.

Sakyma turned to look into the worshipful gazes of his people and the dark, watchful eyes of his sons. Three strong boys stood before him, the first taller than the next. Shale, Tonaka and Ni'zin, these were the sons of his hearth and he would imbue within them with the same power that he now wielded.

Nothing would stop his conquest of those that were too weak to stand against him. The sound of Sakyma's laughter was drowned out only by the cheers of his people.

CHAPTER ONE

"Do you know how the river came to be?" Denoa sat at her father's knee listening to his words, just as she had from the time that she was a young child until now.

"I am listening." In this way, Denoa respectfully waited for her father to bestow his story to her listening ears.

Narin inhaled with a harsh rattle that hurt her ears. Denoa struggled to listen to her father's voice and she searched past the thick sound of his words until she caught the thin thread of the man beneath. Narin had once been a strong hunter, but that time had come and gone.

Their people survived by harvesting food from the land. They stayed within the sheltering confines of the red rock canyons that rimmed the land for as far as the eye could see.

Her father had changed gradually over the time of long cold and he had not recovered his health. With each passing day, Narin continued to fade away on the inside, though his body was physically unmarred. Denoa feared that her father's mind was irreparably changed, damaged in some unfathomable way, for he was not himself.

Narin shared the stories of their people with his only daughter, not because he feared death, but because he embraced a life fully lived.

"There was a time when our people wandered across the desert sands, seeking a place of shelter, food and water. They did not carry the seeds of the land in their pouches, they did not press these seeds into the ground and give them water and sound to make them grow. These things were not known to the first men to walk this land and catch sight of the red rocks." Narin coughed and choked for a moment before catching his breath.

He spoke as if his daughter did not already know this particular story, when in truth, Denoa knew it well. Patience was inherent within his daughter's spirit and she listened as if hearing the story for the first time. She knew that each day spent with her father was a gift. Each word spoken from his lips was welcome in her heart. Through the stories of their people, he would be remembered and if she listened and remembered each word that he spoke, he would always remain with her.

Denoa sat with her knees bent beneath her and her eyes slightly closed. She listened with her heart just as her father had taught her. Only those trained to become future storytellers could listen without hearing and look without seeing. Denoa treasured the gift given to her and she did not resist the heady pull of her father's voice.

"Their salvation came from one of their elders. A woman that had lived upon the land all the days of her life. During that time, the old ones were treated with respect for they were the ones that knew where to go to find water and when to stop and make a shelter. They knew the ways of the sun and moon, they knew the ways of the night stars and so it was that one young hunter stopped to listen to the one that they called Ani', Grandmother.

"Where will we go to find water? The streambeds are dry and only the tracks of animals rest there. Yet, we do not see the buffalo, deer or even the small rabbit." The young hunter was a powerful sight to behold and his body was that of an able-bodied man. The people of his band looked to him as their leader, but their belief in him waivered when he leaned down to listen to the oldest member of their band. Many scoffed and a few of the women openly showed their disdain. One of the men thought to challenge his position of authority and a few others encouraged this one to act. Still others remained silent and watchful." Narin opened his eyes to gaze at the face of his beloved daughter.

She was so much like her mother who had been lost to them for more seasons than he wished to count. Denoa's head was tilted just so, as she sought to capture each word and hold it to her heart. With a sigh of contentment, Narin fell back into the familiar cadence of the story.

"The hunter inclined his head to Ani and she told him the secrets of the land. He listened carefully, taking in all that she told him with words both spoken and unspoken."

"This is the way you must go. Take the pathway that leads up to the top of the red rock and it is there that you must call forth water. Men will be needed to dig into the mountainside. You will find a small trickle of water there but listen closely, when you find it, do nothing to harm the flow of water. Simply leave an offering and return with men and stone tools."

"The hunter did not allow his impatience or concern to show upon his face. Most of the water skins carried by their people were empty or nearly spent. His own water had been given to a young child who shared the precious liquid with his siblings.

The people built a shelter to keep them while the young hunter walked a far distance until he found the spring hidden deep within the red rocks. It was not easy to find, but the animals and birds led him to it. He left his hunting knife, bow and arrows behind as an offering. These things were all that he had to defend himself and hunt for his band.

If they did not have water to sate the thirst of their entire band, they would all die. The next morning he returned with the men of his band and together they dug deep into the red rocks.

Their hands against the stone were useless and their stone tools barely made an indentation. It was only when the young hunter wedged a flat slate into the crevice that a larger hole was made."

"In this way the rock began to crumble and fall until water crashed through the red rock, creating the river that runs near our village to this day." Narin opened his eyes once more and he caught his breath at the beauty of his daughter's smile.

Denoa smoothed the hair away from her father's face and offered him a sip of the healing brew that she had made earlier. The liquid was hot and even though the day was almost unbearably warm, he drank deeply. Rivulets of sweat built upon Narin's brow and he wiped them away with the actions of a man who had always known such hardships.

"The time of long cold is almost upon us. Soon days of warmth and burning sunlight will become a distant memory." Denoa busied herself with the cleaning of her father's dwelling.

The inside of her father's lodge was narrow, opening up to a circular seating area. Her sleeping place rested on one side of a low burning fire and his on the other.

She was a young woman of rare grace and several of the village hunters had already offered much to her father in hopes of joining with her as lifemate. Denoa turned her head away from the young men that she had grown into adulthood with and her father did not force the issue.

At times, she watched the jungle that rimmed the edge of the canyons with a look of expectation upon her face. She never told her father what she hoped to see there amongst the sparse growing trees. She never told anyone, but the desire was still there.

In the secret place within her heart, she dreamed of finding her true mate, a man that was not only a hunter and harvester of the earth, but also a strong hunter and protector.

The people that gathered within the shelter of the red rocks were composed of several bands and family groups. They were driven together by desperation. They had no leader that stood out amongst them. Denoa was Narin's only daughter and she knew that soon she would be forced to choose a mate whether her father demanded it or not. Her time of becoming a woman had come and gone.

Other women her age were already expecting their first child and still she waited. She often wondered why she yearned for something more than she could name or describe. How long would she be able to hold on to the hope for something more, something different from that which she was accustomed?

Denoa was thankful that her father did not press her to accept the offer of one of the young men that vied for her attention.

He was content to let her make her own choice in the matter, though she would not try his patience. If the time of long cold came and went and she did not take a mate, their hope of surviving the time of long cold would fade. Denoa knew that she must seek out a mate soon, but she often dreamed of finding someone that stood apart from the other men.

Was it wrong that she wished to join her life with someone like the strong hunter in her father's stories? Was it wrong to yearn for someone that would remain steadfast despite what others thought of his actions?

Denoa had more questions than answers but though she was only seventeen seasons of age, she knew well the ways of the heart. The heart wanted that which the heart wanted and it would not be swayed by the words or the thoughts of others.

Denoa recognized her father's stubbornness and resolve in herself. Yet, she was her father's daughter and she would not have it any other way.

"If he lives, he will come to me. I have only to wait." Denoa spoke the words in a murmur, as a mere exhalation upon her lips. "May it go well with you, daughter." Narin's eyes sparkled with merriment as his daughter looked up from her task, caught unaware, held transfixed by his perceptive gaze.

Denoa couldn't stop the smile that blossomed upon her face as her father easily read the deepest secrets of her heart. Instead of words that scolded, he readily offered his blessing.

The Legend of the Sundancer (Book One)
Available now on Amazon.com

**KENNEDY PUBLISHING
TITLES BY KARAH QUINNEY:**

The Whale Hunter
Pillar of Fire (Book One)
Sacred Fire (Book Two)
Sacred Path (Book Three)

The Great Land
The Seeking Star (Book One)
Shadow of the Moon (Book Two)
Light of the Sun (Book Three)

Sundancer
Legend of the Sundancer (Book One)
The Last Sundancer (Book Two)

Warrior
The Warrior's Way
Daughters of the Sun
The Cloud Forest – New Release

KARAH
QUINNEY